Gretchen McCullough's latest ᴜᴜᴜᴋ ᴄᴀᴘᴛᴜᴜᴇs ᴛʜᴇ magic and absurdity of the city and its people with a humour few local writers have managed to achieve.
    —*Egypt Today*

Novel look at Egypt: history, mystery and just plain quirky for your bookshelf.
    —Kate Durham, *Egypt Today*

McCullough displays all the idiosyncrasies of Cairo in a slightly comic, non-dramatic tone. Cairo is endless amounts of fervor, hoopla, commotion, confusion and turmoil. For all its corruption, pollution, noise, havoc, chaos and double standards, Cairo is still endearing for both foreigners and Egyptians and they long for it when they leave. This is what McCullough captures best.
    —Sherine Elbanhawy, *Scoop Empire*

Gretchen McCullough is an American academic who has lived and worked in Cairo for several years. The Cairo she writes about is full of bizarre, anarchic, extraordinary characters—a scissor-throwing Swedish belly-dancer, an man known as Ugly Duck with a colorful and very public love-life, a pair of fugitives who sneak back into the country after Tahrir. She writes cracking dialogue and deft dead-pan internal monologue. Read this book. It is very funny stuff.
    —Annemarie Neary, *The Orphans*

Shahrazad's
GIFT

Gretchen McCullough

 Cune

Shahrazad's Gift
by Gretchen McCullough
Copyright ©2024
Cune Press, Seattle 2024

ISBN 9781951082437 (paperback)
ISBN 9781614572800 (epub)

Library of Congress Cataloging-in-Publication Data

Names: McCullough, Gretchen, author.
Title: Shahrazad's gift / Gretchen McCullough.
Description: Seattle : Cune Press, 2024.
Identifiers: LCCN 2023046568 (print) | LCCN 2023046569 (ebook) | ISBN
   9781951082437 (paperback) | ISBN 9781614572800 (epub)
Subjects: LCSH: Cairo (Egypt)--Fiction. | LCGFT: Short stories. | Fiction.
Classification: LCC PS3613.C3864496 S53 2024 (print) | LCC PS3613.C3864496
   (ebook) | DDC 813/.6--dc23/eng/20231017
LC record available at https://lccn.loc.gov/2023046568
LC ebook record available at https://lccn.loc.gov/2023046569

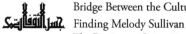

Bridge Between the Cultures (a series from Cune Press)

Finding Melody Sullivan	Alice Rothchild
The Passionate Spies	John Harte
Music Has No Boundaries	Rafiq Gangat
Arab Boy Delivered	Paul Aziz Zarou
Kivu	Frederic Hunter
Empower a Refugee	Patricia Martin Holt
Biblical Time Out of Mind	Tom Gage, James A. Freeman
Afghanistan and Beyond	Linda Sartor
The Other Side of the Wall	Richard Hardigan
Apartheid Is a Crime	Mats Svensson
Curse of the Achille Lauro	Reem al-Nimer

Cune   Cune Press: www.cunepress.com

For my parents,
Anne and Graham McCullough,
who inspired a real love of books and travel

Contents

"Then, Dinarzad cleared her throat and said, 'Sister, if you are not sleepy, tell us one of your lovely little tales to while away the night, before I bid you good-bye at daybreak, for I don't know what will happen to you tomorrow.' Shahrazad turned to King Shahrayar and said, 'May I have your permission to tell a story?' He replied, 'Yes,' and Shahrazad was very happy and said, 'Listen.'"

From the Arabian Nights.

1

The Wedding Guest

ATILDA RODE IN ON A WHITE STALLION. Her legs dangled nicely over his flanks. I had used an Edwardian white sheer corset as a model for her costume, but the black laces zigzagged, like a spider web, across her chest. And yes, oh yes, we had pulled the laces tight to push up her big boobs. A black mask covered her eyes for this 19th-century costume ball—as if she had a tantalizing rendezvous with the Marquis de Sade himself. Her long straight black hair had been teased high and powdered white. All other accessories were a wicked black: garters; very short leather shorts; shiny stilettos.

Our well-heeled guests at this wedding party roared as if they were at a sleazy strip joint on the west side of LA. A gargantuan red tent had been erected on the grounds of the Marriott at *Sharm El-Sheikh,* a swanky resort town on Egypt's Red Sea coast. Egyptian waiters in starched white *galabiyyas* hovered with trays of drinks.

The noise from the clapping and the lights from the blinking cameras had made the stallion jumpy. "Easy does it, boy," I said. God, that's all I needed now: a runaway horse. When I glanced behind me at the tables facing the stage, I noticed the bobbing of scalloped gold hats.

"Waiter!" I called out. I needed a drink—red wine. Even Stella Local beer would do just fine, although I doubted anyone in this crowd was drinking beer.

Our last crisis had been the lost suitcase at the *Sharm El-Sheikh* airport— the costumes for the show. Batilda was pissed. "Luv," she said in her Manchester accent, "You're fuckin' dead if you don't find it." I was used to her foul-mouthed temper tantrums. I had experienced much worse in Hollywood.

Bunny Rasheed, the American queen who had commissioned us to do this gig, stood in front of me, like a statue. She whispered in a throaty Lauren Bacall imitation, "Darling, we're excited you came all the way from Odessa." She was smiling, but her blue eyes were vacant. No expression.

"Odessa?"

"West Texas, honey. Don't call her a cowgirl 'til you've seen her ride."

The horse was about to bolt. I had told Batilda she shouldn't get the cheapest horse at the Pyramid stables, but she had not listened—that broad could squeeze blood out of a stone. Unlike me, she was a shrewd businesswoman.

The stallion lurched toward the guests' tables. This was not the way we had rehearsed it. Shit! The waiters dove out of the way.

My hands shook. I lit up a cigarette. "We hope your guests like the show, Bunny."

I was fleeing creditors in LA. Production companies didn't pay their bills. This was my second stint in Egypt. The first time, I had moved to Cairo because of my Egyptian husband, Kamal, a doctor, a specialist in diabetes. We had met at tango dance lessons at the Stairway to the Starz Dance Studio in Hollywood—he was finishing up his residency at UCLA. He had a beautiful dimple in his cheek when he smiled. Expressive brown eyes.

"You're Dan's new secretary? He said you were pleasant," Bunny said, fingering her expensive pearl choker.

"Who?"

"You know, Dan. Chairman of Oil Rig Hand Jobs."

I giggled. Bunny whispered in my ear, "Just between you and me, hon, he thinks the sun comes up to hear him crow."

So here was a glimmer of the real Bunny. Had she given ol' Dan a few hand jobs before she had snagged Rasheed? Or was it the other way around?

"Remember, I work for Batilda," I said. "The dancer." I gestured toward the stage. "The Turkish bath was my idea?"

If I were honest with myself, it was my most grandiose set design. We had used chunks of pink Aswan marble to mimic a Turkish bath.

I craned my neck to see if Batilda had made it to the stage. She was waving to the crowd. Easy. Easy. Just get off that wild stallion!

"Why, of course!" Bunny exclaimed. "I thought your face looked vaguely familiar."

Bunny had forgotten the temper tantrum that she had thrown at her villa at the Sakkara Pyramids only a few months ago when we met to discuss the show. People were flying in from all over the globe for this wedding on the Red Sea Coast in Egypt: Tashkent, Houston, Sofia, Detroit, West Texas. Millions of pounds were being spent. Bunny wanted spectacle. Fantasy. Something big. This was Bunny's sister's third marriage. I was dying to ask her if we could have a steel phallus on stage. Instead, I had spent days trolling around on the internet on every kind of kinky web site in search of oriental spectacle. Did I really think we could hang Batilda by her nipples upside down? I was saved by the painter Eugene Delacroix—his Orientalist painting of a European woman being tended by a Nubian man at a Turkish bath had been the inspiration for my design.

"Don't you know who I am?" Bunny had said that day.

"Bunny Rasheed," I said. It was odd—an upper-class WASP pet name coupled with her Egyptian husband's family name.

"Most people think I look like Audrey Hepburn," Bunny said. "What do you think?"

I studied her. "Too tall. She was short and petite."

Bunny frowned. Her lip protruded, as if she were going to sulk.

"Grace Kelly, luv. You look exactly like her. Give us a kiss," Batilda said, giving me a wink.

This was a ludicrous lie.

"You don't know the name of the family who founded Exxon Oil?"

"Well, no…"

Batilda shouted at me later, "Luv, just fuckin' kiss her arse! We're making thousands on this wedding."

"Because I didn't know. I'm from California. Not Texas! Do you think I know every damn person in the US?"

After awhile, even Bunny got tired of asking, "You don't know who I am?" Instead, she asked, "How old do you think I am?" I was about to say sixty-seven, but Batilda jumped in before I could speak.

"Not a day older than thirty-five, luv," Batilda answered. She was a bold, confident liar. In the entertainment business, honesty was a real liability. I needed to practice being socially superficial. Unfortunately, it didn't come naturally to me.

Bunny was close to fifty. Give or take two or three years. But she was lithe. Had beautiful clothes. Servants. A black Land Rover. Not that anyone needed a Land Rover in Cairo!

Before Bunny had thrown her tantrum, she had been charming. "Do you know the secret to a good marriage?" she had asked. "Marry an Egyptian playboy."

I had almost spewed fresh lemon juice all over her pristine white sofa. Batilda elbowed me.

When it comes to spoiled bitches, Batilda beats them all, though. Marry me or I'll cut your oxygen supply off! Batilda looks good—maybe not real, but she still looks good. Silicone boobs, tummy tuck, ass job, Botoxed face. Bunny had also had some "adjustments." Her face was pulled so tight, every time she crossed her legs her mouth snapped shut.

But after a thousand hassles, complaints, and changes, we had made it to performance. Bunny waved her hand toward the stage. "If you'll excuse me, I hope you enjoy the show."

"The costume designer made the costumes for Cheech and Chong's movie *Up in Smoke*."

But Bunny still did not recognize me. Who the hell cared? As long as we got paid. She was off her head on something. She floated away. She murmured to herself, "Just because a chicken has wings doesn't mean it can fly."

After my second husband, Kamal, flew away for good with my favorite purple beach towel, I called up The *Price Is Right's* production company and said, "Remember me? Queenie? The gal who made the costumes you were so happy with? I need the cash. I'm so broke I can't even afford a tube of generic toothpaste from Wal-Mart."

To stay in groceries, I was teaching little old ladies how to belly dance at Stairway to the Starz Dance Studio at the Hibiscus Mall. Mostly, I told them embellished anecdotes about movie stars that I found in the *National Enquirer*. "Ladies, have you seen the size of Melanie Griffiths' lips?"

The production agent at *The Price Is Right* said, "Who is this?"

"Queenie O'Connell," I said.

"Who?"

"Queenie O'Connell."

"Never heard the name," she said, hanging up on me. Another one who claimed she didn't remember who I was. Yet six months before, she had taken me to lunch at the most exclusive restaurant in Hollywood. "Chocolate mousse or raspberry cheesecake, dear? That's a novel concept. Show how women can be empowered by their sexuality, not victimized by it..." I was making belly dancing costumes for the gals who pointed to the washing machines on *The Price Is Right*!

Of course, if Batilda hadn't wired me the money for a plane ticket to Egypt, I might still be sleeping in my blue Mustang in the Hibiscus Mall. I am the only one who knows that her parents run a tiny inn in the wilds off the coast of Sweden. They keep insisting that she return home to change sheets. Batilda tells everyone she meets that she trained in the Ringling Brothers and Barnum and Bailey's Circus!

A tiny, gnome-like woman was sitting next to me. From behind many folds of skin, she peered at me with intelligent blue eyes. Her white, curly hair was wild. A tuft of hair stuck out from her head, like a feather.

"Golly, would you look at that. Bless Patsy!" the shrivelled woman said, blowing smoke out from her nose. She was probably around eighty.

I laughed.

"Don't you wish you had a body like that?"

"It's carefully constructed," I said.

"Of course it is!" She pulled out a cigarette from her packet of Kents. "You belong to the bride or groom?"

"I made the costumes," I said. "Designed the set."

"You're mighty talented." The old lady guffawed. "Juicier than a *Harlequin Romance*! You sure don't get your ideas from *McCall's*!"

"Underwear advertisements on the internet. Are you one of Bunny's relatives?"

"No. I'm on a package tour. This looked more fun than the Pharaoh party. I sneaked away. Well, did you ever...? That horse is well-endowed."

She was right. The horse had an enormous, fat, red cock. Some of the men in the front row were pointing at it as if they were fourteen-year-old boys. "Yee, doggie!"

Batilda was sliding off the stallion. She wobbled slightly on one of the stilettos. She almost lost her balance.

I took a cigarette out of my pack. "Christ, why did I insist on the stilettos! Too risky!"

"It's obvious," the old lady said. "Sex appeal."

But as soon as Batilda straightened up, she took off her stilettos, kissed each one, and tossed them to the middle-aged men in the front row, as if she were a rock star. A howl rose from the audience. Two men were fighting over her shoes.

"That wasn't in the script!" I said.

The old lady laughed. "She knows how to egg on the crowd. Some men have a foot fetish."

More than twenty Nubian men with ostrich feathers fanned around her in an arc on the stage. She turned around to face the audience and raised her arm, as if she were Cleopatra hailing her army.

One of the Nubian men stood behind her and untied the mask. The drunken men in the front row whooped. She threw the black mask out into the crowd.

"She's a pistol," the old lady said. "I ran a high school drama club a hundred years ago. Some people are just natural hams. And some are just like blocks of wood."

"Yeah," I said. "She's a drama queen, all right."

"Is she a polecat offstage?" the old lady said. Beneath her droopy eyelids, two blue eyes shone with mischief.

"Well…" I said. Why was I confiding in this cute little old lady? She was on vacation and wanted to have fun.

"One would expect so," she said. "I'm sure she's no angel."

Of course, I was grateful not to be still sleeping in my car, who wouldn't be? Those rescued by Batilda should understand they were the tiny garnish on a plate of Swedish meatballs. Besides her cats from the street (Swink, Pout Face, and Julia Childs), there were the wounded, the crippled, and the crazy: me; Jimmy Doyle, the lush; Gary, the American professor; and Gabriella, the penniless Italian painter.

Suddenly, two turbaned men in Arabian Nights–style costumes appeared on the stage. Batilda beckoned to the one with the bigger muscles. The other feigned displeasure and drew his sword.

The audience yelled, "Kill him. Kill him."

"A tale of woe and perfidy. That'll make a good story," the old lady said. "Yes sir."

"If you're not the one being had," I said.

I had heard about Batilda poaching men from wives and girlfriends. And really, why should I have been surprised when she did it to Gabriella?

Late that evening, after Batilda had danced in front of a crowd of fifty at her own apartment, she said to Fathy, Gabriella's lover, "Luv, would you mind filling this tub up with water? My feet are so tired," she said, leaning forward in her black lace-up camisole so he could see her nipples, large as sand dollars.

"*Wallahi. Begadd,*" he said. Seriously?

"Fathy," Gabriella said, pulling at his hand. "No." But Fathy's eyes were mesmerized by Batilda's outrageous boobs.

Batilda sighed and said, "Gabriella, luv, when he's finished massaging my feet, he'll come to your bed. I need his services more than you."

"Massaging feet?" Gabriella asked, puzzled. She was a talented painter who drew charcoal sketches of haunted faces of pharaohs from the Egyptian Museum, but her English was broken.

"I'll make it worth your while, luv," Batilda said to the young man, who was an impoverished painter.

He smiled. "*Mish fahim.*"

But it was clear the handsome young man understood.

"For crying out loud, Batilda. Can't you control yourself?" I said. Did she have to prove to us that she could seduce every man?

"Why should I?"

When Gabriella realized at last what was happening, she stamped her feet and said, "*Putana!*"

"Gabriella, luv, of course we're still friends," Batilda said, smiling. "I'm just borrowing him for a short time. You can have him back soon. Kiss. Kiss."

"*Porca!* Fill your belly. Stuff your mother! *Putana!* You cheat me! Eat caca!"

"Let's be rational, pet. European-minded. This is called multiple partners," Batilda said. "There's no need to be uncivilized about this. It's a fair exchange for all the meals you've eaten here, isn't it?"

"*Porca! Putana!*" Gabriella screamed. "Aaaay. Aaaay." She wailed. She had enjoyed the attention of Fathy, her first lover since her divorce. I felt sorry for her. On the other hand, why wasn't Fathy more loyal?

"Gabriella…" I said, extending my hand to her. What could I say?

Gabriella brushed away my hand. "*Porca! Putana!* Every one of you a cheater. Liars! I stay in this garbage country for my son, Marcelo."

I heard glass shattering. Gabriella had overturned Batilda's goldfish tank on her way out.

"Queenie, pet. Save my darlings! Ringo Starr! Benny Hill! John Cleese! There's a bucket in the kitchen. Underneath the sink," Batilda said. "Don't forget to sweep up the glass."

I was on my hands and knees, picking up those helpless goldfish who flopped between shards of glass, as if I were Batilda's maid. Only John Cleese, the angelfish, didn't make it. Aquamarine pebbles crusted under my fingernails. My nails were chipped and jagged; I badly needed a manicure. Batilda had spent a fortune on coral for her tank—I set the coral away from the broken glass. "I want the place to be comfortable for my wee babies," she'd said.

Why had I obeyed? Because I was under her spell, like everyone else in her life? When I went to report that John Cleese had died, she was no longer sitting in front of the tub, soaking her feet. Her bedroom door was shut. I put my ear to the door: ecstatic moans of pleasure. A few drunken guests lingered in the living room. They were interested in mooching the last of the Scotch and couldn't care less about the coupling in Batilda's bedroom.

Unable to stand it a minute longer, I had gone downtown to the bar, *El-Horreya*, the Freedom Café, which specialized in pickled lupine beans and cheap beer. I had gotten plastered. The last thing I remember was Jimmy Doyle quoting poetry to me in a slur: "Things fall apart; the center cannot hold; mere anarchy is loosed upon the world."

Now, Nubian men swirled around Batilda, fanning her with large ostrich feathers. The man who won the sword dance had disappeared and another admirer appeared. Oh how wonderful to be like Batilda—to be admired, adored, and desired!

"Are you married?" the old woman said.

"Divorced twice."

I wanted to forget the past. Neal, a drummer for the Doors—a druggie. Heroin. And Kamal, the Egyptian doctor, who loved to dance. In the beginning of our marriage, he had led me across the kitchen floor in a tango. I was not a good judge of character—that was always my problem.

The old woman put her liver-spotted hand over mine—such a tender gesture for someone who didn't know me. "You've just gotten some bad apples, my dear. Someday you'll meet a nice man."

I started to cry. My life had been full of bad apples—men and women. But why had I suddenly become maudlin?

"There, there," the old lady said, patting my arm. "You're probably just exhausted from the work on the show."

"No kidding. I'm a basket case. Working for that broad. Did twenty designs before we came up with the corset. Then, the damned suitcase got lost. I spent six hours at the airport!"

Batilda was unlacing her corset. The men in the front row were almost jumping out of their chairs.

I felt the tears rolling down my cheeks. The old lady continued to pat my arm. "Anything underneath that skimpy corset?"

"Silicone," I said.

The lady giggled. "That's the fashion these days. I was horrified to hear that my granddaughter had implants when she was seventeen. She was just precious before that…"

"Traveling by yourself?" I asked.

"Yes, sweetheart," she said. "Patrick's been gone a year. Spinal cancer. Be a lamb and pour me some more wine, would you?"

"Happy to," I said. I filled her glass to the brim.

"I'm so tiny that I can't drink the way I used to," she said. "I have osteoporosis. Terrible disease. Your bones crumble. Don't forget to drink your milk, sweetheart!"

"Was your husband a nice man?" I asked.

"Oh, Lord, yes. He was a doll," she said.

"How did you meet?"

"Patrick was good people. Originally from West Texas. He was doin' graduate work at Chapel Hill—history. One day he was sitting under a tree with some other students, talking about the Trail of Tears—which was quite serious. I covered my mouth and started whooping like an Indian. He didn't think I was very funny," she said, giggling.

I giggled, too.

"My, he was handsome. He had a fine physique. Rudy Valentino except with red hair and green eyes. So proud. Stood tall. He wasn't afraid of anyone or anything."

On stage, Batilda was arranging the wine glasses for her next act. She would balance on her bare feet on wine glasses.

"At first, we were going to get married in a year. And then six months. And then we just couldn't wait any longer. Young people in the heat of passion."

Neal and I had also ended up at the courthouse after a six-week romance, but our marriage had lasted only two years. And when he had left, he had taken all of my B.B. King tapes, my favorite hippy-dippy lamp, and my ten-speed. A set of wine glasses from Tijuana. Really, why did I care now?

"How long were you married?"

"Forty years," she said, taking a sip of her wine. "It wasn't all roses. There are bound to be a few dead skunks in the middle of the road. How does your dancer keep from breaking the glass?"

"Balance. It's a trick."

"Yes, sir. Life can throw you off balance. Of course, when we moved to West Texas from North Carolina I cried for a year. His people were different. There were no trees and my hair went flat."

"Your hair went flat?"

"It's dry in West Texas."

I felt emotionally dry.

"And it wasn't easy being married to Patrick. He was a good man, but he never could say he was sorry. One day we had a fight. Instead of saying he was sorry, he bought me a refrigerator. I said, 'You know, honey, money doesn't grow in the bathtub. Wouldn't it be easier to say you're sorry?' At that time, we were both teachin' school in Lubbock. That was the Depression. And our salaries were in scrip!"

"One of Batilda's lovers bought her a refrigerator," I said. "Another one—an Italian arms dealer—bought her a white Maserati…"

"An arms dealer!"

"Batilda has a lot of admirers," I said.

"Expect so. She's an attractive girl." The old lady smiled, but seemed distracted. "You know, I don't care about things anymore. Maybe that happens when you know you're not long for this world."

"Surely…" I was embarrassed. Did she know that she was going to die? "Are you okay?"

"For now," she said. "I love tearing the house down. When I was in boarding school, I got punished for dancing all night."

"Bunny says that the secret to a good marriage is a marrying an Egyptian playboy."

The old lady snorted. "Who's Bunny?"

"The sister of the bride. She hired us to do the show. You're from Texas. Maybe you know of her. Bunny Tushman. Her family founded Exxon Oil."

"Don't know the name. We lived in a tiny town near Lubbock called Loop. After the war, we moved to South Texas. Way down next to the Mexican border."

"What's the secret to a good marriage?"

"Oh, pooh. There are no formulas," the old lady said, sucking on her cigarette. "But there might be a few key ingredients, just like making good buttermilk biscuits. First, there should be chemistry—that's your butter. That's what holds you together. Being a straight shooter. Being kind. Being able to say you're sorry."

The Egyptian waiter swooped down and took away my plate. I had only taken a few bites of my filet mignon. "Excuse me. Excuse me. I'm not finished," I called out. "Good meat shouldn't be thrown away."

Her mischievous blue eyes became sad.

The crowd was stomping their feet. While Batilda was standing on the wine glasses with her bare feet, she was balancing a flaming sword on her head.

To my surprise, the old lady's blue eyes welled with tears. "To have to feed him with a spoon. We even had a pulley lift to get him into bed. When I couldn't lift him anymore."

"I can't think of anything sadder," I said.

When I looked up, though, her tears had vanished. "I have to say, I didn't have any tears left when he died," she declared. "When I go, I want to go in my sleep. Like a lamp that suddenly blinks out."

"Egyptians always thank God for good health."

"Nothing truer! Here's the little prayer I have in my bathroom. Right above the commode: 'God grant me the serenity to accept the things I cannot change; courage to change the things I can; and the wisdom to know the difference…'"

"That's beautiful," I said. I wasn't hanging around much with people who recited prayers.

"My son wanted to give me the money for a face lift, but I said, 'Son, if I've got a little time left on this earth, I would like to see Egypt.'" She leaned forward and whispered, "Don't tell anyone. I'm on the loose. My son forbade me to leave the country. I ran away. No one knows where I am."

I couldn't help but laugh. She was so much fun.

"After Egypt, I'm headed for the Galápagos. I'm a birdwatcher. Want to get a few more birds for my life-list."

At last, Batilda took her bow. The crowd was clapping. She waved her hand toward the band and bowed again.

"Of course, I miss Patrick, but life is for the living, my dear. The brave ones," the old woman said, picking up her ebony cane. A lion peered at me from the handle. I glanced down at her swollen ankles.

Was I a brave person? I had always thought so, but now I was not so sure. On stage, the band was packing up their instruments.

A posse of middle-aged men surged toward a triumphant Batilda. She was most herself in an audience's gaze. She hated silence. If she was alone in her apartment, she turned up Jerry Springer at full blast. Her favorite show was *Secret Mistresses Confronted*. She loved it when they threw chairs on stage.

"Batilda, just this one picture." "I want mine with Batilda and the horse." "Batilda." "Please, Batilda." She beamed into the camera. Each time, it was pure novelty.

"Queenie! The show was fabulous. Just fabulous," Bunny called out. She embraced me as if we were long-lost friends and then kissed me on both cheeks.

"Thank you," I said.

"The whole thing was so....so.... fabulous! You know, one of my friend's daughters is having a birthday party for her seven-year-old. Do you think you could make the costumes for the clowns? The pony is going to ride into the lobby of the Sheraton."

"Well, I...We'll see. You know, I enjoyed talking with...." I said, gesturing to the old lady. I had never asked that wonderful lady her name.

She was being escorted out of the enormous tent by an Egyptian waiter. Her white hair bobbed in the crowd.

"You will think about making costumes for the pony party?"

Bunny drifted off to another guest. I heard her saying, "Wasn't she fabulous?" And then I saw her pointing toward me. We had finished the show at last, but I was not happy. Just flat. Drained.

The next morning, I searched for the old lady everywhere. At last, I recognized the Egyptian waiter at the front desk who had escorted her out of the tent the night before. "The old lady from the wedding? What was her name?"

"What?" he asked.

"You helped an old lady out of the wedding last night."

He looked confused. "I'm sorry, madam. But I didn't help an old lady. I was serving drinks. I never saw an old lady. I served you many times."

Was I drunk? Had I lost my mind?

"There was an old lady sitting next to me. I swear to God, you escorted her out of the tent."

"*Wallahel-Azeem*. I never saw any old lady," he said, cupping his hands together. "Have a nice time."

I spent the rest of the morning by myself at the pool. The place was attractive, but felt artificial—bar stools, shaped in the form of tree trunks, in the pool. Batilda was off in the desert, riding horses with some of the wedding guests. I wished the old lady were lounging beside me. My Bloody Mary would have tasted much better in her company.

Later that afternoon, I had to give Batilda a fitting. She was going to dance again for the wedding party. At this performance, she was wearing a more conventional belly-dancing outfit: a simple bra-bodice for a top with a short skirt—decorated with shiny red beads.

"I look like a pig. Look at this cellulite. Do something!" Batilda said.

I dared myself not to flatter her. All I had to say was, "Of course you're not fat. You're the most beautiful woman in the world."

"You thought the costume was fine before," I said.

"Take the bloody beads off."

"We don't have time," I said.

I could always make costumes for the other belly dancers in Cairo. In fact, the famous belly dancer *Lulua' el-Bahar*, Pearl of the Sea, had called me the other day, begging me to make her a costume. I had put her off. She might be worse than Batilda. Suddenly, I heard the voice of the old lady, "Life is for the living, my dear. The brave ones." I could have sworn the old lady had whispered in my ear, but there was no one in the room but Batilda.

I was adjusting the thin spaghetti strap over her shoulder in the mirror. I had a pin in my teeth. I glanced in the full-length mirror. Batilda was admiring the curve of her neck. I got another pin from my pincushion. When I looked up, she was smiling at me.

"Kiss. Kiss," Batilda said. But when she smiled, her face did not move, as if it were a mask. "Don't you think you should go on a diet? You've really let yourself go."

I remembered how the tiny, wizened lady had described her love for her husband, Patrick, the night before. "For better and for worse." Debilitating illness fell on the side of "for worse."

"You know what?" I said, handing Batilda the scissors. "I think I'm going to throw in the towel."

More than anything, I wanted to spend a month on the Egyptian peninsula of Sinai—where you get up early and sit on the white sand all day long, eat fresh grilled snapper when you are hungry, let the sand run through your toes, pick up driftwood and pieces of curled shells, bob in the water like a cork. The salty water buoys you up when you float—makes you feel light. Carefree. And when your ears are under the water, you are soothed by a slight hum.

"You're being ridiculous. We haven't finished the job," Batilda said.

"This is the last show," I said. "You don't need me. The costume is fine."

"Queenie, luv," she said. "You can't go. Not after all I've done for you."

"We're more or less done," I said.

"I'll dock your share if you walk out now," Batilda said.

I shrugged. I had a stash in my drawer at home. Money under the tile, as the Egyptians would say. Enough for six months at a Bedouin camp.

"You're nothing without me," Batilda said.

"Fuck off!"

"You'll do what I tell you," she shouted. She threw the scissors at me.

I imagined I was floating on my back, buoyed up by salty water. I heard Batilda's cursing, but this time, it didn't touch me.

I closed the door and skipped like a kid down the red carpet of the Marriott hallway—no more bordellos. No more shiny red beads. No more cursing.

Instead, I dreamed of bobbing in the Red Sea.

2

The Empty Flat Upstairs

KEIKO HEARD DRILLING UPSTAIRS. SHE ALSO heard banging early in the morning. The maid next door was beating carpets. When she asked the *bawab*, the porter of the building, about her neighbor's maid, he told her that the maid did not come every day. Besides the drilling, the beating of carpets, the knocking of the water in the pipes in the building, she could hear the man who lived between the buildings, clearing the mucus from his throat, and the wailing of his wife when he beat her. The people upstairs also wore hard shoes, which made a clacking sound when they walked across the floor.

The *bawab* insisted no one lived upstairs.

She was sure that she heard drilling and the clacking of shoes. How could she concentrate on Arabic grammar with so much noise? She had a difficult time imagining herself teaching Arabic to Japanese businessmen in Tokyo. It seemed too late to quit the course now, though. The earplugs she bought at the pharmacy did not muffle the noise.

Late at night, she also heard cats meowing and raucous laughter from above. Did the people who clomped across the floor own cats?

She called the Egyptian landlord, a doctor who was teaching in America. No, he said, no one lived in the flat upstairs, although the flat belonged to his cousin. It was the only flat in the building which was not rented.

"Aaah so, but does your cousin let anyone else have the key?"

Like the *bawab*, the landlord insisted that no one lived in the flat.

Keiko complained so much about the drilling that her foreign neighbors concluded that she must be crazy. Maybe she should go back to Japan. Maybe she had been in Egypt too long. Maybe she needed psychological help. Her neighbor across the hall had even given her the number to the counseling service. For her kindness, Keiko had given the woman a small summer bell to ward off evil spirits.

She had not gone for counselling. She was sure she heard drilling. Anyway, the doctor would also tell her that she did not hear drilling, like the *bawab*, like the landlord, like her neighbors.

Keiko was disturbed, but it was also true that the *bawab* had a spare key to the flat.

Batilda had made a special arrangement with the *bawab* to rent the flat without the landlord's knowledge. (Even though he was more honest than most and did not cheat the landlord on the rents he collected for him, he could not refuse Batilda's generous offer. He had three unemployed sons in the village.)

Officially, no one was living in the flat upstairs.

The drilling that Keiko heard was the hum of a sewing machine. Keiko's hearing had been damaged from five years of living in downtown Cairo, next to many mosques. Now that she lived in Garden City, which was quieter, some noise was amplified; other noise mutated into something else. When she spoke to the *bawab*, she banged her hands on the table and shouted because she knew he was lying about the flat upstairs. Did he think because she was Japanese, she was stupid? Could be fooled by his facile assurances? She was sure no one told the truth in Cairo.

If she had been bolder, she would have marched upstairs and banged on the door when she heard the drilling. Found out about this never-ending construction project.

Batilda had given the key to her American friend, Queenie from LA, who made belly dancing costumes for a living. Queenie had been tipped off that there would be a raid on her flat on the Pyramids' Road and she would have to pay taxes for having a business in a residential zone. If she made the costumes somewhere else, she could deny that she had a business. Queenie was strapped for cash and could not afford to pay taxes.

Naturally, Batilda wanted to help out Queenie because she made costumes for her. Queenie also made costumes for other famous belly dancers and other minor entertainers in Cairo. (They rarely paid their bills and materials were expensive, but Queenie could not see herself back in LA.)

When Queenie was not sewing, Batilda used the landlord's cousin's flat. Keiko heard other noises besides the drilling.

For example, Batilda usually used her own flat for assignations with businessmen and as a place to relax. However, in her flat there was now a hole in her bedroom ceiling. (A plumbing leak and the constant jouncing of her bed had plunged her bed through the ceiling to the next floor onto her middle-aged neighbor, Dr Gary, a professor of environmental biology, a specialist on the water of the Nile.)

Batilda had not really minded if Gary heard what was happening in her flat, but recently he had started shouting up obscenities and paranoid things like:

"Go ahead, fuck your brains out!"

"They're poisoning the water!"

"Don't eat fish from the Nile!"

Batilda had decided to use the landlord's cousin's flat for her assignations with businessmen or even Big Boy, the black Caribbean bodyguard for the famous Saudi Arabian princess who lived in a hotel downtown. When Keiko heard the clacking of high heels, it was not her imagination. Batilda wore gold stilettos. The Egyptian businessmen were usually fat and wore expensive Italian leather shoes with heels.

Keiko complained to the *bawab* about the clacking and clomping of shoes overhead.

He said, "So now the drilling has stopped. You are hearing ghosts?"

"Do ghosts wear shoes?" Keiko asked.

The *bawab* twirled his Turkish-style moustache. He was a little afraid of losing his monthly supplement from Batilda. What if this persistent Japanese woman discovered the truth?

He shrugged. "Maybe the noise is coming from the street or from somewhere else."

"No. Here are the noises from the street. Call to prayer at five-thirty. ALLAHU AKBAR. Every morning some man starts his Volkswagen early in the morning to warm it up. The Egyptian lady in the building across from us has a bird that makes an ugly sound. The man who washes the cars shouts 'Good morning' to the *bawab* in that building. Sometimes, they quarrel."

"Okay. Okay. Is Tokyo a quiet city?"

"Japanese don't love noise. Stillness is a value in our culture."

"Maybe you need a holiday. You are tired."

"I just came back from Japan. One month ago," Keiko said.

Other times, Keiko heard loud meowing from the flat upstairs, as if hundreds of cats were having a wild bash. She knew this was impossible, but she heard the meowing. How could there be hundreds of cats in that flat if it were unoccupied?

Even shrewd Batilda did not know that her cats used the spare flat as an escape pad on the nights when she had a show. Her lead cat, Swink, had discovered where she kept the key. Pout Face and Julia Childs were happy to come along. As a joke, Swink nicknamed the bar "Lucy's Cat House," after the most docile of all the cats who lived in the building, a plump black cat with green eyes, who hardly moved from the sofa. If other cats could escape from their owners in the building, they joined the fun. They enjoyed themselves immensely. Fat Louie played the piano; Sasha played the drums; while neurotic Caesar looked at himself in the mirror. Self-centered, diabetic King Farouk complained that he was tired of eating bland chicken breasts and bored everyone with details of his love affairs. Sacco and Vanzetti played ball.

The *bawab* said, "So not only do the ghosts wear shoes, they meow?"

Also unbeknownst to Batilda, the landlord, and the landlord's cousin, the son of the landlord's cousin had made a copy of his mother's key. The son was an indifferent law student at Cairo University, who used the flat whenever he wanted to have sex with his girlfriend. He bragged so much about this flat that his friends began to pester him for the key so that they, too, could sleep with their girlfriends.

After Keiko turned on her rice cooker every day, she kept a log of sounds which she heard from the empty flat upstairs: Drilling. Knocking of the bedposts. Meowing. The sound of the piano and the drums. Clacking and clomping of shoes. Hooting. The television. Arabic music. She needed to track the noises to see if certain noises happened at certain times of the day. Or on certain days. Then she could present her evidence to the landlord.

"Aaah, so. Hanky panky upstairs. I think many different people have the key to that flat. So much noise. So much activity for an empty flat, aaah so. Doesn't make sense."

The landlord called the *bawab*. "Is this true?"

"She is crazy. I told you. She hears things. Makes up stories. Thinks everyone is out to get her. She even thinks someone is drilling a hole in the ceiling upstairs to spy on her."

"It would be better if her flat was empty," the landlord said. He was halfserious when he said this, because he did not mind the rent money. "Is she bothering the other tenants?" he asked.

"I don't think so," the *bawab* said.

"Well, then. She will not stay in Cairo forever," the landlord said.

The noise from the flat upstairs continued to nag Keiko. She had to have some quiet so she could study for her Arabic Linguistics exam. The university library was not an alternative place to study because it was noisy there, too. The continual ring of mobile phones. Raucous laughter.

This once, she dared herself to go upstairs and confront whoever was making noise.

To Keiko's surprise, Batilda opened the door. She was wearing a silk robe; it was only loosely tied. Keiko could see her breasts. Were they real? As if she is a Japanese courtesan, Keiko thought.

"Excuse me. So sorry," Keiko said, bowing. "The noise. I am trying to study."

"What is it, luv? What can I do for you? Do you want to take belly dancing lessons? Looks like you could lighten up a bit," Batilda said.

"Oh, no, I couldn't. Sorry to disturb you," she said, bowing, backing away from the door.

"We are watching my performance at last year's belly dancing festival. Don't you want to come in and see?"

"So sorry," Keiko said, backing further away. She was sure they were watching lurid pornography.

"Don't be ridiculous. We would love to have your company, wouldn't we, Big Boy?"

Keiko was terribly embarrassed. The muscular black man was not wearing a shirt. He was wearing a pair of flimsy shorts. She could not tell whether they were shorts or underwear.

He was so black. Keiko could not imagine sleeping with him. She wondered what it would be like.

So the flat was not empty! Keiko decided not to show the *bawab* her hand, completely.

"I know that salacious, immoral things are happening in that flat," Keiko told the *bawab*. (This was a good chance to use the old-fashioned Arabic vocabulary she was learning in her Arabic Linguistics class.)

"So the ghosts are now taking off their clothes?" the *bawab* asked.

Keiko became embarrassed and backed away from him, with her hand over her mouth. Most improper! Was he making suggestive remarks that she…? She turned and headed for the elevator. What kind of woman did he think she was? If the *bawab* continued to treat her with such sarcasm and disrespect, she might tell the landlord that he had forced his way into her apartment.

One week, Keiko realized she had not recorded any drilling in her log. (Queenie had gone back to LA to sell her costumes to Bette Midler. She no longer needed a place to do her sewing.)

Three days after, the clacking and clomping stopped. (The hole in Batilda's ceiling was repaired.)

Soon after, the meowing tapered off. (The cats did not use the place for a bar anymore; instead, they use Lorenzo the Italian's balcony as a place to hang out. It was simply easier to get there. Another bonus: someone in the building had thrown hundreds of mackerel cans on his balcony. The cats could have a mackerel cocktail party, rather than drinking vinegary Egyptian white wine.)

The thumping of the bedposts stopped altogether. (The landlord's cousin's son broke up with his girlfriend. She had taken the veil and refused to sleep with him anymore, unless he married her.)

Keiko told the *bawab*: "This is not a quiet building, like you say. Stories. Lies. There is something underneath. I know what I hear."

However, when Keiko went to record noises in her daily log, there was no longer anything to record. She was sure she had heard the drilling, the meowing, the clacking, the thumping of the bedposts, the piano music. Where had all the people gone?

The *bawab* shrugged. The less he said, the better. But he shouldn't have worried. No one believed Keiko. The foreigners in the building knew him to be a good, honest man.

When Keiko called the police in the neighborhood and complained that there was a prostitution ring in the building, they did not take her seriously. They knew the *bawab*. And they were not about to arrest Batilda, a popular belly dancer in the city.

They knew this *Yabaniyya*, Japanese woman, was crazy. Tired in her head.

3

A Little Honey and a Little Sunlight

Take, for joy's sake, from these hands of mine
A little honey and a little sunlight
As the bees of Persephone once ordered us to do.

—Osip Mandelstam, *Poem 116*, November 1920.

"GIVE ME THE SKINNY, DOC," I SAID, as if I were a real swashbuckler. Not the moment of reckoning, the last hurrah, the final goodbye, the diminishing hourglass. He was shining a slender flashlight, the size of a cigarillo, into my eyes. For a moment, I saw a wondrous rainbow. But when I blinked again, Dr Ivanov's violet blue eyes were scrutinizing me. Instead of my ratty blue jeans with the Grateful Dead patch over the bum, I was wearing a crinkled paper gown. Otherwise, completely starkers, except for my yellow boxers.

"I'm sorry, Joe," Doctor Ivanov said.

My mother gasped, "Jesus." Her old-fashioned black purse, which she usually carried with her to Mass, was hooked through her arm. Poor mom. Dad had dropped dead of a heart attack the year before when he was watching the final bout of *World-Wide Wrestling: The Masked Marvel vs. The Mighty Zorro.*

I giggled. I had smoked a joint, instead of wolfing down Lucky Charms cereal for breakfast.

"Too bad," I said, as if I had just lost a few bucks on a Maryland lottery ticket, not been given my notice. "Hey, Doctor Ivanov, what do you do for stress?"

Teachers tell students they are going to fail; bankers tell customers they don't have any money; traffic cops tell drivers they are going too fast. A doctor at the Johns Hopkins Medical Center has to say: Sor-ry, but tick-tock goes your clock. You have three months. Six months. Maybe a year. Even a trainload of gold wouldn't make up for having to deliver such bad news. I didn't enjoy shouting at my Egyptian students, "You're plagiarizers. Cheaters. I told you a thousand times to cite from your sources. You don't listen." Or did I?

"Marathons," Ivanov said.

"Maybe you ought to try something lighter. Say, ballroom dancing? Or spinning? You ride and ride on a stationary bike and don't go anywhere. Personally, I would love to learn the tango with Marilyn Monroe."

Neither my mom nor Doctor Ivanov laughed.

"Doc, do I have time to go back to Cairo for my guitar? A Washburn. My Dad gave it to me."

When I was not writing poems about Egypt, I was plucking out folk ballads.

Even in the spring, I had a queasy feeling that the *old boy* had returned. Your words begin to slur and you become a tadpole swimming in a thick, brackish pond, who is trying to come up for air, but can't. Can't. Can. It. I(t). Tah. Aah. Aah. Syllables dribble out of your mouth, like snot—a profound punishment for a poet. I felt so lousy in the last month before I left Cairo that I simply dropped wads of dirty Kleenex on the floor of my apartment. Left hundreds of McDonald's bags on my dining room table.

When there wasn't a single Rigatoni left in my apartment and I couldn't drag myself to the store, I called McDonalds for a Happy Meal. I overtipped those Egyptian slobs. "Buzz off, pal," I'd say, before I slammed the heavy wooden door in the delivery boy's face. Immediately I regretted it, when I saw the hurt look on the kid's face. Why was I behaving like such a lout? Considering what a runt I was (all one hundred and thirty-five pounds), I'm surprised no one punched me in the face. But like so many expatriate losers in Cairo, I enjoyed lording it over the locals.

Shortly after I wolfed down the Bargain Bonus, I barfed it up. Sometimes, I didn't make it to the toilet. Afterwards, I crawled into bed and closed my eyes and slid back into the brackish pond, a tadpole again. Curled up in the fetal position. Going back, back, back. Wished Mom would cover me with a blanket, like when I was a little kid. Make soup with homemade dumplings. I toyed with the idea of strangling myself with my Flintstones tie, but frankly, I didn't have the energy. Instead, I picked up Mandelstam's poems, which were dog-eared on my bedside table:

> Take, for joy's sake, from these hands of mine
> A little honey and sunlight
> As the bees of Persephone ordered us to do…

All we have left to us are kisses
Sheathed in down like tiny bees
That die as they scatter from the hive...

I should have visited those gargantuan statues at Abu Simbel in Egypt, a tribute to one man's desire for immortality. I should have lived every day as if it might be my absolute last.

After my return from Egypt, I was shuttled off to the Johns Hopkins Medical Center. The lights were too bright—atmosphere sanitized. I was bundled up in a crinkled paper gown, which made me feel like a blob of toilet paper. Doctors and nurses wear green, shapeless outfits with papery shoes, as if they are on the space shuttle. Everything was disposable. I longed for the chaos of Egypt. Emotion was messy, like the wads of Kleenex that littered the Egyptian apartment I left. I wished I could apologize to all those McDonald's delivery boys.

Ivanov was giving me the Latinate medical terms for *the old boy*. Why was he going through the motions? The correct medical terms were gratuitous information.

In the middle of this sleeper, I said, "Tell me, Doc, are you related to any famous ballet dancers?"

"Joe, please," my mother said. It was the exasperated voice she used when I lay down in the middle of *Piggly Wiggly* and threw a tantrum if I didn't get a *Hershey's Kiss* when I was five. Of course, there were worse things in life than not getting a Hershey's chocolate kiss at *Piggly Wiggly*. Feeling ugly. Never getting a single one of your poems published. Never having a girlfriend. Losing your job. You would never, ever, go to St Petersburg, the city of your dreams.

"This is the treatment we can offer," Doctor Ivanov was saying. Even though his voice sounded professional, his blue eyes were sad.

In a flash, I know I won't return to Cairo, even for my Washburn guitar. Never finish my project of learning all of Peter, Paul and Mary's ballads. Never finish my collection of Egyptian poems. Never have another party with my pals. I see myself in Cairo on the roof of my apartment building, plucking out "Puff the Magic Dragon Lived by the Sea" for my drinking buddies. There's Big Tulie, my two hundred-and-twenty-five-pound sidekick; Margarete, a good egg; Carter and Rachel, my pothead pals, old hippies. Carter shouts, "Yo, Joe, play Puff again." They lean against the satellite dishes, drinking Egyptian beer, Stella Local, out of the bottle. The sky is the color of lapis lazuli, and the

Pyramids perfect in the distance. A blue sky, so rare in Cairo. The sky was usually a tepid yellow from pollution. In March, the *khamaseen*, the dust storms, whirl through, blowing boards and crates off the roofs of buildings. From one of my Egyptian poems:

> October, farmers burned cane in faraway fields
> bitter smoke spirals and rises in this wild city
> I yearn for grainy, pink cotton candy at the Maryland
> County Fair...

No happy ending, dear reader. Sorry that as an author, albeit an unpublished one, I cannot deliver delusion. However, if you keep reading, I promise I won't give you too much sadness, although I can't promise absolute hilarity, either. (April Fool!) I barfed a lot. I dreamed Sylvia Plath was a champion boxer. Would she approve? This is funnier, though, than *The Bell Jar*. (Although that wouldn't be too hard!) Sometimes, I made patients laugh, by pretending to be a mummy. Other times, with my red bandana wrapped around my head, I was Snoop Doggy Dog. One day I got carried away, impersonating Osama bin Laden, and caused a national emergency on the floor.

"9/11. 9/11. 9/11. Terrorist on the floor," I shouted.

How ridiculous could that be? I was a one-hundred-pound shrimp sporting an IV, not a tall Saudi with a beard.

An Indian orderly, named Gopi, said in all seriousness, "Yaaar, Mr Pulaski, don't make jokes about 9/11. This is a very serious matter, isn't it?"

"I'll make jokes until I'm dead, pal," I said.

"I am sorry, Mr Pulaski," he said, wagging his head.

"Does that mean yes or no?" I asked.

"I must escort you back to your room, Mr Pulaski," he said, wagging his head again.

"I'm just like any Joe. Call me Joe, Gopi," I said.

But he never did. I was always Mr Pulaski.

Occasionally, I tried to write poems, but I could not thread the words together, each word a lone pearl.

One day Ivanov brought me a guitar, a Gibson. Mom was watching *As the World Turns*. (Helen was sleeping with her best friend's husband and had just discovered she was pregnant.)

"Wow! Incredible, Doc. Thanks," I said, admiring the rosewood on the back of the guitar. I plucked a string. My fingers burned to play.

For a minute, Ivanov smiled.

"Hey Doc, have you read Mandelstam?"

"Both the sea and Homer—all is moved by love.
To whom should I listen? Now Homer falls silent,
And a black sea, thunderous orator,
Breaks on my pillow with a roar."

"Very cool, Doc. An American doctor would never quote poetry. Most American doctors talk about golf. Their investments. How high their malpractice insurance is. They're bores."

Ivanov shrugged.

"Why did you come here?"

"You have heard of the American Dream?'"

"Nice sense of irony, Doc. But you know, no one would die for poetry here."

"Opportunities. Better jobs. We wanted a better life. Why, everyone wants to emigrate to America."

"So what? Have you seen how many street people we have on the streets of Baltimore? It's a fuckin' disgrace."

"Joe. Watch your language," Mom said.

"Hey, Mom. No big deal. The f-word," I said. "Am sure Doc has heard the word before."

"Sometimes, we miss home. Speaking Russian," he said, suddenly waving his hands, expansive. "On long winter nights, we drink vodka and eat caviar and sing with our friends…"

"Sure," I said, remembering the evening on the roof of my building in Cairo with Tulie and Carter and Rachel and Margarete.

"Do you have any kids, Doctor Ivanov?"

"One daughter. Natasha. She's eleven," he said.

"That's a nice age. Before they become teenagers," Mom said.

But I noticed she had one eye cocked on *As the World Turns*.

"Maybe you can play me a song, next time, eh?" Doctor Ivanov said, smiling briefly.

I was not fooled. His eyes were pensive.

One day shortly before my finale, I dreamed I was at the circus in St Petersburg. The ceiling is gilded with gold leaf, flecked with silver stars. No lions. No elephants. But acrobats soar through the air on trapezes. Their courage is breathtaking. Clowns are higher still, riding bicycles back and forth, as if they are tiny bees on a thin gold thread. At the same time, they are dropping sheets of blank paper into the vast net below. Are those my poems they are dropping into the air? Who will catch them?

> Take, for joy's sake, this wild gift of mine
> This uninviting desiccated necklet
> made of dead bees that once turned honey into sunlight.

Dear reader, there will be no artifacts. No sheaths of poems, wrapped in pink ribbons. No manuscript to be published posthumously. No *Confederacy of Dunces*. None of that glory and fame for me. Nyet. Nein.

Cut to the next scene in this script. I am nine feet under. Dry as dust. Departed. Deceased. Extinguished. Ex-tinct. (An aside: I gave away my heart, my eyes, my kidneys, and my liver for transplants. Needless to say, other parts weren't up for grabs. They chucked the rest. Along with the crinkled paper gowns and the disposable shoes.)

When Grandma Pulaski died, we had to chuck a lot of stuff from her attic. "Hey Mom, is there any reason we need to keep all these sequined purses?"

We laughed a lot about those sequined purses. Just how many sequined purses did you need in a lifetime?

Very cool were the rubber-banded rolls of hundred-dollar bills tucked everywhere. Underneath the cushions in her couch. In her panty hose. In jars of Ajax under the sink.

Mom let me keep the cash for helping her clear out the junk. I bought plenty of lids of pot and other goodies with Grandma Pulaski's stash. Pleasure, instead of insurance. So, don't save your acorns for the winter. By the time winter arrives, you might already be eaten by the big, bad wolf. (I preferred the three little oinks.) Thanks, Granny. When I was naughty, Granny P. chased me around with a pancake turner.

A professional packer, a lady named Zahra ("flower" in Arabic) with a mummified-looking face and a few teeth, will go through my stuff. Flotsam and jetsam. It is her job to pack people. Of course, my circumstances are rather odd in that I am not going on to the next job. But to the next state: Ca-da-ver.

In Cairo, the housing office will have to hire a locksmith to bust open the lock. (No one has a spare key, not even my close friends. I was manic about my privacy.)

Ladies and gentlemen, here is what was left:

Moldy Rigatoni with oregano and ant sauce still in the strainer in the sink. (Not my mother's homemade dumplings.)

Hundreds of packets of sugar in the kitchen drawer. (Zahra is a first-class forager. A scavenger. Read my lips: a crow, not a flower. Packets of sugar are enough to cause her orgasmic delight.)

Kitchen drawers: packets of plenty from McDonalds. Natural incense. Trick birthday candles. A lemon squeezer. Plastic Handiwrap. Ziploc bags. Receipts from Sun Lite cleaners. A bottle opener. One jar of unopened pepper. (Worth fighting over, eh? I was a lousy housekeeper.)

One very doleful microwave. (Never bothered to wipe up the coffee inside.)

They will spend two hours looking for a shortwave radio that I got at the Saint Anthony's charity sale in Baltimore for twenty bucks.

A Beatles suit. Very straight style. Blue. Chinese collar. A matted wig. (I wore to Tulies' Halloween costume party. I was a skinny Ringo Starr. *Love me like that, yeah, yeah, yeah.*)

Wide ties with goofy designs. Yellow elephants tiptoe through the tulips. *Scooby-Doo. The Flintstones.* Yabba Dabba Doo. The Sphinx. (Loved to be a goof.)

A pair of faded Levis, left on an unmade bed. Waist 30". *Grateful Dead* patch sewn on the back pocket. Who in this world could have such a tiny waist? Give to one of those skinny traffic cops in Cairo. (They won't.)

One very handsome guitar, leaning against the couch. (Dad gave me the Washburn the year before he died. His favorite Johnny Cash song: "I Walk the Line." We begged to differ on musical taste. And although he never understood the appeal of poetry, he loved music. Close enough?)

One well-thumbed copy of *Playboy.* Silicone boobs, pressed flat under the mattress. (Who will kiss me?)

> All we have left to us are kisses
> Sheathed in down like tiny bees.

A cigar box, bursting with promising poems-in-progress, written on matches from Harry's Pub, bills from Sun Lite cleaners, and Fourth of July napkins.

Passels of sheet music on a rickety music stand: Peter, Paul and Mary. The Beatles. Bob Dylan.

Books from my smallish library: Dostoyevsky's *Crime and Punishment. The Gambler and Other Stories.* Joseph Brodsky. Anna Akhmatova. Bulgakov's *The Master and Margarita.* The brilliant Russian poet, Osip Mandelstam. Sentenced to the Gulag and exile for his ode to Stalin:

> At ten feet away you can't hear the sound
> Of any words but "the wild man in the Kremlin,
> Slayer of peasants and soul-strangling gremlin."
> Each thick finger of his is as fat as a worm.

Mandelstam's wife, Nadezhda, and the poet Anna Akhmatova and friend, Natasha Shtempel, preserved his manuscript in pillowcases and saucepans. Reconstructed fragments from memory—the sacrifices of love and friendship. For the love of poetry. But who loves words in America? Clichés: the bottom line. *If you are not for us, you are against us.* After 9/11, Terror Twaddle. Fiddle-faddle. Tomfoolery. *George Sprat, a man who liked no lean.* W. was Humpty Dumpty who sat on the wall.

Publishing in America is a bazaar, like the Khan il-Khalili in Cairo. Where they sell hubbly bubblies and brass trays and alabaster statuettes and Muski glass and bottles of oily perfume. *Special deal for you, my friend.* But here's the deal—as a dead boxer of no great fame or notoriety, who is out of the ring, I can offer you this advice: Under no circumstances hang rejections on your fridge under a corny cow magnet.

Read this beauty, if you are suffering from insomnia:
From Tristia:

> … Who can know from the word goodbye
> What kind of parting is in store for us,
> What the cock's clamor promises
> When a light burns in the Acropolis…

Lights burning in the Acropolis. In Egypt, lights blink on and off. Keep a candle in a jelly jar in your kitchen. Just in case. Although it is more fun than you can imagine, to cook pasta in the dark!

I am no Osip Mandelstam. Nyet. Just plain Joe Pulaski. I have no girlfriend who will memorize my poems. Who will kiss me? No one will save my beauties in pillowcases and saucepans. (They are in the cigar box. A better conceit.)

But the university will ask Margarete, a friend of mine, to be present while they pack up my possessions. Witness to Zahra the mummy lady and her entourage. Witness to the flotsam. *Could you please sign here?* We did not snitch the McDonald's sugar, even though we lusted after it in our hearts. We did not filch the handsome guitar. We did not loot the Beatles suit. We did not filch the worthless microwave. We did not pocket the clock. (I tore off the hour hand for obvious reasons.) We did not hock the faded Levis. We did not purloin the Peter, Paul and Mary sheet music. We did not hook the Russian books. We did not pinch the poems in the cigar box.

We have an announcement to make:

There will be no memorial service, no wreaths of flowers, no chocolate sheet cake, no spaghetti casserole, no booze, but wait, wait, wait. Sssssh. I hear some murmuring. Listen:

"Poor Joe." (So what? Everyone's a poor Joe. Or a poor Mohammed, if you are in Egypt.)

"He must have suffered." (You don't know the half of it. I mean, that adage about walking in someone's shoes is garbage, unless you have an imagination.)

"Didn't he write a poem for you?"

(From one of my poems: *Phallic column in a stone-pit*
below the level of the river on Roda Island
measures river's rise and good fortune for the Nile Valley…)

"His behavior was outrageous." (So, I wasn't dull?)

"I just couldn't renew his contract. His behavior was so unpredictable." (I agree with the boss, even if she wore the most ridiculous high heels. It was stupid to shout at the top of my lungs at a security guard at the Ramses Hilton. I don't know why I took my class to the Ramses Hilton mall. Er, no lesson plan?)

From one of my poems: "*Your last minutes are gold dragoons*
you lasso jokes and swagger like a cowboy…"

What isn't sent to my parents in neat boxes, but tossed in a green garbage bag: packets of sugar, mustard, mayonnaise, ketchup, a checkered lunchbox without a latch, a cracked coffee thermos, rusty wire in the form of a figure eight, a box of Band-Aids and a giant jar of orange-flavored Tums. Who doesn't suffer from heartburn?

Margarete will lug all that detritus down the stairs and give it to the *bawab*, the porter of our building. He is as happy as if someone has given him a big Chevy. Ashraf will say, "Iowa." Yes, in Arabic, sounds like the state, Iowa. I only learned "Aiwa," and "Laaaah", which means, "No." Just say No to Arabic. Yes to Russian. Once I tried to tell Ashraf, the *bawab*, "Look, pal, I'm fluent in Russian." But he just looked baffled. How to explain: I never really wanted to live in Egypt.

The housing office sent the handsome guitar home. We're late for a very important date. *Could you please sign here?*

It will be at least a year before Mom will sift through the flotsam. I didn't win any trophies in high school, no letter jacket, no prizes. I was not a macho jock with sinewy muscles and wide shoulders. Not the Most Athletic. Not the Most Handsome. Not the Most Popular. Not the Most Likely to Succeed. However, Mom had framed the certificate with the gold seal from the National Council of English Teachers. A literary prize, for a short story I called "*The Loser*," about a pimple-faced pipsqueak who was so lonely he read Yeats' "*The Second Coming*" to his pet turtle, Jimmy Hoffa. Mrs Sweetman, my eleventh-grade English teacher, had said, "Joe, you're so talented. You ought to write. I see great things for you in the future." Her idealism and kindness were intoxicating. I started dreaming about taking down her silky, brown hair from the small knot at the back of her neck.

I was even mean to my cat, Frankie Kafka. Although maybe *the old boy* affected my behavior more than even I might admit. Was *the Joker* pressing on my kingpin, my wizard, my Einstein? Making me act like a jerk?

I wasn't even nice before I got sick the first time. And don't think I'm telling you because I'm afraid of God. Even though we're Polish Catholics and we had purgatory crammed down our throats at that crummy school, Saint Anthony's, God is for the buzzards. I believe in Nothingness, the Existential Void, the Blank. Camus is my man. After Mandelstam, of course.

The Peace Corps sent me home from Uzbekistan. I was so drunk on vodka that I picked a fight with a border guard. I broke his thumb. He broke mine, too. Tit for tat.

I always hung with a guy named Big Tulie in Cairo. (Yeah, he's white. Last name is Tulip.) Big dude. And everyone used to call us Mutt and Jeff. Don't get me wrong, he wasn't dumb. He just wasn't as sharp as I was. He thought Steinbeck was one of the greatest writers of all time. And every time we had passed the tenth Stella beer, he brought it up to needle me. "You don't know shit about writing. You're a fraud, pal," I said. I threw beer in his face and stormed out of the Last Pyramid Bar.

Another thing: we had an environmental nut, Dr Gary, in our building, who went loopy about the water in the Nile. He even dumped a ton of his contaminated fish at the gate of the university. They hauled him away to the loony bin. I used to call him up and say in an Egyptian accent, "Fuck you, mister."

Here's the good me:

I saved a street cat with a gouged-out eye.

I used to give a few pounds every day to the one-legged beggar on Kasr el-Aini street. Granted, I didn't say "God help you," in Arabic, but mean stuff, like, "Hey man, why don't you buy yourself a peg leg?"

I listened to Biljana wail when her diabetic cat, Rumi, died. Biljana was a goofy Serbian painter who lived on the top floor. (Even though I was tempted to tell her there was no Cat Heaven, I did not.)

The day before I left Cairo, I jerked off in front of my she-cat, Frankie. I was remembering the doughy middle-aged woman from my host family in Uzbekistan. Boy, was I surprised when she came in my room in the middle of the night and went down on me. I am thirty and I have never really had a girlfriend. No Nadezhda for me. (Her name means Hope in Russian. Good, eh?)

Afterwards, I opened the kitchen door. "Go," I said. Frankie looked at me, as if she were surprised.

When she refused to go, I stomped on her tail.

"Find true love," I said.

I wandered into the bathroom and looked at myself in the mirror. A few black whiskers sprouted from my chin. I looked like a stray. "Loser," I said, examining my whiskers. Didn't even have full beard. I wiped the tears away with my hand. Even my fingers were slender. Looked feminine.

But I heard my high-school English teacher's voice, Mrs Sweetman. She was saying, "Joe, you're so talented." What happened to her after she moved away? Was she still alive? How was it that people who were so important to us just slipped out of our lives?

That night I had boiled Rigatoni for my last supper. When the Egyptian driver, Hassan, came, I wasn't packed. I thought I would be leaving the following night. In the middle of our row, the electricity went out. He shone a flashlight on my ticket; he was right. He was surprised when I didn't take a suitcase. "Bags?" he said. "No bags? No *shunot*."

"No *shunot*, pal," I said, slamming the door to my apartment, as hard as I could. On the way to the airport, he didn't say a word. But when he left me next to the road, he said, "*Terouh wi teegi bessalama*. May you go and come back safely, Mr Joe."

I felt my eyes well up with tears. Why was I crying? I didn't know the guy. He was peaceful. I was not.

But suddenly, Ivanov was shining a light in my eyes. I was in the hospital. Not Egypt.

"You worry too much, Doc. You should take up ballroom dancing."

Did I say that? Or was that another time? I have to get a new punch line for the ole Doc.

"Can you hear me, Joe?" Ivanov was saying.

But I am far away, in the Tsarkoe Selo, the imperial palace designed by Rastrelli for Tsarina Elizabeth. I am gluing amber panels back onto the walls in the Amber Room. And no, the Germans didn't abscond with the amber during WWII. The Russians desecrated their own palace and stole the loot. I am reciting Mandelstam, while I glue the amber panels back onto the walls of the palace:

> Take, for joy's sake, from these hands of mine
> a little honey and a little sunlight...

It is a noble project, renovating the Amber Room. As noble as writing poetry that will never be published. As noble as playing ballads, however imperfect, on the guitar for my friends in Cairo. As noble as listening to a loony Serbian woman who is sad because her cat died.

Mom is handing me a panel of amber. I am saying. "Don't be sad, Mom. Take this necklace of dried bees. Once upon a time, those bees turned honey into sunlight. I promise you. This necklace is much finer than one of Grandma Pulaski's sequined purses."

But I cannot speak now, the syllables won't form, even though I hear my own poetry:

> The eye of exile is violet blue, my dear friend
> Nostalgia defies reason, as it should.
> The sweetness of your gift, a guitar, rich rosewood.
> Since of course, you knew
> my fingers would refuse…

Bubbles of oxygen float to the surface of the brackish pond, as if they are in slow motion. One of the amber panels has fallen to the bottom of the pond. I want to touch the luminous amber. I feel light and free. Almost weightless.

For Jim Schultz

4

Taken Hostage by the Ugly Duck

THE DAY AFTER HODA WAS HIT IN the ear with a rotten egg thrown by her British neighbor, she adopted a blue heron. Complaining to her friends had not been enough, complaining to the landlord and the *bawab* had not been enough, complaining to her husband had not been enough. She had never suffered such humiliation! She had marched to the Friday bird market and bought the bird with the harshest call. The terrible yawing would surely torment her British neighbor, whom she had nicknamed "The Ugly Duck." He was a balding man in his late fifties with spindly legs.

When she came home with the enormous bird at three o'clock in the afternoon, her husband, Fahmy, who was still in his pajamas, said, "Don't you usually pluck your chin hairs on Fridays?"

Hoda was too busy now, watching the Ugly Duck, to waste her time on vanity. She and Fahmy rarely had sex anymore. And when they did, it was a lackluster and cursory affair; he rolled off her quickly and starting picking his teeth.

Every Friday, while she was looking in her hand mirror, plucking her chin hairs, she sneaked a glance behind her at the Ugly Duck in the building opposite hers. On warm days he often strutted nude on his balcony, with a gaggle of young Egyptian men. Where was his wife? Such an unashamed parading of sensuality enraged her. When she had finished watching the Ugly Duck and his entourage, she prayed and recited the Quran in front of the sheikh on the television.

Now, her husband, Fahmy, glared at the blue heron. "Why didn't you adopt a kitten? There are plenty around the neighborhood," he said.

"You hate cats," Hoda said. She had begged him to have a cat for years, but he always refused.

"The heron is going to ruin our gold furniture," Fahmy said.

"Maybe the bird will turn into a cat."

"Herons eat fish. This isn't a very practical pet. Where are we going to keep him? With Amir here, we have hardly any space," Fahmy complained.

"Amir will have to find another place to live," Hoda said. "He is thirty-five years old."

"But Hoda, he's not married. You're going to give his room to a bird?"

Hoda was transforming. Internally, she had not changed an inch for years. However, two events had happened to distract her from her persistent delight in matchmaking and speculations about the price of gold: the day her precious Amir had slapped her in the face because he couldn't watch *il-Limbi*. Who would marry him? He was a fat lug, who sprawled out on her marital bed, watching television, hour after hour. She and Fahmy had spent thousands of pounds on private lessons to get him through the faculty of Engineering at Cairo University, but he had never gotten a job. Every presentable girl she had brought to the house had left in tears.

But even worse than her son Amir was the Ugly Duck, in the building across the way, who taunted her with his unnatural, lascivious sexuality: the obscene gestures, the hooting, the loud, raucous music. Some singer always whined, *"Diggin' the dancin' queen."* On Fridays, the young Egyptian boys would take turns, kneeling in front of the Ugly Duck, sucking his thing. He sat, legs splayed open, as if he were a king. His eyes were closed.

Why didn't anyone in the neighborhood call the police?

Once the Ugly Duck mooned her with his hairy haunches when she was watching. Another time, he whipped his thing out and sprayed it at her. She flicked on the bright lights of her chandelier, which were almost as strong as police searchlights.

There were no screens on her windows. Late every night, she hung out the window, watching the Ugly Duck's apartment. Egyptian soap operas were a bore compared to the nightly scenarios on the Ugly Duck's balcony.

A young man with beautiful black curly hair appeared the most frequently on the Ugly Duck's balcony. He wore royal blue turtlenecks and tight blue jeans. She guessed he was about seventeen and she nicknamed him *Faris*, Knight. She wondered what it would be like to have such an energetic sexual partner. Her only sexual partner had been Fahmy and he was lethargic and unoriginal. She had heard from her women friends that there were many other variations that would increase pleasure.

Now instead of her son lounging on her marital bed, the blue heron yawed at Egyptian toothpaste commercials, or a veiled woman in a pink headscarf putting laundry into the washing machine.

One day, after a stormy row with the blue heron over a pillow, Amir had suddenly moved out and settled with his paternal aunt, who had no children. Undeterred, the heron soon learned how to turn the television on and off. And he even asserted his rights to the large marital bed. He flapped his wings between Hoda and Fahmy.

Naturally, they quarrelled. Fahmy complained about the bird in his bed. He complained about the smell of rancid fish in his flat. He complained about the bird feathers in his dresser drawers. The smell of bird shit permeated the flat; no amount of cheap Egyptian cologne could dispel it. He complained that she was not making stuffed squash or béchamel pasta for him anymore.

"You're jealous of the blue heron?" Hoda said. She was incredulous.

"You don't love the blue heron," Fahmy said. "You *hate* our British neighbor."

Of course, she relished the intensity of her feud with the Ugly Duck. She enjoyed hating the Ugly Duck, much more than loving a man or even the blue heron. Could love be this intense, too?

The Ugly Duck retaliated by buying a colorful Amazonian parrot. He taught it to say things in English, like:

"You can dance. You can jive."

Did he mean with her?
Or, "*Wait a minute, Mr Postman.*"
The Postman?
Or, "*I'm on top of the world looking down on creation.*"
The blue heron and the giant parrot competed yawing in the cul-de-sac. The cawing of the birds muted the call to prayer, the squealing car horns, and the wails of cats in heat.

The tall, slim *bawab* from Aswan reported to her: "All the neighbors are complaining. The bird calls are terrible. Nobody can bear the noise. It's even louder than the call to prayer."

As if the parrot had overheard their conversation, he even started to imitate the call to prayer. "*Allahu Akbar.*"

The parrot alternated "*Allahu Akbar*" with "*Wait a minute, Mr Postman*" or "*You can dance. You can jive.*"

The sheikh at the neighborhood mosque complained to the *bawab*, who then told the Egyptian landlord in America, Dr Hossam, about the blasphemous parrot. The parrot's call, "*Allahu Akbar,*" was quashing the muezzin's call, which was amplified to screeching point. This colorful parrot was the work of the devil. The Israelis had planted the parrot in Garden City to destroy the missionary spirit of this small neighborhood mosque.

The landlord, a successful surgeon, began to dread making the frequent, expensive phone calls to Egypt, and listening to the complaints about the blasphemous parrot at the British man's apartment in his building.

He called the sheikh at the mosque himself, directly. "I mean no disrespect, Sheikh Abdou," he said. "Do you really think the Israelis would waste their time on a little mosque in Garden City?"

"Never underestimate the power of the Zionists," Sheikh Abdou said, cryptically.

"Maybe the parrot was planted by the Copts in the neighborhood. There's a Coptic Orthodox church just right around the corner from the mosque," Dr Hossam said, offering another conspiratorial explanation.

"I never thought of that," Sheikh Abdou said.

"Haven't they been asking you to turn down the volume at Friday prayers for the last five years?"

"Well, yes…" Sheikh Abdou said.

Dr Hossam promised he would call the British man about the blasphemous parrot, but because of his busy work schedule at the medical school, he forgot. He was teaching wholesome blonde American medical students from the Midwest how to do tummy tucks and boob jobs.

One night, the atmosphere at the Ugly Duck's apartment changed. Instead of wild, ecstatic couplings on the balcony, Hoda heard shouting. Bodies being slammed against walls. The crunching of bones. Cursing. *Motherfucker! Cunt!*

The rage in these words was more terrible than the parrot's monotonous calls, "*Diggin' the dancin' queen.*"

The next time Amir came to lunch, she asked, "What does 'cunt' mean?"

He almost choked on his fried drumstick. "Why do you want to know?"

"No reason," she said, not wanting to discuss the Ugly Duck with her son. Had Amir spurned the idea of marriage because he was like the Ugly Duck? She pushed this unpleasant thought out of her mind—it wasn't natural.

More and more, the Ugly Duck sat on the balcony alone, a ragged ice pack on his bruised face. He was no longer the king on his throne. He seemed as pitiful as a one-legged beggar on Kasr el-Aini street. But hadn't the Ugly Duck brought this upon himself? God's punishment for his depraved behavior?

If the Ugly Duck saw her staring at him, he shouted, "Stick it up your ass, sister." He made a gesture with his hand; she was sure it meant something dirty.

Soon after, the loud Amazonian parrot disappeared.

Hoda thought the landlord had called from America, to tell the Ugly Duck that he had to get rid of the parrot, but the *bawab* offered another explanation:

"The Ugly Duck gave all his money to the handsome young boy with the curly hair. The Ugly Duck doesn't even have a piaster for a bean sandwich. He sold the parrot to a local pet shop for grocery money."

"But isn't he working as a financial advisor? Doesn't he have a good salary?" she asked.

Who were these foreigners who came to Cairo?

Hoda hinted to the *bawab* that she would tip him extra for information about the Ugly Duck. He obliged her with rumors, his own speculations, and the occasional fact: she heard that the Ugly Duck's appetite was so voracious that he had sex with the thin peasant guards who sat guarding the embassies in the neighborhood. She heard that the Ugly Duck propositioned a hustler in the neighborhood. He was beaten up and tied to a chair and robbed of thousands of British pounds. Why was he keeping so much cash at home? For a week, she didn't see the Ugly Duck.

Had he moved?

No one seemed to know.

Every night she stayed up late until the early hours of the morning, hoping for a glimpse of the Ugly Duck on his balcony. Hoda was concerned. Had something terrible happened to the Ugly Duck? Had one of the Ugly Duck's lovers taken revenge upon him?

"I think the Ugly Duck has been murdered," Hoda told her husband.

"Your whole life has been taken hostage by our foreign neighbor," Fahmy said. "Can't you think about something else? You are neglecting your wifely duties."

He certainly did not mean sex, but the wondrous creation of béchamel pasta. She had no time to cook. She had to find out what happened to the Ugly Duck. Did she know anyone, anyone at all who worked at the foreign bank?

Although they weren't close anymore, Hoda had a childhood friend, Thoraya, who was a secretary at that foreign bank. When Thoraya came over for tea, she droned on about the achievements of her children, who had immigrated to Cleveland, Ohio, and were driving Toyota Land Cruisers. Of course, this annoyed Hoda and reminded her that her own son was doing nothing except watching *il-Limbi* comedies, even at his aunt's flat. She listened for three hours to the tiniest mundane details about Thoraya's grandchildren, too. At last, Hoda ventured, "We have a neighbor who works at your bank."

She didn't even know the Ugly Duck's name.

Thoraya yawned, like an overfed cat. "I can't keep all these foreign advisors straight. They come. They go."

"I think something terrible might have happened to him. He just disappeared," Hoda said.

"He probably left the country. Was he a special friend of yours?" Thoraya asked, giving her a wink.

Hoda was alarmed—Thoraya could not keep her mouth shut.

"Not really," Hoda said, trying to sound casual.

"You know, British people are not like us. They're not sentimental. They're cold," Thoraya said. "Listen, I've enjoyed seeing you, but I have to go. Moustafa wants calf-feet stew for lunch. You know how much time that dish takes."

Hoda feigned a laugh. "Yes, these men take up all our time." All those hours with smug Thoraya had been a dead end.

The next day, the *bawab* reported that the Ugly Duck had moved to another flat in Garden City. Two days later, he told her that the Ugly Duck had returned to England.

She became suspicious. Suppose the *bawab* had been telling her stories the entire time?

"How can the Ugly Duck be in Cairo and England at the same time?"

The *bawab* swore that he had seen the Ugly Duck riding in a taxi, late one night, two large suitcases tied to the roof of the car.

After the summer, another man moved into the Ugly Duck's flat. The new man never opened the windows in his flat and the curtains were always drawn.

Hoda even bought an expensive pair of binoculars, but it did her no good. She could not see through the heavy brown curtains. It was just not the same. This new man was dull compared to the Ugly Duck.

Once the new man with the goatee appeared on the balcony. Was he Spanish? Italian? Why had the man with the goatee come to Cairo? Did he like young boys like the Ugly Duck?

Another time, the new man flung open the doors to his balcony and noticed the empty parrot cage. He started to sweep up the sand and bird shit on his balcony, but went back inside after five minutes of sweeping. Lazy boy! Just like Amir. The pink broom leaned against the shutters for weeks. Unlike the Ugly Duck, he never sat on the balcony. His flat was shut like a tight bubble. The empty parrot cage swung in the wind. She missed the laughter and loud music from the Ugly Duck's days. What were the songs? She sang, "*You can dance. You can jive.*"

One Friday, when she was staring over at the empty balcony, Fahmy said, "Now that our British neighbor is gone, you can get rid of the blue heron."

"No," Hoda said.

"If you don't get rid of the bird, I'll divorce you," Fahmy said, in a menacing voice.

She yawned and ignored the threat.

Three days later, the blue heron disappeared.

She tore apart her apartment, searching for the bird. In every closet. In all the laundry baskets. Under every bed. But why would the blue heron hide, when he had reclined so comfortably on her bed?

The heron must have flown. Nothing remained except for the smell of fish, the bird droppings, and feathers.

She even dug through the bottom of the garbage chute. She found: empty plastic mineral water bottles, Domino's pizza boxes, bits of string, dead red roses, the rinds from honeydew melons, coffee grounds. She had almost given up when she found the heron, wrapped in a paper bag from a Lebanese restaurant. There he was, buried with white plastic containers of eggplant and hummus. Red pomegranate oil dripped into his eyes. *Ya meskeen.* Poor thing!

Someone had strangled him. He would no longer yaw. She was stunned that someone had murdered the bird. At the same time, she did not wish for him to return to life. Fahmy was right. She had never really loved the blue heron, but had bought him for revenge. But even revenge against the Ugly Duck had turned into something else.

She used the paper bag as a shroud to cover the limp face of the blue heron. She even said a prayer for him.

"Someone killed my bird," Hoda told the *bawab.*

He was surprised. "Really? I thought he would live forever."

"Do you know who killed him?"

"Hard to say," the *bawab* said, scratching his chin. "Might be someone in your family. Might be one of your neighbors. Excuse me for saying this, but the noise was unbearable."

Hoda climbed the stairs instead of taking the cage-like elevator, which somehow reminded her of the Ugly Duck's cage for his parrot. Her husband, Fahmy, was not at home. She opened the door to her bedroom and looked in. A few of the blue heron's feathers had settled into the center of their marital bed, where the bed sagged. She was glad that Amir was not lounging there. Waiting to be served his tea, like a pasha. She had spoiled him. Things might have been different if she had had another child. But she would never forget the joy she had felt when he was born. He was so tiny, so vulnerable. Such a happy baby! When he smiled, there was a cute dimple on his chin. She could never resist kissing him on the chin.

That was a long time ago.

5

Fatma's New Teeth

"THAT'S IT, POPPY," VARTAN, MY ARMENIAN DENTIST, said, "not much longer, Poppy," spraying water into the hole of my tooth.

Since I was his captive I couldn't tell him, "My name is Mary Beth." He had opened the tooth to drain the abscess. Every time I visited his office he put in a tiny swab of medicated cotton and then sniffed it to see if the smell was "bad." Shortly after he first drilled the hole the tooth broke when I was trying to crack open a pistachio nut.

I made countless trips to Vartan Migoian, with his shock of snow-white hair and black bushy eyebrows, the year after 9/11. Newspaper headlines echoed in my head: FLIGHT PATH OF FOUR HIJACKED PLANES. To get there I had to pick my way through piles of trash and mewling feral cats, dodge groups of men with greasy hands working on chewed-up Chevrolets, sidestep others playing backgammon on the sidewalk. His office was in a gloomy building across from a café where the regulars sucked on their hookahs as if it were opium. The toothless *bawab*, the gatekeeper squatting in front of the building, leered at me with olive-green eyes. "Madam," he said, gesturing toward the dirty stairs as if I were going up to a brothel. An Egyptian colleague had cornered me at the elevator after 9/11: "Did you know all the Jews in the World Trade Center were warned before the attack? They stayed home."

As I picked my way up the dark dirty stairs, I wished I could have stayed home. I didn't trust the rickety elevator. ELEVATORS: DISASTER WITHIN DISASTER. In bright red letters above one door: "Import/Export. Automobile Parts." The door was open, but there wasn't even a desk inside.

"This won't hurt a bit, Poppy, he said, holding a savage-looking metal contraption. I felt as if I were a victim in a bad Frankenstein movie.

9/11 COMMISSION REPORT WARNS OF BIOLOGICAL THREAT.

At least I had a full set of teeth, unlike my maid, Fatma. We all knew Fatma would feel much better about herself if she had a set of new teeth. When she smiled she looked like a jack-o'lantern. She had served us loyally for years, even though she once put a backgammon set in Oliver's washing machine. And that's not counting the broken sherry glasses from Prague, the cracked Fabergé eggs, and the shattered *mashrebeyya*, mother-of-pearl inlay mirror. If she didn't slap at the dust with her dirty rags, sweep the balcony, beat the carpets, change the sheets, order the groceries from the Blue Nile, we would have had to do it ourselves.

Better to have an honest maid with every human frailty under the sun than a thief. You have to be tolerant and accommodating. That's what you learn about the locals after so many years in Cairo: real accommodation. When I was covering the civil war in Beirut, I used to advise rookie journalists, "Don't run into a mob. Wear comfortable shoes. Tie your shoelaces. Most importantly, carry extra packs of cigarettes." You could always get through a militia checkpoint if you offered the guard a cigarette. PLO. Phalanges. Israelis. It didn't matter; all those miserable soldiers were always longing for a cig, especially in the winter—they never resisted that temptation.

AIRPORTS NEED HELP. HOMELAND SECURITY ADMINISTRATION CREATED.

If we could pool a nest egg to help Khaled, the man who parked cars next to our building, to get his taxi repaired, then we had to help Fatma who is missing almost all her front teeth. After I came up with the idea, it took a month to coordinate our all schedules for a meeting. Oliver was correcting the proofs for his new book, *A Field Guide to the Mammals of Egypt*. Louise was playing in a tennis tournament at the Gezira Club—the times for matches varied from day to day and changed sometimes in the course of an hour. Mary rode her horse at the Sakkara Club on Tuesday and Thursday; Monday and Wednesday she had a standing appointment at Dr Wafik's for a cat with feline leukemia.

Vartan barked orders in Arabic to his assistants, Mustafa and the woman who covered her head with a pink veil, Zahra. She looked like a carnation; the lovely pink material around her head went well with the starched white lab coat.

Zahra handed Vartan a thin pencil pick. Vartan roared something in Arabic. Stupid? No! No! Quickly, Mustafa produced a set of gargantuan, shiny pliers.

"What are you going to use those for?" I asked.

9/11: GETTING OUT ALIVE.

"I have to break off the tooth, Poppy. Are you ready? This won't hurt a bit. Do you feel anything where I gave you the shot?"

He didn't wait for an answer, just plunged the pliers into my mouth. I closed my eyes: better not to know.

WHY WAS CIA UNPREPARED FOR 9/11 ATTACK?

"Rinse, Poppy!" Vartan said. "You see, it wasn't so bad."

I watched my blood and spit swirl down the white basin. Zahra offered me a Kleenex to wipe the residue from my lips.

US HAS BLOOD ON HER HANDS. SANCTIONS. INFANT MORTALITY RATE IN IRAQ AT 40%.

Vartan deposited the shard of tooth in a jar with the delight of a child who has caught a firefly.

"I have others," he said. "Would you like to see Omar Sharif's?"

MORE SURVIVORS' TALES. SEE US NEWS AND WORLD REPORT.

"Omar Sharif is your patient?"

"We play bridge together. He's a gambler. Not like me. I'm very cautious. I wouldn't risk a single piastre of my hard-earned money. Once, the group insisted that I put something down to bet. I gave them one year's worth of free visits to my clinic."

"What's he like?" I asked. "I loved *Dr Zhivago*. Sharif was so handsome."

"Charming, Poppy. Perfectly charming. But he's a terrible loser. He is miserable when he loses."

"Most men hate to lose."

A famous journalist once blew cigarette smoke in my face at the Ali Baba Bar in Beirut after I had scooped him on the Flight 847 story. The Organization for the Oppressed of the Earth, a Lebanese group, had hijacked the plane. They flew it to Beirut, then to Algiers and back to Beirut, again to Algiers and back again a third time to Beirut.

Vartan put Omar Sharif's tooth back in the jar. "That solves the mystery."

MANY PIECES OF PUZZLE FROM 9/11 SOLVED. STILL QUESTIONS LINGER.

"The root was dead because the tooth was cracked. That's why you didn't have any pain. But you had that bump in your gums. That was your body trying to tell you something was wrong."

EUROPEANS POINT TO US FOREIGN POLICY AFTER 9/11.

Our group met at the Nile Hilton swimming pool to discuss Fatma's new teeth. Much more pleasant than lying in a drab green dentist's chair, my mouth stuffed with bloody cotton. Luxuriant green trees hung over the hotel garden. With a perfect blue sky and cheerful sun shining down upon us, how could we not feel optimistic? Egyptian waiters ran to and fro adjusting the wide-brimmed yellow umbrellas that looked like floppy summer hats lying on the trimmed green lawn.

We all knew that Fatma would look much younger and more attractive with a set of new teeth. It was hard to believe she was only forty. But she had had a hard life. Poor nutrition. Illiterate. A husband who poked out her eye with a knife and then deserted her. She raised three daughters by herself and lived in a tiny apartment in Imbaba, the slums, on the other side of the Nile.

At our first meeting the group fanned around me in the shallow end of the pool like baby ducks. I lay against the pool's edge, sipping my drink.

"I've never understood why Fatma doesn't wear a patch over her eye," Mary said, making the motion of the breast stroke with her wrinkled arms. Did someone say she used to be an aerobics instructor?

"I think the eye is gone for good," Oliver said, bobbing up and down like he was on a pogo stick.

"Her husband poked it out with a knife," I said. Most men were bastards. My husband had gambled away every cent of my salary at *The Houston Chronicle*.

BUSH SAYS TERRORISTS WILL PAY.

"That might just be hearsay," Oliver said.

Ever rational, the Brit with his Cambridge degree, tiny waist, and bird-like legs.

"I have a cat missing an eye," Mary said." I named her Pirate. She has such a sweet temperament."

"We're talking about a human being," I said.

"Shouldn't we ask Fatma if she *wants* new teeth?" Louise asked, smoothing back her thick wet hair.

As a veteran journalist, I always caution, "Pick your translator wisely."

Sometimes you'll find that the translator skews the message to suit their own agenda. Choosing Louise as a translator for our project was a mistake. Not only did she think she was Michelle Pfeiffer in her hot pink two-piece bathing suit, she was a big know-it-all.

"Yes, shouldn't we find out if Fatma *wants* new teeth?" Oliver echoed, still bobbing up and down.

"Why wouldn't she want new teeth?" I said, taking a sip of white wine. "Waiter! I need ice! Ice!"

We were giving Fatma something permanent, something that would improve the quality of her life.

Vartan was saying, "If you don't floss and gargle with salt water and use hydrogen peroxide, you could make your periodontal problems worse. If you do your homework, Poppy, you won't need scaling. That will cost you a fortune."

He held up a plastic model of a set of teeth. With a bulbous forefinger he pointed to the gum line.

"There is an acceptable gum line. Too far below is not good."

Was that how Fatma had lost her teeth? Poor hygiene with disastrous results?

RUDEMAN/HART REPORT: NEXT ATTACK COULD CAUSE GREATER CASUALTIES IN AMERICA

Vartan was often peevish with Muhammad and Zahra. When Muhammad and Zahra left the room, he said, "If you're too soft with them, they take advantage."

Vartan once told me how he came to Egypt from Palestine after the 1967 war. His father was a jeweler and had stayed behind in the West Bank. Vartan was fluent in Armenian, Arabic, English, and French. He could probably pinch-hit in Italian too.

"Do you speak French?" he asked one day when my mouth was full.

"Ah, yes. Excuse me for saying, Poppy, but the Americans and the French are the worst at learning languages," he said, peering into my mouth.

"*Hola, que tal?*" Seventh-grade Spanish with Mrs Weed. The Pablo-and-Maria dialogue.

I wanted to say, but couldn't because his fingers were in my mouth, that learning Spanish was far more practical in the US.

US MILITARY IN DESPERATE NEED OF ARABIC SPEAKERS.

Of course, if my workload with the student newspaper had not been so heavy, I would have worked more on my Arabic. I knew my numbers and a few amenities: peace, good morning, carnation, a thousand thanks.

Since Louise knew the most Arabic in our group, she was delegated the task of speaking to Fatma. She reported back that Fatma had said it was "a beautiful idea." *Fikra jameela.* "Maybe she doesn't want to offend us."

A beautiful idea—that was enough for me.

That was how Vartan had described my new tooth. "I will make you a beautiful new tooth out of acrylic, as if I'm an artist. I'll use acrylic because it's much cheaper than porcelain."

Mustafa filled out a card for me. "Miss Mary Beth," he wrote alongside, "Please Advice Twenty Hours Before Cancellation." For crying out loud, why didn't Vartan proof his appointment cards?

"Should I pay now?"

"No," Mustafa said. "Next time."

"But I think maybe she was being diplomatic," Louise said. "Like she didn't want to offend us."

BUSH DECLARES: IF YOU ARE NOT WITH US, YOU ARE AGAINST US.

Completely unrelated to my broken tooth, I split an old filling on one of my back molars when I was chewing on a piece of sesame candy, spitting out tiny bits of metal afterwards.

On the way to Vartan's I passed cars with open hoods like patients with their jaws open double-parked on the crowded street. Loops of heavy tires decorated the pavement. A single bulb beamed from underneath a purple-colored Fiat. A small boy hawked limes in front of Pirelli Tires, my landmark for Vartan's: turn right at the next street after. The smell of garlic was overpowering. Were mechanics wolfing down *koshari*, Egyptian-style spaghetti with lentils and rice, in between engine jobs? Shiny new mufflers hung outside one shop like slabs of beef.

IRAQI BABIES DIE FROM LACK OF MILK. POOR NUTRITION.

Vartan poured liquid metal into a small mortar and pestle and then snapped his fingers at Mustafa. On cue, Mustafa turned on the water.

After he finished the filling he said, "Now, Poppy, make sure you wait two hours before you eat. You can't feel your tongue. You could bite it off!"

I wondered if I did bite off my tongue whether he would pop it into a jar of formaldehyde for his collection.

Mustafa again said, "No charge." I became suspicious. Why was he being so generous?

Later that evening when I tried to eat lentil soup, it dribbled down the side of my numb, heavy cheek. Did Fatma only eat mashed potatoes and beans with her limited dental capacity? Wouldn't she be happier if she could chew?

Once we decided to get Fatma new teeth, we had to choose between implants and dentures. I asked Oliver if he would research prices, but he had been asked to go on a field trip by the Egyptian Environmental Ministry to search for gazelles in the Western Desert, who were near extinction. Mary volunteered, but then reneged.

In the end, it was easier for me to do the research myself. Luckily, I met an American-educated doctor named Fouad at the pool who specialized in implants and dentures. "Implants will cost up to LE 70,000. Good dentures will cost anywhere from 5,000 to 10,000 LE."

The amount of money needed was staggering. The higher range for dentures would cost us $1,500. This was a much bigger investment than I had bargained for. As it was, the university had only given us only a two percent raise, about $70 a month.

US SPENDS THOUSANDS ON AIRPORT SECURITY.

"You should make sure she really wants them. Once, I had a Saudi patient who was furious that his son paid so much money for implants. When he found out how much the implants had cost, he stormed into my office and insisted that I take them out. Sophisticated procedures for sophisticated people," he said.

Fouad was a competent swimmer, but I passed him on the breast stroke on the third lap. In water I felt light and fast, though I was sluggish on land and avoided looking at my body in the changing-room mirror. A tanned, sleek Italian greyhound positioned herself in front of the mirror so she could dry her hair. "Excuse me," I said, trying to get into my locker, but she hardly moved. "*Excuse* me," I said. She continued primping and admiring her voluptuous breasts without the slightest self-consciousness. I wrapped a large towel around myself and hurried to the bathroom before she could see my thick, flabby waist and floppy legs.

Shortly after my conversation with Fouad, my beautiful new tooth came loose. I had a bad habit of sucking candy when I was proofing the students' articles at the *Daily Mirage*. CLUSTER BOMBS IN AFGHANISTAN. PALESTINIAN DEADLOCK. STUDENT UNION DEMANDS MORE PRAYER SPACE. I had to make yet another trip to Vartan so he could cement it back. He had to squeeze me in between appointments, so I had to wait in his tiny waiting room. I picked up a red ashtray in the shape of a boot. How I loved the tasty panini sandwiches in Rome! If I had enough money I'd go back to Italy, but the dollar was very weak against the euro. There was also a plastic globe with snow on the bottom. I turned it over: Niagara Falls. On a bookshelf was a small figurine of a matador. A stuffed toy leopard squatted next to some small potted palms. In between photographs of family gatherings with Vartan posing as the paterfamilias hung prints of Gaugin: nude, exotic women in Tahiti. I imagined the tanned Italian greyhound strolling in the buff through the road of mechanics and the riot that would ensue.

PALESTINE DEMONSTRATION IN CAIRO TOMORROW. US EMBASSY SAYS AMERICAN CITIZENS SHOULD EXERCISE CAUTION. VARY THEIR ROUTES.

Was there a way to Vartan's clinic other than through the road of mechanics?

"Miss Mary Beth, Dr Vartan is ready for you."

AMERICA READY FOR NEW THREATS TO HOMELAND.

I opened my purse and fished out a black velvet jewelry pouch.

"Lucky you didn't swallow it," Vartan said, studying the acrylic tooth between his two weathered fingers.

AMERICAN CITIZENS CONCERNED MORE ABOUT SECURITY THAN FREEDOM.

In late October the weather started to get cooler. Not everyone continued to turn up at the pool. When she did, Louise left early to play tennis at the Gezira Club. I found her sitting on a lounge chair in a lime-green jacket and black warm-up pants. Once I had a figure like that.

MICHIGAN WOMAN SAYS HER HUSBAND IN JAIL BECAUSE HE IS ARAB. HIS FAMILY EMIGRATED FROM SYRIA ONE HUNDRED YEARS AGO.

I suggested to the group that we opt for dentures. I knew they wouldn't want to spend any more than that on teeth for Fatma, no matter how much they liked her. Fouad had given me his card, so that day I called to make an appointment. It occurred to me that if Fatma had a ride to her appointment, she might be even more amenable to the idea.

"Oliver, could you take her in your jeep?"

"I don't think Fatma wants to go," Louise said.

"We've gotten this far," I said. "Why not go ahead and do it?"

US NAMES AXIS OF EVIL: SYRIA, IRAN, AND NORTH KOREA.

"I could take her in my car, but my horse just died," Mary said, her eyes tearing up.

"I'm sorry to hear that," Oliver said.

"How long did you have her?" Louise asked.

"Ten years," Mary said, drying her eyes with a dirty red bandana.

We needed to get back on track. Why did I always feel like I was moving backward in this country?

BIN LADEN ELUDES CAPTURE.

"Bad kidneys?" Oliver asked.

"Cancer. I had to ask the vet to put her down because she was in so much pain. She was arthritic too. Could barely stand in her stall. Not to mention that she had bad teeth. I had to pay someone to look after her full-time."

I was wondering how to get them back on the subject of Fatma's new teeth without appearing callous. Say a prayer for the dead horse?

MORE MEMORIAL SERVICES PLANNED FOR VICTIMS OF 9/11.

"The *bawab* told me how Fatma lost her eye. A fungus. Untreated. By the time her parents took her to the doctor, it was too late," Louise said.

"I always wondered, but it seemed impolite to ask," Oliver said.

"I'm sure it was her husband. We ran a story about cases of spousal abuse. There are hundreds of such cases in Egypt. Those are the facts," I insisted. "I know I'm right."

BUSH SAYS IRAQ IS CLEARLY LINKED TO 9/11 TERRORISTS.

"Why would the *bawab* lie?"

"Sour grapes," I said.

"I can vouch for him. Once one of my cats got loose, and he searched everywhere for her. On the roof. In the elevator shaft. Eventually we found her on the roof of a building across the street," Mary said.

SURVIVORS TELL OF HARROWING ESCAPE FROM WORLD TRADE CENTER.

"Could you find out when Fatma is free so you can take her to the appointments? Perhaps you and Oliver could coordinate?"

"Her schedule keeps changing. She works for Oliver on Tuesdays now. She works for the Joyce scholar on Wednesdays. But he asked if he could switch with me. On Thursdays she goes to Zamalek."

"I didn't know we had a Joyce scholar at the university. So many people come and go, it's hard to keep everyone straight. Have any of you ever read *Ulysses*? I never could get through it."

BUSH POOR STUDENT AT YALE. PARTY BOY.

"My Russian jeep, the Neva, is still in the shop. Anyway, I'm taking a group out on the Nile to look for the Kuhl's Pipistrelle bat. We have a bat scanner," Oliver said.

"Can't we get any consensus here?"

US CAN'T GET CONSENSUS AT UN AGAINST IRAQ.

"The *bawab* told me that once she had lost her eye her father was so afraid no one would marry her that he organized a marriage with her cousin. Fatma was not beaten by her husband. And *she* left *him*. They're separated, not divorced. They haven't lived as husband and wife for years."

"None of this helps with the question of Fatma's schedule," I pointed out.

When I asked when we should meet again, Louise and Oliver moaned about midterm grades. Mary was presenting a paper at the University of Idaho: Blogs in Information Technology. And I was already overworked teaching five courses.

"We'll keep in touch by email," I said.

Emails flew around like sparrows trapped in a chimney. Much to my surprise, when I saw Fouad at the pool he told me Fatma had not been to see him once in the last few months.

She canceled every single appointment I had made for her.

In the meantime, my beautiful new tooth was irritating my gums, which were raw as hamburger meat. No amount of gargling with salt water helped.

MORE HEALING RITUALS AT GROUND ZERO. CANDLELIGHT VIGIL HELD.

I wished I could cancel my appointment with Vartan. Every morning, though, I looked in the mirror and studied the raw gums around the beautiful tooth, which made me look like a vampire. As much as I hated it, I would have to go downtown to Vartan's clinic, pick my way past the leering men and the toothless smirking *bawab* with the olive-green eyes.

AMERICA RAW AFTER ATTACKS.

Vartan seized a thin pick and vigorously scrapped off the plaque. When I started to gag he ordered, "Rinse!"

I spat blood into the white basin and watched it spiral down the drain. Was this my punishment for never learning Arabic? For trying to help Fatma get new teeth?

BUSH URGES ALL COUNTRIES TO WORK TOGETHER TO PREVENT WORLDWIDE TERRORISM.

After the endless scraping, Vartan took a tweezer and picked out medicated cotton from a small brown jar.

"Open, Poppy!" he said, stuffing the cotton around the acrylic tooth. The peroxide in the cotton made me gag. "How much longer?" I felt like a prisoner in Guantanamo Bay.

PRISONERS HELD AT GUANTANAMO DENIED LEGAL RIGHTS.

At our last meeting in January the sky was gray and the wind whistled through the trees. Without the sun, a chilly gloom settled over the green garden. The pool was deserted except for a few serious swimmers. Fouad was not there. Oliver was dressed for a bird-watching expedition in a tan safari jacket with hundreds of pockets. A pair of small expensive binoculars hung from his neck. Louise turned up in a fashionable royal-blue warm-up suit.

"You're not swimming?"

"Too cold," Louise and Oliver said at the same time.

"But it's heated!" They were sitting so far away from the pool, I had to shout. "Fatma keeps canceling the appointments I make for her. Can you talk to her? Couldn't you all come closer so I don't have to shout?"

Mary put one toe in at a time at the shallow end of the pool.

"The water is perfect once you start swimming. Don't be such a baby."

"I think I pulled a muscle when I was riding the other day. The sauna will feel better."

BUSH SAYS REVENGE WILL MAKE US FEEL BETTER.

"But we haven't had our meeting yet," I said.

Mary picked up her towel and headed for the cave-like sauna in the health club downstairs.

"Mary," I called. "Mary!"

UGLY INCIDENTS CONTINUE AGAINST IMMIGRANTS AFTER 9/11.

Instead of dealing with the issue of canceled appointments, Louise told us what the *bawab* had told her: Fatma was worried about how she was going to pay for her daughter's wedding. Her husband, who lived in Aswan, rarely sent her any money.

"You seem to have a lot of time to sit around and drink coffee with the *bawab,*" I said. "Don't you have any school work?"

"That's how you find out what's happening," Louise replied, bouncing a ball on her racquet, then flipping the racquet and bouncing the ball on the other side.

CLINTON TRACKED 9/11 TERRORISTS. INTELLIGENCE IGNORED BY FBI AND CIA.

"Could you please stop doing that?"

"Maybe you should get somebody else to translate," Louise said.

I could see I would have to eat crow and flatter Louise because she was the only one with some conversational Arabic. I wished I did not need Vartan, either. But we all had to go to the dentist sometime.

My gums were still so sore from the new tooth that Vartan finally decided to replace it with a porcelain one. Because I gagged so much or bit too hard he had to redo the wax mold fourteen times. Of course, he had to contain his rage with me, so Mustafa and Zahra bore the brunt of it.

"Poppy, just bite down normally. That's a good girl, Poppy. Steady," he said, putting yet another wax mold into my mouth. Was this how my cat felt when I tried to cram a pill down her throat?

ISRAEL ROLLS TANKS INTO GAZA. US TURNS BLIND EYE. AMERICAN MEDICAL ASSOCIATION RELEASES REPORT OF THE EFFECT OF ANTHRAX ON THE BODY. TINY SPORES ATTACK THE LUNGS.

After that, our group did not meet at the Hilton swimming pool again: they all had excuses:

"I am waiting for my kit from America to see if my cat has feline leukemia. The delivery man from DHL is coming any minute."

"I'm under a deadline for an article on the White-Tailed Mongoose for *Egypt Today.* Why don't we just give her the money?"

Louise said she had an important tennis game.

Soon after, Mary and Oliver completely disappeared.

TERRORISTS WANTED BY FBI GO UNDERGROUND.

"Since you speak Arabic, it's your job to see that she gets to her appointments," I told Louise.

"We can't make her get new teeth."

"I'm overloaded with work," I said. "I don't have time to go with her to her appointments."

Finally, even I was worn down and gave Fatma her teeth money in a sealed white business envelope with her salary. I asked Louise to tell her that the money was specifically for a pair of new dentures.

"I really don't have time. I have to finish this summary on identifying suicide bombers through DNA in body parts."

"Please," I said. "This is the last time."

Fatma smiled and nodded, yes, yes yes. *"Shukran,* Miss Mary Beth," she said, pointing to her teeth. Mustafa called to say my porcelain tooth was ready. I made yet another pilgrimage down that awful street with the leering men and the toothless *bawab.* Did I want to end up with one front tooth like him?

The brass plate said: Vartan Migoian: Specialist in oral surgery. How did I know he was a certified dentist except for someone's word at the university?

US SAYS THEY HAVE PROOF OF SADDAM HUSSEIN'S WEAPONS OF MASS DESTRUCTION.

"Now, remember, Poppy, don't eat before the anesthesia wears off or you could bite off your tongue."

"My name is Mary Beth," I tried to say through a mouthful of cotton.

"What, my dear Poppy?"

I took the cotton out of my mouth. "Is it okay to drink?"

"Why, of course, Poppy," he said, grinning. "Do you drink Scotch or gin?"

"Listen," I said. "I hope this is the end of my troubles with my teeth."

"Mustafa," Vartan bellowed. "Another appointment for Miss Mary Beth."

"Why?"

"I have to see if the porcelain tooth takes."

All the dental work cost me five hundred Egyptian pounds, not even one hundred US dollars. I wondered if Fouad was a better dentist than Vartan. But Vartan was so confident and explained everything so thoroughly. He was certainly not overcharging me. Even so, what if he was just a carpet seller who had fled Palestine and set up as a dentist in Cairo?

Traffic was gridlocked in the center of the city—President Mubarak was hosting an important conference on Terrorism in the Middle East.

MUBARAK WARNED US OF TERRORIST THREAT BEFORE 9/11. US IGNORED WARNING.

One of my journalism students was supposed to cover the conference, but I had no credit left on my mobile phone, so I couldn't check up on her. No taxis were available, and I had to walk home from Vartan's clinic. After I flipped on the light in my apartment, I spied a pair of shoddy dentures on my dining room table, covered with a starched white cotton tablecloth that reminded me of Vartan's white coat. Fatma had not gone to Fouad, the American educated dentist, the slim swimmer, but to someone much cheaper. The teeth were not even straight. They probably hurt as well--which was why she had left them on my dining room table.

My mood worsened when I discovered I was out of white wine. I was flat broke. How stupid I had been!

"For crying out loud, why didn't you tell us she didn't want new teeth?" I shouted into the phone at Louise.

"I've been trying to tell you for months."

How many times had I been fooled?

"She spent the money on her daughter's wedding. They had a nice party. She's embarrassed by such generosity. She doesn't know how to thank us. 'A thousand thanks.' *Alf is-shukr*."

"A wedding," I said. "A one-off?"

"It was important to her," Louise said. "Look, I gotta go."

**US BEEFS UP ARABIC LANGUAGE PROGRAMS. SURGE OF
INTEREST IN MIDDLE EASTERN STUDIES IN US UNIVERSITIES.**

Fatma would rather go around looking like a cross between a jack-o'lantern
and a pirate. She'd have to eat jello for the rest of her life. Why was I getting so
involved in her problems?

**XENOPHOBIC ATTACKS ON IMMIGRANTS IN US CONTINUE
AFTER 9/11. PAKISTANI MISTAKEN FOR ARAB KILLED AT 7-11 IN
OHIO. HIS WIFE SAID HE ONLY WANTED A CHERRY ICE.**

The phone rang.

"I forgot to tell you," Louise said. "Fatma's daughter was very happy. They
used some of the money to get Fatma an eye patch. With her new outfit, the new
eye patch, and a new hairdo, she looked great—the perfect mother-of-the-bride."

6

The Charm

I WAS STANDING ON THE MARBLE COUNTERS on the tips of my toes—it is very
hard to reach the dust close to the ceiling. I was straining high to brush off
a patch. And what do you know? Spiders had woven a web in that far corner—those rascals!

The door slammed. Dr Sheri ran in the kitchen, shouting, "It's the end. It's
the end."

I didn't like the wild look in her eyes. Her clothes were soaked to her skin—it rained only occasionally in Cairo in November.

I put my foot carefully on the chair and got down. I set the pole with the bushy pink top against the counter. "Is it raining?"

Dr Sheri didn't answer, but started sobbing. She sat down right in the middle of the kitchen floor.

"No. No," I said, helping her to her feet. "Not here." I led her into the living room to the couch. I ran to the bathroom to get a towel to dry her off.

As I was drying her hair, I said, "Now, dear, tell me what happened."

She covered her face with her hands. "They hate us."

"Who hates you?"

"The Egyptians," she said.

"Don't be silly. Of course they don't. Nobody hates you, Sheri," I said. "This is about the government. Not you."

"No, no. Zeinab, this time it's different," Sheri said. "They're out for blood."

I waved my hand. "Not at all. Foolish talk. We're not a violent people. You know that."

"I was running for my life. They chased me down a street, for God's sake! I ran smack into a water cannon. Look, I'm telling you. They pretended to aim the cannon at the youth. And then they turned it on me. They were laughing their heads off."

"Listen, these things blow over. You've lived here how long? You know, people are always demonstrating in this country. If it's not one thing, it's another." I kept drying her hair. "We need to get you out of these wet clothes. You'll catch a cold."

"No," Sheri said, shaking her head back and forth, like a rag doll. "This is it. Mark my words, Zeinab. The day of judgment."

"Nonsense. The war's in Iraq. Far away. Believe me, dear, it'll blow over. People'll go back to worrying about how to feed their children."

Dr Sheri knew all about my problems. My husband, who spent our money on cards. My neurotic daughter. The son who squandered money on hash. She had been a very sympathetic listener and helped me a lot. Sudden loans when I was in a pinch. Advances on my salary. The unexpected chicken or a kilo of meat.

"Are you an expert on Iraq?" Sheri said.

I laughed. "Of course not. As you know, I left school at twelve."

"They were about to rip off my clothes," Sheri said, pulling a wet strand of gray hair away from her eyes. "Hoodlums. Thugs. Monsters. I could have been raped."

"Come on, now. You're upset. I'll make us some tea." I went back to the kitchen and lit the gas burner. For a moment, staring at the flame, I wondered if it was a good idea to leave Sheri alone at all. She was disturbed.

"They screamed, 'Bawk, bawk, skinny chicken. Bawk, bawk, skinny chicken.'"

"Is that all they said? Come on. They could have said something worse. Why didn't you tell them to get lost?" I shouted.

I opened the refrigerator. A single cup of yogurt sat alone in the first shelf. A jar of mustard. No wonder she was a stick—she wasn't eating, either. At least she had milk, but it was skim. No taste. I'd do without. She liked her tea milky. Five sugars for me without milk. I put the mugs on a small tray and brought them into the living room. I wondered if I had a pack of biscuits in my purse. She wouldn't buy them for herself, but would eat them if I offered them to her. That might make her feel better. I rummaged in my purse. Ah, yes. I had a few cookies left—creamy chocolate icing in the middle.

"Why didn't you shame them?" I said, handing her a mug of tea. "Your Arabic is good enough. You know what to say when people behave badly." I offered her a cookie.

"I don't know," she said, nibbling at the cookie. Her left eye started to twitch. She was crying.

"You would have done that before when you first came. You told yourself how you cursed a guard who said something improper to you. You're not getting enough to eat. I'm worried about you."

She was silent for a moment. Suddenly, she said. "I want Dudie." She stuck out her bottom lip. "Dudie! Dudie!" she shouted.

"He's on the curtain ledge in your bedroom," I said. "Where he always sleeps."

Of course, her cats were everything to her. I didn't mind feeding them, but we had agreed that I wouldn't have to clean out the boxes. Dudie was the white cat with the pink eyes who hid high up on the curtain ledge. Shushu, the other one, a fat black cat, usually hissed at me, like a snake. I had seen nicer cats in my day, but Sheri adored them. She treated them like her children.

She got up and dragged herself into the bedroom. I followed her. "You'd better get those clothes off. Otherwise, you'll catch a cold."

I helped her lift her blouse over her head. She stripped off her clothes and handed them to me. She was much too thin—her bra just hung on her. No breasts now. Starving herself. But why? Maybe I should bring over some okra stew with a bit of meat for her.

The monster, Dudie, appeared. "Dudie," Sheri shouted, clapping her hands. Dudie jumped into her lap. "Come to mommy."

When I first started working for her, she had told me a lot of intimate things about herself. When she came back from America, she had brought me bars of chocolate from the duty-free shop. Nibbling on the delicious chocolate, we had lounged on her bed and flipped through her photo album. She had showed me photographs of herself: a much fatter and lovelier-looking woman than she was now. Her wedding dress had hundreds of beaded pearls! Her husband, Mazen, had bushy eyebrows and a strange-shaped head, but he smiled at her with such adoration. Anyway, handsome men often thought too highly of themselves. "He looks very nice," I said.

"You know," she said, giggling. "We fell in love in Arabic poetry class. We recited poetry to each other."

"How romantic!" I said.

She asked, "Have you been in love?"

I laughed. "No. Anyway, you know, love is a luxury for us."

"No one at all?" Sheri said. She was so eager to know about me in those early days.

"There was my cousin," I said. "We liked each other. But he's dead. He's been gone a long time. Fifteen years."

"What happened?"

"Well, he was killed in a minibus accident."

"I'm so sorry," she said, touching my hand. Despite the fact that she was odd, she had been very kind to me.

Suddenly, Shushu, who had been under the bed, emerged and hissed at me. Foul creature. I ducked into the bathroom and put her wet clothes into the laundry basket. Could it wait? If I put the wet clothes in the washing machine,

I would have to wait until the cycle finished before I could leave. No, that's all right. I'd do the laundry next time.

"Come to mommy," Sheri said, speaking baby talk. Shushu approached the bed, warily, as if she were hunting. "That's a good girl."

Shushu leapt up on the bed, and nuzzled her neck. I could never understand these relationships with animals.

"Give me your mug. I'll finish up in the kitchen," I said.

"Thanks for being so good, Zeinab. It was a distressing day," Sheri said.

"No, it's fine," I said. "You'll feel better tomorrow."

I had other colorful employers. Kharalombos was a huge Greek man who taught movie stars how to dance. I spent hours vacuuming his flat because he dropped Kentucky Fried chicken crumbs everywhere. Batilda, a Swedish belly dancer, often asked me to help her dress before she performed.

The day after the huge demonstration in Tahrir Square, everything went back to normal in Cairo. The US invaded Iraq as we expected. They were powerful and did as they liked. I was already tired of the inconvenience of blocked streets and security trucks. I hoped that Dr Sheri would be fine. The experience had not been pleasant for her, but she had not been harmed physically.

When I turned the key in the door, she was waiting for me. "I'm having a terrible day," she said. She was nervously tapping her foot. "Everything has gone wrong."

"Good morning. The roads were blocked. The president was passing through the city. You know how they block the roads when he moves."

"Sure. No one can move for hours. My students at the university always use this excuse."

"Are you all right? Are you feeling better?" I asked.

"I'm not going to the university today," she said.

"Why not? What's that smell?"

"The washing machine caught on fire," she said.

"Oh, dear," I said. "Why don't you hang the clothes outside? They'll get the fresh air." I started picking up the clothes. Wet clothes were draped over the couch and the dining and living room chairs.

"No. They'll get dusty," she said. "When they're dry, they'll be dirty again. We must wash them again." She was chewing on her fingernails; they had been chewed raw.

"Ya Doctoor Sheri, don't pick at your nails like that. Have you called the university? Maybe they could have an electrician come and look at it," I said. I started taking out the pins in my veil.

Her eyes narrowed. "I don't trust anyone."

"They do their work well. Just phone them," I said. "Or it might be that you just need a new washing machine. Haven't you had this one for seven years?"

"Everything is shit in this country. Nothing lasts," she said. Suddenly, she wandered away from me and gazed out the window. "Nothing lasts," she murmured.

Thieves weren't clustered in the university housing office. She was in a state like this before. Two years ago, she had mentioned for days that the vegetable seller had overcharged her for onions. I wandered into the bathroom. She followed me.

"Don't touch the machine," she snapped. "I don't need a flood. I've just had a fire!"

"I've switched the water off," I said.

I turned the knob. It made an odd whirring sound, but refused to spin. "Maybe the *bawab* knows someone who can repair it. I'll go downstairs and ask him."

"Don't you dare! That *bawab* is a busybody. He gives me the creeps. He reports everybody to the secret police."

I chuckled. "A broken washing machine? Not very interesting intelligence."

"I'm sure he reports my every move," Sheri said. "They think I'm a CIA operative."

I retreated into the small bathroom and took my cleaning clothes off the hooks from the door—an old tee-shirt and a pair of warm-up pants. Today she announced that she would clean with me, as she sometimes did. "Oh, it's all right. Listen, don't you have any work to do for the university? Papers to grade?"

"I can't," she said. "I feel like doing something mindless today."

Sheri never called the housing office to come and look at her washing machine. She spent her time gazing out the window. I found granola bar wrappers and apple cores under her bed. In the end, I started washing out her clothes, the linen, and the towels in her bathtub. Other things started to break. Her screens needed to be repaired—I cut my fingers on the torn mesh. We suffered from a plague of flies and mosquitoes. The plumbing went awry. In both bathrooms, water backed up. The toilets refused to flush. Sometimes water with brown sludge flooded onto the floor and I had to clean it up. All of the handles on her windows broke. When it was windy, the windows flapped back and forth. All of the light bulbs went out, one by one, and weren't replaced. I lit small tube candles, so I could see.

Her only expeditions were to the pet shop downstairs. She loved to see what was new in cats' toys. She bought ear wipes, hair brushes, and dental treats for Dudie and Shushu.

I began to dread going to Dr Sheri's. She was becoming completely unglued. But I had to go to work: I needed the money. To my surprise, she stopped ranting about thieves and her washing machine altogether. In the meantime, Baghdad fell. Sheri didn't even mention it. I had to take my daughter to a psychiatrist. My son continued to stay out until dawn and sleep all day. My mother needed a kidney transplant. I was calling every relative we had to see if we could scrape up the money.

When I opened the door, Dr Sheri was holding a cat cage. "Zeinab, forget about cleaning," she said. "We've got to get Shushu to the vet."

"Ya Doctoor Sheri, why? What's wrong with her?"

"She's not eating. I'm worried about her."

We lured Shushu into the kitchen with some cat herbs. Shushu followed her nose and went straight into the cage. But when I tried to close the door of the cat cage, the peg wouldn't go into the hole. Shushu dug her claws into my hand. "Awwww!" I pulled back. For a minute, her claws just hung on my hand! In a flash, she let go and squeezed past the door.

Blood oozed from my hand. My hand was on fire. I ran to the bathroom. Held my hand under the tap.

When I returned, Sheri was cooing, "Now, Shushu, be a good girl and come down from there." Shushu had leapt up onto one of the counters.

At last, Sheri coaxed her to come down with the herbs. Grabbing her by the scruff of her neck with one hand, she held her by the bottom with the other. "In you go. Bad Shushu. Bad pussy," Sheri said, giving her a spank on the bottom. Then she shoved her into the cage.

I picked up the carrier. Actually, Sheri was too weak to carry the cage herself, which she would have done a few years ago.

When we arrived at the vet, a confident Egyptian woman spoke to us in English and showed us into the waiting room. I was thinking about how else we might raise the money for the kidney for my mother—I had a cousin in Kuwait who was making a good salary as an accountant. Shushu yowled in her cage. This clinic for animals was very shiny—we had never been to this one before. The walls had been freshly painted. On every wall were photographs of animals in slick black frames. Fashion magazines in English were stacked on the coffee table.

Look at that girl with the transparent white top. No sleeves. I could never wear that. I used to have a figure like that years ago. The lady with the tangerine nail polish. Nice sandals, too. I love the way the beads wind through her toes. Look at that tiny dog peeking out from a golden purse—he looks like a rat! That plump girl over there is showing her belly. She's smiling at me. She has a diamond in her tooth. Is that her dog? Look at that huge, skinny dog with black spots. Oh, my God! He's licking his privates! Oh, that must be the doctor walking through the waiting room—white coat. That Egyptian boy is wearing a warm-up suit with the colors of the Egyptian flag. He's wearing braces. My gums bleed. I should go to the dentist. I've got no money for that. Is that fluffy ball of cotton his cat? Those people must be Americans.

A door opened and shut, in the blink of an eye. That must be the doctor's office.

The lady with the tangerine fingernails spoke to the attractive confident Egyptian woman who was ushering people in and out of the doctor's office.

"Please tell Dr Girgis I'm here. He knows me. Madame Georgette," she said. She studied her fingernails.

Sheri shrieked, "I heard what you said. I speak Arabic. I'm an expert. A professor of Arabic. Don't you people wait in line? You only came five minutes ago. The rest of us have been waiting here for over an hour. There's a system here. If you think that because of your connections, you're going to jump in front of all of us, you're mistaken. Over my dead body!"

The tiny dog in the golden purse yapped. I'm sure he's a rat.

The Egyptian lady with the gold purse stood up. "I can't sit here all day. I have things to do."

"What? Oh, like getting your fingernails done?" Sheri said.

The boy with the braces giggled.

"What a rude woman you are," the Egyptian lady said. Her dog was barking itself into a frenzy. "It's clear you were brought up very badly."

"Go blow it out your ass. And for God's sake shut that rat up! Push everyone out of the way to get what you want. You're the rude bitch."

Help! I wanted to crawl under my chair. This was very embarrassing.

The Egyptian lady slapped her magazine down on the coffee table and stormed out of the room.

The confident Egyptian receptionist ran after her. "Ya Madame," she called. "Ya Madame."

As soon as the door popped open, the Egyptian doctor in the clean white coat ushered the girl with the diamond tooth into the examining room. We heard her dog barking.

Shushu had the worst diagnosis possible. She had breast cancer and had to be operated on, immediately. After the operation, she tore out all her stitches. She didn't hiss at me anymore. I had never liked Shushu, but started to feel sorry for her. Her eyes were glassy and she was lethargic. She even turned up her nose at chicken breasts. The entire time, Dudie lounged up on the curtain ledge. The only time he came down from the ledge was to eat Shushu's food.

My daughter, Soad, had calmed down and was out having fun with her friends. But I was really worried about my son, Mahmoud. He was hanging out with a bad crowd. Reeked of hashish. Were they stealing, too?

One day, I thought Sheri might be getting better. Fully clothed, she was sitting cross-legged on her bed. She was flicking through her photo album again—it reminded me of the earlier days when we gossiped together and ate duty-free chocolate. "Do you miss him?" I asked.

"Sometimes," she said. She was wistful. "He always made me laugh. These days, I don't laugh."

"Oh, come on, now," I said. "A lot of things in Cairo'll make you laugh. It's a crazy city."

"It's too late. I'm the one who left," she said. "He's long gone. Remarried by now."

"What happened?"

She told me the rest of the story about Mazen. "We weren't married long," she said. "He got a job in Saudi Arabia, but I didn't want to go."

"But why not? The salary would have been good. You would have had a comfortable life," I said.

"No. No. I didn't want to go," Sheri said. "Women in black abayas. I didn't want to live like that. It's a terrible place."

"Oh," I said. Maybe there were other reasons for the divorce. Maybe she couldn't get pregnant.

I was dusting. I noticed the necklace that lay in a tangled heap on the bedside table.

I picked up the necklace. The charm was a small gold rose. "Did Mazen give you this? I have always wondered. It's very feminine."

"No. No. My grandmother gave it to me before she died. A graduation present for finishing the university. My grandfather gave it to her when they got engaged. It's an antique."

"I'll put it in your jewelry box. That way it'll be in a safe place for you."

"Yes, that's a good idea. I had it out. I rarely wear it." Sheri said.

One day when I came into the flat, Sheri was sitting in one of the heavy armchairs in the living room. She was crying. I had hoped she was getting better. Her hair was dishevelled. She had that same wild look in her eyes.

"Ya Sheri, what's wrong? What's that smell?"

She began weeping. "She's dead," she said. A pile of used tissues had been thrown on the floor. "Dear Shushu was always there for me."

"I'm sorry," I said.

"Really? You're sorry. I bet you are. Don't lie to me. How dare you! You must have known," Sheri said.

"What? Known what? What are you talking about?"

Sheri's eyes narrowed. "Don't you lie to me. You cleaned the room. Why didn't you tell me?" She sobbed.

"My dear, she was alive when I left."

"LIAR," Sheri said.

"Look, I know you're upset, Sheri. You know I'm not a liar," I said. "Where is Shushu now?"

"Under the bed," Sheri said, blowing her nose into a Kleenex. "I couldn't deal with it."

"Since my last visit? Why didn't you call the *bawab*? Why didn't you call me?"

"I'm scared of death."

After I had taken off my street clothes, I put on the old tee-shirt and stretch pants that I wore for cleaning.

"I'll deal with this," I said, carrying the broom into the bedroom. Sheri was behind me. "What are you doing with that broom? You aren't going to sweep Shushu into the trash?"

"My dear," I said. "I know how much you love cats." She needed help. She needed to see a doctor.

Sheri sobbed. "Shushu was special."

I knelt down on my knees and peered under the bed. Shushu was right in the center underneath the bed. The smell was horrendous. I wanted to gag. I couldn't throw up now. I would have to mop up the vomit!

"Maybe we should get the *bawab* to help us?" I said, poking the soft corpse with a broom.

"You'll hurt her," Sheri said.

This was ridiculous. I wanted to escape from this task and dump it on someone else!

"The *bawab* will throw my beloved Shushu in the garbage," Sheri said. "You know he's a scoundrel and he reports on us to the secret police."

"I'll need two towels. A small one and a big one. Come on, don't just stand there."

Sheri disappeared. I kept poking Shushu with my broom; she was on top of one of the winter carpets. Why didn't I think of that before? Pull the entire carpet out from under the bed. I tugged at the heavy carpet.

"Here," Sheri said, handing me the two towels.

"Look, help me. Just pull on the carpet," I said.

With the two of us, the carpet slid out from underneath the bed. And there was Shushu. The wound from her breast operation had never healed, where she had torn out the stitches. Tiny black things were crawling all over her. "My God," Sheri said, "Shushu is being eaten."

"She's dead," I said. "Haven't you ever seen a dead creature?"

Shushu stared back at me. Her eyes were now a fluorescent black, covered with blue flies. You could see her teeth. It almost looked as if she were smiling, but I knew better—that was the smile of death.

"Give me the towel," I said. God, I needed gloves. But we didn't have any. I lay the big towel next to her on the carpet. With the broom I edged her corpse onto the big towel. Using the small towel, I rolled her corpse onto the bigger towel—the movement was enough to rupture her decomposing body. Her entrails spilled out. I suppressed my nausea again. The smell was ungodly.

"Wait! You can't just throw her away," Sheri said.

"No, I'm not. We aren't going to throw her away," I said. Quickly, before the maggots escaped from the corpse, I folded the white towel around Shushu. I knotted each end, the way we did with a shroud.

Of course, we buried people the day after they died. But Shushu wasn't a person. Three days with any creature was a disaster, even in the autumn.

"What should we do with her?"

"We should bury her. At the club," Sheri said.

"The club?"

"They have a pet cemetery there," Sheri said.

"Will it make you feel better?" I asked.

"Yes," Sheri said. "Yes, it will." She seemed more in control.

I carefully put the white shroud into a cloth shopping bag. We hailed a taxi outside of Sheri's building and asked for the club. The taxi driver made a face. "*Ya hagga*, what's that rotten smell?" I put my palms face up, as if I were praying. Mercy, please. When he glanced at Sheri, he understood. Sheri started to weep again, so I said, "The entrance of the Gezira Club, please."

We wandered around the vast grounds of the club—we circled around the horse stables, track, tea garden, and the tennis courts. But still we couldn't find the pet cemetery. I suggested we ask the guards.

But Sheri didn't want to talk to anyone.

"They hate foreigners here," Sheri said. "I feel alien here. Everyone stares at me."

I wondered if people might also stare at Sheri in America. She looked strange.

"They don't hate foreigners," I said. How could I tell her that I felt like an alien here, too?

After what seemed like hours trying to find the pet cemetery, Sheri gave up and decided to dig on the edge of the golf course.

"I don't think it's a good idea," I said.

But Sheri wasn't listening to me. She pulled the spoon out of her purse furtively, as if it were candy. And then she knelt down on the grass, tucking her long legs underneath her so she could dig. As she was hacking at the earth, she grunted like a deranged child.

Suddenly, two security guards were making their way toward us.

"Sheri," I said. "Look out!"

But she didn't look up and continued hacking at the hard earth.

The older guard with a streak of gray in his hair, stood in front of me. "What are you doing here? What's going on here?"

I explained to them that we couldn't find the pet cemetery. Sheri's cat had just died and she was still very upset. "That's too bad," he said.

The other guard with the mustache said, "No problem. We'll take you and the lady to the cemetery."

"Sheri," I said, touching her arm. "They'll take us to the pet cemetery."

But Sheri was digging even more furiously. She wasn't listening. Her stringy salt-and-pepper hair had fallen into her face. She badly needed medical help—I was very sorry for her. She was all alone and far away from her family.

"Madame," the older guard said, very politely. "You are spoiling the grass. It's against the rules of the club."

Sheri brushed a few strands of her hair out of her face and narrowed her eyes. Then, she cursed them both in the foulest Arabic I had ever heard. I was embarrassed—this was terrible. "I'm very sorry," I said to the guards. How insulting!

Jumping to her feet, she dropped the spoon and ran toward the exit. "Sheri. Sheri. Sheri, dear," I called, running after her. But when I reached the entrance, she had disappeared.

I returned to the guards. They were staring at the bulky towel, which contained Shushu's corpse.

"I'm sorry," I said. "She is..."

The older man said, "We'll help you. What do you want to do?"

"Bury Shushu," I said. "Bury the cat."

The dignified old man insisted on carrying the bundle for me. The cemetery was behind the track. No wonder we had never been able to find it.

Weeds had grown up here. A few graves had actual stones, engraved with the names of animals. The ground was hard. The younger guard knelt on his haunches and dug with one of his keys—it took some time to dig a hole. He explained, "We have wild dogs here." At last, the hole was deep enough. The older guard lay the cat's corpse in the grave and covered it with dirt. I found a piece of loose cardboard and scribbled on it, "Shushu. The cat of Doctoor Sheri."

I thanked the kind men and left the club. On my way home, I called Sheri, but she didn't answer. I resolved to call her the next day, but my mother was dangerously ill, and I forgot.

Miraculously, a kidney had appeared. The doctor assured me that everything was legitimate. My cousin had given us a huge loan. We needed more money. I had no other choice but to ask Sheri. She had lent me money in the past. It had been two days since I had buried Shushu. I needed to check on Sheri.

This time, when I dialed her mobile number, I got the message, "The number you have dialed is no longer in service." I tried the landline. No answer. I dialed again. Had something happened to Sheri? I phoned later in the day. I let it ring twenty times. Imagining the worst, I rushed over to Sheri's apartment. Or maybe they had taken her away. But who were they? Did anyone but me know how bad the situation was? She seemed to have no contact with anyone but those two cats. Well, now just one cat, Dudie.

Anwar, the *bawab,* waved to me on my way into the building. He was sitting on a small stool in front. His son, Nasser, was washing a black Mercedes with a faded pink rag.

"What happened? Did something happen to Doctoor Sheri?"

Anwar shrugged. "Gone." Anwar was not a big talker—we had only exchanged greetings in the last seven years I had worked for Dr Sheri. I couldn't believe he was an informer for the secret police.

"What? Where has she gone?"

Anwar made a gesture with his hand, like a plane going into the sky. "America."

"She's not well." At least she had not harmed herself.

"You're telling me," he said. "She destroyed the flat."

"Oh," I said. What had she done? "I did my best. But she refused to let any repairmen into the flat."

"I'm not blaming you," Anwar said. "We have to clean up the flat for the next tenant. The landlord wants you to clean it. We'll pay you extra."

"Now?" I asked. I wasn't prepared to work. I couldn't leave my mother for that long.

"The new tenant is coming in two days."

"When did she leave?"

"Yesterday," Anwar said. "Her brother took her back."

"Her brother?" She had never told me she had a brother. She had given me all the details of her marriage with Mazen, but had not mentioned a brother. I remembered a conversation about a sister, who had three kids in some place that I had never heard of—only corn fields there.

"He didn't look like her brother," Anwar said. "But what do I know? They looked funny together."

I was baffled. "What did she do with her cat?"

"They took it away in a cage," Anwar said.

"She didn't leave anything for me? No leaving money?" I said. My voice cracked. How was I going to get the extra money for my mother's operation?

"No," Anwar said. "Sorry." One of his boys was watching television at a screeching point in the small room where they slept in the front of the building. The television host said: "Who wants to be a millionaire?" Anwar shouted, "My son, turn it down!"

My eyes filled with tears. "She wasn't a bad person," I said. "Just disturbed." I had tried very hard to please her. To help her. The episode with Shushu was terrible.

"I'm sorry," Anwar said. "Can I make you some tea?"

"No," I said. "I can make some upstairs."

"May your burden be lightened," Anwar said. "One of my boys can help you."

"No," I said. "I can work faster if I'm alone."

The flat smelled different—as if the *bawab* had tried to cover the smell of the dead cat with fake jasmine spray. Sheri was asthmatic and had hated those sprays. I made myself some tea and sat in the living room chair, instead of the stool in the kitchen. I put my feet up on the coffee table. Nice to have this spacious flat to myself. I flung open the doors to her wardrobe—she had left so many sleeveless flowery and polka-dotted dresses. Lovely. But I could never wear those dresses anywhere but inside the house. Masses of shoes. I picked up a pair—dark blue with tiny, glittery stars. They were three sizes too big for me, but I slipped them on, anyway. They were so big that I clomped when I walked. I was hungry. But I knew what to expect from Sheri's refrigerator. I opened it anyway. One shriveled carrot. What was a book doing in the vegetable bin? Strange. I flipped through the pages. Arabic poetry. The Arabic was indecipherable.

Something tucked in the book dropped on the tile floor. Something shiny. I picked it up—it was tangled. Ah, the rose-shaped charm! Tiny diamonds decorated the gold rose. How had it gotten here? She had gone off and left her grandmother's graduation present—she would be sad when she realized she had left it behind. Would the *bawab* or the landlord have her address? But even if I wrapped up the necklace and tried to send it to her, I could not afford the postage. That wasn't a good idea, either. If I relinquished the necklace to Anwar, he would hock it. He had to provide for six boys. Suppose Anwar gave the necklace to the landlord, who was so stingy he refused to change the pipes in the building. Once the brown sludge had even burst through a pipe, gushing onto the kitchen floor. I had seen all the gold chandeliers and gold frames of the Virgin in the landlord's flat. Neither the *bawab* nor the landlord would send Sheri her necklace. No one had ever given me such a beautiful necklace. Even my wedding ring had been cheap silver. Why not me? No! The necklace didn't belong to me—that was not the way I had been raised.

I knew that the cat's box must be full of clumps of shit, yet I avoided facing it. Ugly! Did they want me to pack all of Sheri's clothes or put them in garbage bags? I still had to put on my cleaning clothes before I scoured the place. Instead, I stood in the middle of the kitchen and untangled each tiny knot on the delicate chain. Wearing Sheri's starred shoes, I clomped toward the large glass window in the living room so I could see the necklace better. Who would ever know? Like finding lost coins on the street. And the gold would help me pay towards the operation. I wouldn't have to beg quite so much from my relatives. I had to stop thinking this way: it would take me hours to clean up this mess. I had to get to work.

But it was hard to ignore the diamonds that glistened in the waning sunlight.

7

Ice

ALTHOUGH I HAD PLENTY OF ICE TRAYS IN MY FREEZER, I had used up all my ice. I waltzed over to my next-door neighbor, Lorenzo, on the pretext that I was informing him about the suicide bomber near the Egyptian Museum, who had just lost his head. The situation was a great deal more serious than last week's *khamaseen,* sandstorm, when I had also appeared at his door. Lorenzo was a handsome Italian American man in his thirties with a PhD from Brown University, who was teaching Ottoman history. After I had described the suicide bomber, who had escaped from the Egyptian secret police by hurling himself off the 6th of October bridge, I parroted the American Embassy warning, "Vary your routes." He didn't laugh.

I offered advice to the other American professors in the building, who had never lived abroad before. I had worked as a stringer for the *Trib*, the *Christian Science Monitor*, and the *Houston Chronicle* in Lebanon during the civil war— this teaching gig was a cakewalk.

I should have remembered from the week before: Lorenzo didn't own a single plastic ice tray. If his guests wanted alcohol, they had to drink local Egyptian beer out of the bottle. A case of Stella Local was stacked in the first three rows of his refrigerator.

I ran my forefinger across Lorenzo's dusty dining room table. "Hmm," I said, "I see you still haven't cleaned your apartment since last week's *khamaseen.* My maid Fatma's free on Tuesdays. And she's honest. Listen, not all of them are. I heard of one maid who stole her employer's sexy underwear."

"I had a terrible week at the university," Lorenzo said. He picked up a cigarette and rolled it between his fingers. "There's no discipline. The students are all spoilt brats and their phones are always going off in the middle of my lectures."

"Give a pop quiz when a phone goes off. It works." I plunked myself down on his sofa.

Lorenzo shrugged and stroked his goatee. He wasn't a big talker—and defied every stereotype about Italians. "That's an idea."

I plumped one of his pillows. "You know, the most terrible week of my life was in Beirut. 1982. Went to Paris for the weekend. When I came back, my apartment building had been pulverized. Just a pile of rubble."

That wasn't true—I was taken captive by the Organization for the Oppressed and Pitiable of Earth. I was lucky to escape alive.

"Yeah, you mentioned that before," he said. He held the cigarette between his thumb and his forefinger, as if he were Humphrey Bogart. For a historian, he had an astonishing lack of curiosity.

"What I didn't tell you. I was on Hezbollah's Most Wanted List. Along with Robert Fisk."

Lorenzo put the cigarette in his mouth and lit his cigarette with an expensive lighter. I stared at his lips. Was he from a wealthy family? The antique lighter had a family crest.

"Robert Fisk? The famous reporter?" I said, trying to get a reaction from him.

Lorenzo stood in front of me. Impossible not to notice the bulge in his crotch. Instead, he said, "Look, a lousy cat bit my finger," he said. He held out the bandaged finger for me to inspect. "I haven't started frothing at the mouth yet."

I couldn't resist touching his finger; a few brown hairs sprouted from the skin. I could now completely understand why an older professor might be tempted to sleep with his sexy young students. In fact, since I had divorced my husband, Marty, I had had a few affairs with married men with monstrous bellies. Loneliness had overcome every principle or scruple I once had.

"You probably don't have rabies," I said, holding his swollen finger. "But I'd get a tetanus shot, if I were you. Have you been to the university clinic?"

"No."

"I'd get it checked out. Dr Marwa. The one who wears the turban."

I wanted to stroke his finger, but instead, patted him on the shoulder. He was much too young for me—robbing the cradle. Ha! I bet he had a wonderful, hairy back.

"When's your girlfriend coming to visit you?" I asked, now pretending I was his mother. At least, someone I knew was having sex. My best friend Sharon and I complained a great deal about the "slim pickings" of expatriate men in Cairo.

"Isabella's coming soon," he said, retreating to his office chair. "We're engaged," he said, swiveling backward and forward. The chair made a squeaking noise, like the rhythm of a rocking bed.

I swallowed and raised my empty wine glass. "Cheers." I would have to continue my quest for ice elsewhere.

If Sharon had lived in the building, I could mooch ice off of her. Unfortunately, she lived three blocks away. I couldn't pad down the street in my house slippers.

I would ask my neighbor upstairs, Rose, on the excuse of informing her about the suicide bomber. My reasons for knocking on Rose's door in the past few months were various: white pepper, a whisk, Quaker oats, chocolate chips, the name of Rose's painter.

I leaned my shoulder against the doorbell. I was holding my mobile phone in one hand, my wine glass in the other.

The door burst open. "Hello, darlin'. Need raisins for your gingerbread men?"

Rose had an unlit cigarette, between her long, red fingernails. The contrast to these red fingernails was a spiky, militant short haircut.

"Thought you should know there was a suicide bomber at the Egyptian Museum. According to my source."

"Yeah, sweetheart. This ain't my first rodeo." Rose said. "What can I do for you, darlin'?"

"Oh. Well," I said. 'Damn,' I thought. I scrambled for another excuse. What might sound reasonable?

"'Preciate your concern, darlin'. We heard it on the BBC," Rose said.

"I was just trying to keep you informed. I'm the Deputy Warden. In case of emergencies. Crises. I was appointed after 9/11."

God, this gal was shrewd. I might try to get ice from the two librarians from Arkansas, upstairs. I had recently borrowed their DVD player so I could see the latest film on Ed Murrow—that was three weeks ago. I might have stretched their patience.

While we were talking, I had edged my foot into the middle of the doorway. Surely, Rose would not slam the door on my foot. I was wearing a pair of Easy Spirit sandals.

"One of our student reporters happened to be at the scene," I said, stretching the truth. So what? That's how it worked in the business. The new faculty advisor, Prue, had gotten tipped off by one of her cronies at AP and Prue had told me.

"Think that's safe for the kids? Being on the scene," Rose said, her hand on her hip.

"Well, you know, we try to teach the kids to go for the story," I said.

"Yeah, Sure. Journalism 101. Took it at University of Alabama," Rose said. "Before I starting writing fiction."

"By the way, bet you don't know that Lorenzo was attacked by a mob of feral cats last week during the sandstorm? You should see his apartment," I said.

Rose swung the door open wider. "You don't say."

What other tidbits could I tell her about Lorenzo? His finger was bitten by a wild cat? The mysterious girlfriend?

Bill, Rose's husband, peeked out the door. "Sure you don't want to come in, neighbor?"

I positioned myself even closer to the heavy wooden door. "I was just passing by," I said.

The last time I had visited Rose and Bill to return three rusty nails and an empty molasses jar, I had stayed seven hours. As soon as Rose opened the door wider, I shot in the apartment. The image of a weasel darting under a car appeared in my mind. I brushed aside this unpleasant memory.

"Now can I get you anything, Mary Beth?" Bill asked.

"Ice, please," I said in my most pleasant, courteous voice. After I had handed my glass to Bill, I marched into the living room. Rose had hung an enormous brass tray from the local market on the wall—I admired her good taste. But the living room was almost the color of blood, maroon-ish. I remembered the mangled corpses I had seen near the Green Line in Beirut. The tiny babies covered with white phosphorus burns from cluster bombs. A Lebanese doctor with his arms covered in blood. Militia soldiers at checkpoints with cigarettes behind their ears, as if they were pencils. I had scooped the story of Flight 847 in 1985, when the Lebanese group, The Organization for the Oppressed of the Earth, had hijacked a plane from Athens to Rome and flown to Beirut and then to Algiers, three times. As one of the few women journalists at that time, I had so wanted to belong to the boys' club. I had expected claps on the back from my male colleagues at the Hotel Commodore in West Beirut. Instead, a well-known journalist I had admired, who was drunk, had said, "Nice tits, doll." "Jump in a lake," I'd said, throwing beer in his face. Later that night, when I was alone in my tiny basement apartment, bombs overhead, I had wept.

Rose ran her long fingers through her spiky hair. I wondered about her history with men. I had heard that Bill was Rose's second husband.

I waved my mobile phone. "There was also an attack somewhere else in Cairo."

Was Bill making wine in the kitchen?

"So, Lorenzo was attacked by a mob of feral cats last week during the sand-storm. Strange, we never heard about it," Rose said. She popped the cork from the Shahrazad.

"I told him he should get his finger checked out at the clinic. By the way, what happened to my ice?"

"Bill, darlin'. What happened to Mary Beth's ice? Did you fall asleep in there?" Rose called out.

"Plumb forgot," Bill called back from the kitchen. "Making the tomato sauce."

Bill's enormous belly hung over his loose blue gym shorts. He was wearing a white tee-shirt. Emblazoned on the front was a picture of a political prisoner, blindfolded: Support Amnesty International: It is better to light a candle than to curse the darkness. Not only had I been blindfolded, but I was chained to a radiator.

"Here's your wine, Mary Beth," he said, handing me the wine glass. I brushed the thought of Rose and Bill entwined in bed away. Was I jealous? I fantasized about Lorenzo. Although what would we talk about? I mustn't gulp my wine. Slow down.

"Thanks," I said. "Could you top me up?"

"We have plenty of beer. Red wine? Oh, that's right. You don't drink red wine," Rose said. She blew smoke out through her nose. "That was our last drop of white. A shame."

I started coughing. Rose knew I was allergic to smoke; she also knew I didn't drink beer and red wine. The Shahrazad red gave me terrible heartburn. I preferred the local white, Bent Pyramid.

"I'll get my own bottle. If you don't mind," I said. I left my glass and my phone as insurance so I could get back into their flat.

"Not a problem," Rose said. "Watch this, Bill." She was blowing smoke rings.

"You're a piece of work," Bill said.

"My ass," Rose said, putting her toe in his crotch.

The moment I returned with my bottle, Bill asked, "Can I get you anything, Mary Beth?"

Rose drove her foot further into Bill's crotch and asked, "Are you fuckin' listening to me? Well, anyway, so Biljana's cat, Rumi, finally bit the dust. You know, the Serbian painter upstairs."

My mobile went off. "For she's a jolly good fellow. For she's a jolly good fellow."

Rose said, "You were teaching your class that day, Bill—Human Rights, Post-9/11. As I was saying, big crocodile tears were rolling down Biljana's cheeks."

I covered the mouthpiece of my mobile, "Two veiled women shot dead by the Egyptian police."

"Sweet Biljana looked at me with those big, sad eyes and said, 'Rumi is dead.'"

I covered the mouthpiece and repeated loudly, "Shootout between police and women in the City of the Dead, the graveyard."

"What's that, honey, what are you saying?" Bill asked.

"Veiled women associated with bomber who jumped off the bridge? One, his girlfriend? High-speed chase ensued after women shot at tour bus?" I repeated.

"How the hell would I know where Biljana can get her cat cremated?" Rose said, but no one was listening.

"Damn it, Rose You've already told me," Bill said. "I can't hear what Mary Beth's saying."

"Four Italians. Two Israelis. Three Greeks. Two Poles. Confirmed dead," I said. I watched Bill scratch his balls. "Okay, thanks." I clicked off the phone.

"Who were you talking to?" Bill asked.

"A reporter for AP," I said. "Good friend of mine. Would you mind getting me some more ice?"

"Sorry, we're out. Would you like to stay for supper?" Bill said.

"Not even two teeny weeny cubes?" I said, lapsing into baby talk.

"Get with the program. THERE-IS-NO-ICE!" Rose said.

"Rose, is that any way to treat a guest?" Bill said. "I'd like to jerk a knot in your tail."

Rose snorted. "Go right ahead, darlin'. Tie up my tail. And give me a good spankin'."

Bill shook his head. "Mary Beth, we don't have any ice, but stay for supper. You're good value." He turned to Rose. "Should I set the table or bring out the plates to the living room?"

"Whatever is easiest, darlin'," Rose said. "Don't put too much olive oil in the salad dressing. You're always doing that."

Why wasn't Rose concerned about this news?

About thirty minutes later, Bill carried in a huge bowl of pasta to the living room and set the pasta on the coffee table. "Dinner is served, ladies."

"I'm telling you what, Mary Beth. You need to have a man. This is the life. I'm done with Alabama," Rose said.

My phone rang again: "For she's a jolly good fellow, for she's a jolly good fellow…"

"Somers here," I said.

Rose was saying, "You know, Bill. My favorite story of the whole year was the donkey ride by the Pyramids. That fucker copped me for a feel and then wanted to overcharge me for the ride. You just sat there, laughing your ass off."

"You could've jumped off the donkey," Bill said.

I covered the mouthpiece on my mobile, "Rose, can you lower your voice?"

Rose ignored me and hooted, even louder. "Better than the donkey ride was the carpet seller from the Pyramids who told you he would buy me for twenty-five camels."

"He said ten camels," Bill said.

"Did not. He said twenty-five," Rose said. "I'm worth every camel. Don't ever forget that!"

"So, they're a new group. Off-shoots of cells. The Islamic Solution. The bombs were made at a marble factory. From nails," I said. "Don't you guys get it? This is a big story."

"Oh, big stories. I have big stories," Rose said, downing her wine. "But they're about carnie people in Alabama. You ever heard about my novel? Named as an Emerging Writer from the New South."

Curious that she had not mentioned it before. But before I could ask, Bill said,

"Did you know, Rose gives the most wonderful blow jobs?"

Rose sprayed her red wine all over the coffee table, she was laughing so hard. "Bill, darlin'…Don't tell our secrets."

"The news in Cairo. Don't you want to know?" I asked. How long had they been married?

"Of course, we know how to hoe. We're from Alabama," Bill said, smiling. He took a chug from his beer. He was sitting on the floor, with his legs crossed, as if he were the Buddha. I was surprised he was so limber. How on earth did they do it?

"No, darlin', Mary Beth said, 'Don't you want to know?' Wouldn't be caught dead with a hoe. Rather eat nails than hoe cotton," Rose said.

"No, I meant hoe. I was thinking of my father, who was a dirt farmer in Alabama. He just scratched out a living with a mule and a hoe," Bill said, smiling.

"Well, darlin'. We weren't talkin' about your father," Rose said. "He has trouble hearing."

Why was I desperate to be with these people? Maybe it was better to drink my wine alone and lie on the couch, reading Dervla Murphy's *In Ethiopia with a Mule.*

"Heard well enough. Class. Despair. You don't see rich people throwing themselves off bridges," Bill said.

"This story is a real tragedy, not a flip anecdote about a cat or a carpet seller!" I said.

"Whooaa. Back in the knife-box with you, Miss Sharp," Rose said. "I would tread lightly if I were you, sister."

Oh, God, what had I said? I needed to tone it down.

"You have the floor," Rose said. "Have any other news you want to share, darlin'? We're all ears."

"This is nothing. Small potatoes compared to my experiences in Lebanon," I said. "Once I interviewed Bachir Gemayel. A few hours before he was assassinated." They had never heard about my memoir, then.

Rose crumpled up her packet of Virginia Slim Menthols. "What did you say, darlin'? I think you might have to make a ciggie run, Bill."

"Would you smoke Marlboro? I have a pack in my apartment. Leftover from a party," I said.

That way I could get myself another bottle of white. However, when I went up to my apartment for the second bottle, I saw that the case was empty. No more Bent Pyramid wine. I couldn't find the pack of cigarettes, either. Damn! I opened my freezer. The ice cubes were hard. But now I had run out of wine. The elation I felt from getting the story had vanished. Without more of the dreamy, numbing sensation that wine gave me, I felt my mood go sour.

The phone cheeped like a sparrow.

"*Houston Chronicle*," I said.

"Mary Beth, is that you?"

"Who'd you think it would be? John Candy. Fat man of your dreams."

"Don't be a smart aleck," Sharon said.

"No shit, Sherlock," I said. Why was I being mean to my one true friend? Frustrated that the party upstairs was not going the way I thought it should go?

"Did you hear about the suicide bomber at the Egyptian Museum?"

"Yeah. There was also another attack two minutes ago. City of the Dead. A shootout," I said.

"Oh, my God! What happened? Why isn't it on CNN?" Sharon asked.

I was broke. Even if I ordered wine from the Blue Nile, I couldn't pay them.

"Tell you when you get here," I said. "Rose and Bill are having a party."

"They're always having parties," Sharon said. "You're so lucky."

"Tell you what I'll do. I'll call them if see if they mind if you come over."

"Could you?"

I hung up the phone, counted to twenty, and then called Sharon back.

"Rose says you're more than welcome," I said.

"Swell," Sharon said. "I don't know how to thank you."

I recognized Sharon's desperation. Did she sense mine?

"Why don't you mix yourself some martinis? Don't you have a large flask? These people don't drink anything but beer and red wine."

"I'll be over in a jiffy. Thanks, Mary Beth."

"No problem," I said. "By the way, could you bring over a bottle of white for me?"

When I returned to Rose and Bill's, I said, "I hope you don't mind, but I invited my friend, Sharon, to come for supper. She's all alone on her birthday."

Sharon and I had celebrated Sharon's birthday ten days before. We had started drinking at four o'clock in the afternoon. First, at the expatriate bar "Harry's" at the Marriott. Hadn't we met some Russian engineers who worked on the Aswan Dam? "Zzee Egyptian people are nice, but not so good on zzee de-tails," the Russian had said. Fyodor? Boris? I didn't remember his name. Did it matter? Sharon had worn one of her sleeveless camisoles with a plunging neckline. One of the Russian giants with yellow Dracula teeth had started paw-ing Sharon. We had stormed out of the bar after the harassment. Much later, we had moved to the expensive hotel, Four Seasons, for a splurge at an elegant Chinese restaurant called "Spice." I had white wine. I didn't remember how much. "Here's looking at you, sweetheart," I heard Humphrey Bogart's voice. Sharon had alternated between martinis and Bailey's. Sharon had called me the next day at noon, "Mary Beth, we have to cut back. Do you know we spent four hundred dollars last night? That was sweet of you."

"Sweet?" I choked.

That wasn't the adjective I would use to describe myself. Not sweet like Betty Crocker chocolate frosting. Frank. Gutsy. Like a fighter pilot. At least, I liked to think of myself as a fighter, but now I was beginning to wonder.

"Well, I don't know. You said it was a birthday treat. You put it on your credit card."

"Shit! No!"

But sure enough, after Sharon hung up, when I checked my coin purse, there was the receipt from my Visa card. More than four hundred dollars. Five hundred and twenty-five dollars, to be exact. Christ. These binges were killing me, financially.

I would have to cut back on my drinking. But not now. When? I gazed at my empty wine glass. I had brought back a Ziploc bag full of my own ice cubes to Rose and Bill's. Sharon was coming soon with my bottle.

Bill said, "I would hate for anyone to be alone on their birthday. Why don't I run out and get a cake at Mohammed's Sweet Delights?"

"Oh, it won't matter to Sharon. She's easy. Do you have any ice cream? Ice cream will do," I said.

Rose stared at me. She didn't bother to disguise her contempt. "We finished the ice cream yesterday," she said, breezily. "Rocky Road."

"Do you want me to go?" Bill said.

"Whatever…" Rose said. She studied one of her long, red fingernails.

Why had I lied about Sharon's birthday? To have the advantage over Rose, because she had put me down. No. Yes. Maybe I just wanted the bottle.

"But if it's her birthday we should do something," Bill said.

"You can go after we eat. It's not dire, darlin'," Rose said. "Don't see it as a human rights violation."

"I'm going," Bill said. He slapped the dish towel on the coffee table. "It wouldn't be right."

"For crying out loud, do you always have to be so decent?" Rose huffed. "You're not Atticus Finch in *To Kill a Mockingbird.*"

I would have to remember to tip Sharon off. Not more than three minutes after Bill had gone for the cake, the doorbell rang.

"I'm Sharon," Sharon said, extending her right hand. In her left hand was a giant carpetbag.

"Pleased to meetcha, Sharon," Rose said. "Welcome to the 'hood."

"I love the colors!" Sharon said, admiring the colors of each of the rooms. "Mary Beth says you have wonderful parties in this building. I live just around the corner but you know, there's no one in my building to talk to. I live all alone with my two cats, Peter and Pan."

"Sharon teaches mask-making at the university," I said.

"No shit," Rose said. "I'm writing a novel about people who speak in tongues to rattlesnakes." She poured herself some more red wine. "If they don't get bitten by the rattlesnake, then their prayers have been answered."

"Really?" I asked.

Rose sighed. "Yeah…Look, it's bad luck to talk about your novel, when you're writing it."

Suddenly I felt competitive with Rose and started to tell tales.

"Sharon does stock theater in the Berkshires. She's worked with famous actors like Richard Dreyfuss. They did *The Goodbye Girl,*" I said.

"Hmmm, interesting. What's in the bag, darlin'? Planning to spend the night?" Rose said.

I wondered if anything would ever impress Rose. She was not impressed by terrorists. She was not impressed by assassinations. She was not impressed by famous actors and actresses…

"I always say, 'Never come to a party empty-handed,'" Sharon said.

"It's not really a party," Rose said. "Just a few cocktails..."

I kicked Sharon's leg under the table, but Sharon paid no attention.

"You know, Rose, my grandma always said, 'You have to see your cup as half-full. Not half-empty,'" Sharon said, wagging her finger.

Then she snapped open the carpet bag and set two bottles of Bent Pyramid on the coffee table in front of Rose. One large metal flask. And a large bottle of Italian raisin wine. Why had Sharon brought that?

"Gawd, darlin'. Enough sauce for a Roman orgy," Rose said. "Planning to get cootered?"

If Sharon were taken hostage and a terrorist were holding a knife to her throat, she couldn't be subtle.

"Are your kids going to write up the story for *The Daily Mirage?*" Sharon said.

"What do you think?" I said.

"Well, I don't know. You're always talking about reporting the story. Checking sources. The importance of facts," Sharon said.

"They'll report it, all right," I said.

"What happened?" Sharon asked.

I was trying to work the corkscrew into the cork of the Bent Pyramid wine. The cork was stuck in the bottle. The cork refused to budge.

"Jesus Christ, Sharon, can't you see I'm trying to open this bottle of wine?" I said. I put the corkscrew again on the lip of the bottle. "This sucker is going to open."

"Eleven people died," Rose said. "Killed by two veiled women."

"Too bad. In the wrong place at the wrong time. By the way, you don't happen to have any martini glasses?" Sharon asked.

Rose didn't move a muscle. "Santa Claus mugs. Go ahead. Help yourself. First cupboard on the right in the kitchen."

"Ha! There we go. Sometimes these Bent Pyramid wine bottles have the lousiest corks," I said.

"I'm back," Bill said, closing the door. He threw Rose a pack of Virginia Slims.

"You're a peach," Rose said.

I fished into my Ziploc bag for three symmetrical cubes and dropped them into my glass. I poured the wine over the ice. The ice crackled. For a moment, I felt immense relief.

During dinner, Sharon talked about Mustafa, the Egyptian tailor who refused to take orders from her, and her department chair, Bob, who hid in his office, doing tai chi, rather than confront the thorny problems of his dysfunctional department.

"Maybe we could talk about something besides shop," I said.

"Cairo is bor-ing," Sharon announced.

"I don't know what you're talking about, darlin'. I think it's the most exciting place on earth. Every day's an awfully big adventure," Rose said.

"We've had a marvelous year in Cairo," Bill said. "My goodness, the Egyptians are wonderful."

"Well, that may be, but our salaries are too low," Sharon said. "We don't get paid enough for…"

Because I was so focused on opening the second bottle of white wine that Sharon had brought, I did not notice that Bill was standing in front of Sharon with a chocolate cake with lit candles. I did not have time to catch Sharon's eye.

Bill had started to sing, "Happy Birthday to you. Happy Birthday to you. Happy Birthday to you, dear Sharon." He was off-key. Rose was puffing on a cigarette.

"Oh, it's not my birthday today," Sharon said. "Who told you it was my birthday?"

Rose turned to Bill and said, "I told you it wasn't dire."

"Blow out the candles, dear," I said.

"My birthday was about ten days ago. Mary Beth took me out for a night on the town," Sharon said.

"Make a wish," Bill said.

"Blow out the candles," I repeated.

"Well, I don't know." Sharon laughed nervously. "Is this some sort of trick?"

"You could say that," Rose said.

"Make a wish, sweetheart," Bill said.

"Just blow them out!" I said. "Knife?" I used my girly voice.

"This was very sweet of you," Sharon said. "Very kind."

"We thought it was your birthday today. How old were you?" Bill said. He handed me the knife so I could cut the cake.

"Fifty," Sharon said.

"You look terrific. Not a day older than forty." He winked at her. "Nice legs."

I was annoyed that Bill was giving Sharon so much attention. He obviously found her attractive. Sharon was wearing a fitted linen purple dress that showed off her firm calves. Her arms were muscular. The white straps of her sandals twined around her tanned ankles. She seemed so feminine. In fact, if I were objective about it, Sharon had a better figure than anyone here.

"Flattery will get you everywhere." Sharon giggled.

"Sharon!" I said. "Behave!"

"Oh, you sound like a schoolteacher," Sharon said. "You're always scolding me."

"What did you wish for?" Bill asked.

"They say you should never tell your wish or it won't come true," Sharon said.

"Aw, come on. You're among friends. You can tell us," Bill said. He was smiling. I could now see what made him attractive. Even though he was bald and he had a paunch, his brown eyes were lively and he had a sweet smile.

Sharon laughed. "I don't even know you. Why should I tell you my wish?"

"Because it's your birthday. Birthdays are special," Bill said. "It's the day the world was graced with your presence."

"Oh, how lovely," Sharon said. "We never celebrated birthdays in our family. Too many kids."

I handed Rose a large slice of chocolate cake. She shook her head. "Have you heard this little joke? Just a little Alabama wisdom. What do guests and fish have in common?"

"Haven't a clue," I said. "Maybe Sharon can tell us the answer to that one. She always knows the punch lines."

"What?" Sharon said.

"I said, 'What do guests and fish have in common?'" Rose asked. She filled her wine glass to the brim.

"I don't know," Sharon said. She was licking the chocolate icing off the fork. "This is a divine cake. Where did you get it?"

"Down the street. At Mohamed's Sweet Delights," Bill said.

"What's your joke about fish and guests?" Sharon asked. "Is that joke from Alabama? I'm from Oregon."

"They both smell after three hours." Rose said. She hooted.

I found myself laughing, too. My grandmother, who was from North Carolina, used to say that, too.

"For crying out loud, Rose," Bill said. "Do you always have to...?"

"What?" Rose said, running her red fingernails through her spiky hair. "Thought you liked bad girls."

"We're bad," I said. "Are you going to pull down our panties and whip us with a black leather belt?"

"Yeah. Give us a spanking," Rose said. "Dare you." She pointed her finger at him provocatively—the red fingernail seemed to invite him.

Suddenly, I had the image of both myself and Rose bent over with our large naked fannies. Desperate for Bill to fuck us, doggy-style, right then and there. Sharon, the little girl, was watching, her mouth agape, horrified. I did not know why, but this turned me on, more than gazing at pictures of buff-looking men in *Playgirl*. Or even that handsome Italian, Lorenzo, with his hairy fingers.

Sharon set her plate down. "I get the picture."

"Why don't you finish your cake?" Bill said. "It's for you."

"Actually, I think I'll just go home. Hang out with Peter and Pan," Sharon said. "I think they might be better company." Sharon's eyes filled with tears.

Oh, my God. What had I done!

"Rose..." Bill said. "Damn it." Bill picked up one of the dessert plates. A thick wedge of chocolate cake sat on the plate, untouched.

"Why are you looking at me, darlin'? Mr Knight-in-Shining-Armor. Mr Atticus Finch," Rose said. She had put her feet up on the coffee table. She was blowing smoke rings. "Saving Damsels-in-Distress. Sad sacks. Losers."

On impulse, I threw the rest of my wine in her face.

Rose lunged for me across the couch. She scratched at my face with her red claws. I socked her in the eye.

"Motherfucker," Rose shouted. "You die." Rose was tearing my hair.

The lamp on the end table next to the couch crashed over.

"Mary Beth! Stop it!" I heard Sharon saying. "Stop! Please. There's broken glass everywhere!"

"Ladies! Ladies!" Bill shouted.

But now we were rolling around on the floor. My scalp burned. Biker bitch. Why didn't Rose dress in black leather and chains? She bit my ear. I ripped off one of her heavy silver earrings. Too bad she didn't have pierced ears.

"They are going to kill each other," Sharon said. "Do something!"

A whole clump of my salt and pepper hair came out in Rose's fist. Rose spat in my face. I kicked her in the boob. "Bitch," I shouted. She hissed, "Cunt."

Bill was tugging on my arm. "Aawww." He was trying to separate us. "Ladies!"

"If you fuckin' wanted a lady, why didn't you marry someone else?" Rose said. She kicked me in the shin. "Some belle of the ball who wears white gloves."

"Shit!" I went for her spiky hair. Her pride and joy.

"Know-it-all," Rose said. "Fraud! Hack!"

Bill was pulling my right arm while Rose was pulling my left arm.

"Mary Beth! Please. Stop!" Sharon said. She was jumping up and down like a small kid. "You're going to get hurt."

Bill yanked me back so hard away from Rose that we fell backwards at the same time. I landed on top of his large belly. My head bonked him on the nose. "Lord," Bill said. Rose was sprawled out on the parquet floor.

"Jesus," I said. I rolled off of Bill.

"Well…" Bill said. "Are you all right?"

"Yeah," I said. "I'm okay." My hands were shaking.

"Watch the glass!" Sharon said. Shards of glass glittered on the parquet floor.

After Bill stood up, he offered me his hand.

"Aren't you going to help your wife?" Rose said, extending her hand. Two of her fingernails were broken.

"An apology would be in order," Bill said. He ignored Rose's hand. "Is this your idea of Southern hospitality?"

Rose was breathing hard. "You can do what you like, Bill. But I'm done with these bitches. NO MORE ICE!"

"I think we should be going." Sharon was clutching her carpet bag. "It was…."

Rose snorted. "Yeah. I haven't had this much fun since the hogs ate grandma."

"The birthday cake," Sharon said, facing Bill. "Was a sweet gesture…"

"You are most welcome," Bill said. "I'm very sorry that…"

Rose was still lying on the parquet floor. Why wasn't she on the stage?

"I'm sorry I lost my cool," I said. I knew I'd never set foot in their apartment again.

"Hmmph…" Rose snorted again.

"If you can't apologize, keep your mouth shut, Rose," Bill said.

"I don't know what came over me," I said. "I'm sorry, Rose."

Overpowering rage? Could now see how crimes of passion were committed.

"Shake and be friends," Sharon said.

This was a ridiculous suggestion. Did Sharon think she was the junior high school principal? "Well…" I said. "See you at the university."

"Bill. My inhaler. Asthma attack," Rose said. She was wheezing.

"Just curious. What other people in Lebanon did you interview besides Gemayel?" Bill asked. "Any other people who were assassinated?"

"Bill, darlin'. I'm serious. Get my inhaler," Rose said. She was having a coughing fit. Hard to tell if it was genuine or not.

"It was a long time ago," I said. Sharon was leading me toward the door. "I'll tell you another time." I had buried it and rarely talked about being held hostage. The memoir had not sold well. And I had never gone to therapy.

"Good night, neighbors," Bill said. He shut the door gently.

—⟊⟊—

"Mary Beth, are you all right?" Sharon asked, when we got down to the next landing. "You have blood on your face."

"No, I'm not," I said. My eyes felt hot from the tears. "Rose's right. I'm a hack. A loser."

"You are not a loser," Sharon said. "She was drunk. We were all drunk."

"She was just telling the truth," I said. "Something I never do. I've been fooling myself all these years. I'm not Carl Bernstein. Never was. Never will be."

"That's not true. You're doing a great job with *The Daily Mirage*. The kids love you," Sharon said.

"Want to come over for a nightcap? Bailey's with ice," I said.

I knew this was a no-no, but I couldn't resist.

"We have to cut back," Sharon said.

"Just one," I said.

"We have to cut back on our drinking. Maybe we could watch *Survivor*, that reality TV show, instead."

"I don't want to watch *Survivor*. Couldn't you humor me this once?" I felt myself getting peevish again.

"Oh, all right. Just one," Sharon said.

I opened the door to my flat and headed straight for the freezer. Just as quickly, I forgot about my brawl with Rose. Seeing so many plastic trays of ice made me feel airy. Light. Generous. Sorry that I had been mean to Sharon.

I took out one of the trays from the freezer and popped out several cubes. Turning to Sharon, as I had many times before, I said, "How many cubes?"

"Three."

I did not remember what time Sharon left. But the next morning I was woken up by the ring on my mobile, "For she's a jolly good fellow."

"I'm not jolly," I said to the ring tone. My head throbbed. What time was it? I checked the phone number on my mobile. *The Daily Mirage*.

"Okay, guys, take responsibility," I said, as if I were speaking to my journalism class. I didn't answer the phone. Instead, I threw on my white cotton bathrobe and went to my study, which I had painted purple. Copying Rose? I picked up a story I had started about a Mongolian businessman who had lost his bride on a camel trip in the Western Desert of Egypt. I had never sent the story in to the *New York Times*. Too busy with *The Daily Mirage*. Hadn't I been doomed to the farm team my whole career? No big gigs for me. Other reporters I knew had been promoted over me—it had been very disappointing. I had spent many late nights pecking at a typewriter or shouting stories into the phone. Eating cold falafel at three o'clock in the morning. Throwing up my cookies after too much drink. But what I had loved about reporting in Beirut: the absolute thrill of making history. Or was that also an illusion? Once, just as Roy and I were driving away from the Ali Baba falafel restaurant in the company jeep, the place had exploded into flames. Roy had placed his hand over mine. We had driven straight to my basement apartment and made love, even though we were on assignment. Roy had said, laughing, "So they fire us?" Roy had picked up my bikini underwear, which was drying on a lamp, and put it on his head, as if it were a crown. I was eating cold cashew Chinese chicken out of the box. Very tenderly, he undressed me. Lou Reed's

"Walk on the Wild Side" was playing on the radio. Later, Roy had left me when he got his big break with the *LA Times*.

I had fallen in love with fairy tales when I was small—Rumpelstiltskin, the man who spun everything into gold. Why had it taken so long to learn that there was no gold? After my mother read me fairy tales, I had scrawled out stories in purple crayon about a magical place called Wish Pond on butcher paper. But after the twins were stillborn, my mother's eyes were red. On those days, I was shepherded over to my grandmother's by my father—I threaded macaroni and buttons on pieces of green thread at the kitchen table for hours.

The phone rang again from *The Daily Mirage*. "Doctoor, Doctoor, we need you to sign off on the suicide bomber story so we can run it tomorrow," the student said.

"Okay," I said. And then, of course, after the publication of my memoir about being held hostage, I had expected my career to take off. But the *Chronicle* had not promoted me as they had promised. In fact, I was no longer reporting—what I loved most. Some lame excuse about my attitude: you had to hand it to management. A month after, I had discovered that my husband, Marty, had gambled away our savings. I cobbled together a living: during the day, I was Circulation Manager at the *Chronicle*, and at night, I taught Beginning Journalism at a community college. That summer, I drove a Pinto without air conditioning. Unbearable in muggy, sweltering Houston.

"Doctoor," the student said. "Is there something wrong? Are you sick?"

"No, dear, I'm all right," I said. I was staring at my bloated face in the mirror with the scratch marks from Rose's red fingernails. I had always had such a beautiful, smooth complexion.

"We are waiting for you," the student said.

"I'll be there as soon as I throw on some clothes," I said.

"You always say, 'Go for the story.' We checked the facts," the student said. The phone clicked.

Go for the story, I repeated to myself, as if I were hearing that tired old saw for the first time. Check the facts. Even if the story was cruel and sad? What I had learned at journalism school seemed ludicrous. Absurd. Who wanted the truth, anyway? One of the twelve easy steps from Alcoholics Anonymous popped into my head: "Make a searching and fearless inventory of ourselves…" With my hand, I wiped the mucus that dripped from my nose. I could not remember the last time I had been touched by a man with any real tenderness. Once I had had a sleek figure, like Sharon, but now my hips had widened; my tummy had swelled from the wine. Now, I wore stretch caftans—one-size-fits-all outfits—funereal black. Not the bright, cheerful colors I had loved as a child. I felt myself floating towards the kitchen for a cube of ice.

I wished for coolness under my tongue.

8

Shahrazad's Gift

"But morning overtook Shahrazad, and she lapsed into silence, leaving King Shahrayar burning with curiosity to hear the rest of the story. Then Dinarzad said to her sister, Shahrazad, 'What a strange and lovely story!' Shahrazad replied, 'What is this compared with what I shall tell you tomorrow night if the king spares me and lets me live? It will be even better and more entertaining.'"

—From *The Arabian Nights*.

DR SAMUEL PLUCKED OUT THE CROWN FROM my infected gum. He studied the tooth with curiosity, as if it were an ancient fossil, and said, "No one uses acrylic these days. That's why your gums are in such bad shape. I know he would be sued in America."

Well, it probably won't happen here. My gums hurt. I was staring at the skull of a cow taped to the ceiling—Georgia O'Keeffe—Dr Samuel had artistic taste. I should have fired that colorful Armenian dentist, Vartan, in downtown Cairo after the crown fell out for the third time.

"It's terrible work. Can I keep the tooth?"

"Sure," I said. "The fairy godmother isn't going to come and take it from my pillow."

Dr Samuel chuckled. He had intense brown eyes, and a head of full black hair—nicely trimmed. My hair used to be a striking black, but had gone salt and pepper.

"Open," he said. He peered into my mouth. "Can you open wider?" He was probably about forty.

"Have you been to North Carolina? They are good people. *Wilad balad.* Salt of the earth."

"You lived there?"

"That's where I did my PhD in Periodontal Disease."

"My grandmother was from a little place called Pilot Mountain. She made the best fried chicken," I said.

"I know the town. Are you from North Carolina?"

"Texas."

"What are you doing in Cairo?"

"I was a journalist. Mostly in Lebanon. Now I'm teaching."

"When were you in Lebanon? Were you covering the war?"

"Oh, yes. It was grisly. I covered the William Buckley story. Do you remember that one?"

"Sort of," he said, scratching his head. "There were so many. Wasn't he supposed to be CIA?"

"Everyone was accused of that," I said. "I met Buckley with some other reporter pals in the Commodore Bar the day before he was taken hostage. I started to hate my job and put in a request to transfer. My request was accepted, but then, of course, I couldn't leave."

"Why not?"

I laughed. "I was taken hostage myself."

"I read quite a few books on it." He looked at the chart. "Mary Beth Somer. Your name sounds familiar. Wait a minute. Did you write a book?"

"Quite a while ago. Seventeen years, maybe."

"Were you taken hostage with a preacher?"

"Yes," I said.

"I read your book! Couldn't put it down. I was a student at Cairo University at the time."

"Really?" I said. I felt flattered. I wasn't covering many interesting stories lately.

"How do you feel about it now?" he asked.

"I refused therapy," I said. "That was a mistake." *Rope chafes my wrists. They are spitting on me: "Tell us what you know." I am always thirsty.*

"You probably don't want to talk about it," Dr Samuel said. "Sorry, I didn't mean to pry."

"It was a long time ago," I said. And yet? "Listen, Doctor Samuel, do you think I'll lose my tooth?"

"It's not past the point of no return. But..."

Dr Samy seemed like a very sincere guy. Someone I could talk to.

"But...?"

He was serious now. "You have a bad case of periodontal disease. And we have to get rid of all this plaque. Are you ready?"

"No! But I'm sure I don't have a choice."

He held the shiny pick carefully between his fingers. "This isn't going to be a fun ride. I'll try not to hurt you."

After he had scraped for a long while, he said, "Are you all right?"

My eyes filled with tears.

"Take this," he said, handing me a tissue to wipe the blood that was dribbling from my lips.

I still hated the sight of blood. I suddenly remembered an explosion I had covered in Beirut. The tiny hand of a two-year-old boy—severed in the rubble. I had gagged and then run away to vomit.

"Do you floss?" he said, winding the thread around his thumbs.

"Now and then," I said.

"You have beautiful teeth. You don't want to have implants."

"Implants? Lord!"

"Gum replacement."

"Oh," I said. "That sounds bad." This was worse than a B horror movie! I remembered our failed project to get our maid, Fatma, new teeth.

"You probably won't," he said. "You just need to take better care of your teeth."

Dr Samy gave me more instructions on flossing. Then he said, "Why not have a drink with a fan? You probably have a lot of great stories. I don't have any patients who have been taken hostage."

I laughed. "You make me sound like I'm more famous than I am." Although it was true, after the book came out, I was interviewed on radio and talk shows. After ten or twelve interviews, I refused. My agent was peeved. "But why? The book is selling like hotcakes." I had snapped, "Being a hostage wasn't a walk in the park." I couldn't reduce my painful experience to a facile advertisement.

"Good," Dr Samy said. He clacked a set of model teeth at me. "Now, for a lesson on brushing...."

We started meeting on Friday evenings in the Barrel Bar at the Windsor Hotel—a bar with barrel-shaped chairs and an old-world feel. Gazelle antlers were hung on the wall. Dr Samy had suggested it. "It's close to my parents' flat. The old British Officers' Club. It has character."

When Dr Samy came in, I was looking at a framed newspaper article on the wall about the history of the bar. I could imagine British officers puffing on their cigars or smoking their pipes. Now the bar served cheap beer and appealed to "the adventurous traveler." Dr Samy was wearing a pair of khaki pants and a short-sleeve Oxford cloth shirt: practical attire for September weather. Out of his white lab coat, he looked even more boyish.

"Hello, Dr Samy," I said, offering my hand. I gave him a firm handshake.

He said, "Now, that's a Texas handshake. Please, call me Samy."

We told each other about our lives. Or rather, I was telling him about my life. He had not been very forthcoming about his. After a month, I had learned: he was forty-three; he had lived in North Carolina for ten years; he had been back in Cairo for one year; he was teaching at Cairo University. No mention of a woman.

My Irish drinking pal, Gaby, an Irish secretary at UNESCO, said, "Well... if he's that secretive, pet, he's probably married. Men are real bastards. I've been through all the dross until I got the real rubbish at the bottom. You better find out." She knew all about her boss' affairs, and sometimes even had to order champagne and reserve the hotel rooms.

"Don't think so," I said. Samy seemed like a kind, good-hearted person. And he had not really made any insinuating moves, as the married reporters in Beirut who wanted "some on the side" did.

"Care for a beer?" Samy said. The older waiter with the dyed black hair almost bowed. He was dressed in black pants and a starched white shirt. The bow tie was slightly askew. When he smiled, he was missing two front teeth. Uh, oh! Too late for lessons on flossing!

"No fried chicken here. But they have good pizzas. How about a pizza? Go on. You were telling me about what you thought was your last night."

"It was in the book," I said. "Late one night, they had blindfolded us and taken us out to a field. We were forced to kneel. They were shouting, 'This is your last chance. We know you are infiltrators. Spies.' Lucas called out, 'As God is our witness, we're innocent.'"

Samy traced his finger along his eyebrow when he was listening. "Lucas was the preacher who was taken hostage with you. How many days chained to a radiator?"

"Two hundred and five days."

"I couldn't imagine what it would be like to be tied to a radiator for that many days."

"I didn't deal with it. My friend, Lucas, had amazing spiritual strength. He recited stories from the Bible to me. But me, no," I said. "I was a mess."

"Here's our pizza." Samy served me a slice.

I took a bite. "You're right. Not bad."

"And...?"

"They said, 'Tell us what you know.' I was mute. Lucas said, 'Trust in the Lord with all your heart and soul, Mary Beth.'"

"So, you thought it was the end?"

I laughed. "Oh, yes." I said. "That happened more than once. But what about you? Why did you come back to Egypt after all those years of living in North Carolina? You seem to love the place."

"Let's talk about Hosni Mubarak. My Siamese cat in America. I found him under a car in a Kroger's parking lot."

I giggled. "Hosni Mubarak? Funny name for a cat."

"Well, yeah...I was a volunteer for the animal shelter. Saved abandoned animals. But your story is more interesting. Tell me," he said. "What on earth did you do to pass the time?"

"We told stories. Played cards. Recited poetry. If we could remember it.... Lucas had memorized poetry in high school and he could recite it by the ream. That turned out to be a blessing. We only had a few books. *Clan of the Cave Bear* and Chairman Mao's story. Imagine those are the only two books on earth and you are stuck with them? Lucas was better able to detach himself emotionally. He taught me to pray." My eyes suddenly filled with tears. "He taught me to pray."

Samy handed me a hanky.

"I'm sorry," I said.

"It's okay," he said. "You have to cry."

Before I met Samy, I had boozed it up with Gaby on Fridays at Lucky Bob's, a wannabe English pub. In the beginning, Gaby and I fed off of each other's hard-luck stories and I had found her superficial gossip about other expatriates amusing and diversionary from my own problems. But since I had started meeting Samy, I felt more light-hearted and happier. Gaby was sure I'd abandoned her for a man.

Gaby said, "Now tell me, dear, was he wearin' a wedding ring by any chance?" She was pouring herself whiskey as if it were fresh buttermilk. My pleasure was now white wine. I absolutely could not drink the hard stuff anymore. For years, I had tried to keep up with the boys after we had filed our stories.

"I didn't notice," I said.

"Oh, for goodness' sake, dear, what do you mean you didn't notice? Come on, you're the journalist. I thought you were trained to pay attention to details. Look for the feckin' ring."

I shrugged. "Look, he's not sleazy. Anyway, we're just talking. He has a funny way of talking out of the side of his mouth, as if he is going to say something wry. I like that."

"Oh, I don't like the sound of that at all. He sounds a bit iffy to me."

"He's just being playful."

"You better be careful, lamb. You told me what happened with that sweetheart of yours, Roy. That sounded like a nightmare. What on earth possessed you?"

"Water under the bridge," I said. "I've gotten over Roy."

Gaby raised a doubt, though. On the other hand, Gaby enjoyed being bitter. Did I also relish poisonous stories? I had told her how Roy had gotten a big job at the *LA Times*; I had gotten the boot at the *Houston Chronicle*. He had promised he would leave his wife; he hadn't. I never saw him again after his seven-hundred-page memoir was published. Why waste another thought on the guy? Except that we had a lot of sleepless nights, listening to the eerie squealing of bombs. Just once I'd like to call him up and say, "Hey, Bones, are you all right?" We had pet names for each other—he called me Tuff-Tuff, since he said I was "quick on the questions." I called him Bones. Our office at the AP had been bombed when Roy was on night shift; he had lost his eye. He wore a pirate's patch over his missing eye.

At the Windsor, I noticed a young woman with a fat blonde ponytail who was traveling alone. She was scribbling notes into a small black Moleskine journal. Occasionally, she would sip from her glass of red wine. Once upon a time, I had written up my notes in steno notebooks in bars. Was the young woman a thoughtful tourist or a journalist? Did it matter? Self-expression didn't always have to be packaged into an article or a book.

I had stopped jotting things down. I had imagined that the Armenian dentist might make an interesting feature. But he had turned out to be a curmudgeon and almost ruined my gums!

"Who were they?" Samy asked.

"What?"

"The guys who took you hostage."

"A group that had split off from Hezbollah. Organization for the Oppressed and the Pitiable of the Earth."

"Nice name."

"Oh, yeah," I said. "But not Mister Nice Guys. I covered many of the hostage stories. Yet I never I thought anything bad would happen to me! That's how naive I was. It's weird what you think of when you think it's your last moment. I thought of my grandfather. And Roy, for a moment."

"Who's Roy?"

"Roy Wise. He also published a book on Lebanon. He was my boyfriend. He's famous now."

"Never heard the name."

"Oh," I said. That surprised me. Roy had his own talk show now—he had exploited his experience in the US in a way I could not.

"What were you going to tell me?" Samy said. "About the exact moment when they pointed their guns at you."

"Are you sure you're not a shrink?"

Samy laughed. "No. Of course not. I had two courses in medical school. But I already knew what to do. Go on."

"They shouted, 'Tell us what you know.' I blanked. I didn't remember a single word of Arabic. I shouted in English, 'Fire. Fire.' My feet were on fire. I was barefoot. Thorns were cutting my feet. A flash, like the lights of a big truck. South Texas. My grandfather has rigged up a rope across the front yard; he is walking. Without his left arm, he is losing his balance. He will not lose his balance if he holds onto the rope. A sprinter in his time at a small college in West Texas, soon he will not be able to walk. And yet, for a moment he is delighted. A mother armadillo blocks his way in the grass; three tiny little armadillos are fanned around her."

"Go ahead," Samy said. He offered me another piece of pizza.

I shook my head. "Not hungry. I don't remember how we got back to the room. When did they chain us up again? I don't know. It was Christmastime and they gave us a cake in the shape of a Yule log and a few oranges. My ears were still roaring. I shat on myself. It was a mess. They wouldn't even let me wash myself off."

Samy was looking at me with his intense, brown eyes. "*Hiwanat.*" Animals, he said.

My eyes welled with tears. He handed me a Kleenex.

"Lucas and I sang, 'Oh Come All Ye Faithful, Joyful and Triumphant,'" I said. "That song always reminds me of my grandparents. Going to the Presbyterian Church with them when I was little. Not so long ago, my grandmother appeared to me in a dream. She said, 'You don't call me anymore.' How can you phone someone who's dead?"

Samy said, "No, you can't talk to the dead." He was silent.

"Are you all right?" I asked.

"Yeah," he said. "Go on."

"They kept repeating, 'Tell us what you know. Spies! Infiltrators! Imperialists of the Universe. You're liars!'"

Suddenly, Samy covered his face with his hands. "God."

"Samy, are you all right? Did something similar happen to you?"

"Yes," he said. "I don't want to discuss the matter."

"Okay," I said. "Maybe we should get our bill?"

"No," Samy said. He was adamant. "I don't want to go. I want to listen to the rest of your story."

"We can do it another day," I said. "You're upset."

"Go on," he said. He was wiping his forehead with a Kleenex. Even though it wasn't hot in the bar, he was sweating.

I took a swig of beer. "Lucas was cutting the Yule log with a piece of cardboard. He didn't answer me when I said, 'You think we'll languish here forever?' Instead, he said, 'You can have the maraschino cherry.' I said, 'No, you take it.' Even though I said that, I popped it into my mouth, like a six-year-old kid. I repeated, 'Think we'll languish here forever? I'm thirsty.' Lucas answered, 'We have to thank God for our many blessings.' I was angry. 'I'm not blessed.' He looked at me squarely in the eye and said, 'But you are. Not everyone has experienced this.'

"'Like what? The story of two people who were forgotten by the world?'

"'No,' Lucas said. 'That's not what I want to hear. You have not been forgotten. Pretend you're sitting by the fire. For each link in our chain, you must tell me a story about someone you love. It's exactly like a prayer.'

"'I'm sick of pretending. It's freezing. I'm thirsty. I have to pee. I can't read *Clan of the Cave Bear* again.'

"At that moment, the door opened. The boy with the stutter sneaked us fresh honey and labna. 'It's your feast day,' he said.

"Lucas said, 'You see, this is the story of the loaves and fishes. We have to see the miracles in daily life.'

"I think I said something sarcastic. I can't remember. But Lucas was right."

"Did you tell Lucas a story?" Samy asked.

"I told him the story of my grandparents. He had told me stories about his wife and children."

"That wasn't in your book?"

"No," I said. "My editor cut out the story. I didn't insist. I'll tell you if you really want to know. I'd like a glass of white wine."

Samy called over the waiter and ordered another Stella beer and a glass of white wine.

I could pretend I was the young woman with the fat blonde ponytail, optimistic. Maybe she reminded me of myself.

The waiter returned with one Stella and a glass of wine and a plate of peanuts from Aswan.

"Love these," I said, scooping up a few Aswan peanuts in the palm of my hand. "Are you sure you want to hear the story?"

"Yes," Samy said. "I'm curious." He nibbled on a peanut.

"Once there was a young man from West Texas who grew up in a dugout. He was very poor. At first, he hitchhiked to Tennessee to the Peabody School for Teachers, but he didn't like what he saw. And then he carried on farther until he came to the University of North Carolina and he settled there and the school saw he had talent and gave him a scholarship and he ate one meal a day at the boarding house. He fell in love with a curly-haired woman whose father worked on the railroad. She was studying Latin and she liked to dance."

"'I want an inspiring story,' Lucas had said.

"In the first year of their marriage, a mysterious monster settled in the nerves of his shoulder. The curly-haired woman who liked to dance felt as if a boxer had pummeled her in the stomach. She was twenty-four. But the doctor took her aside and said, 'Don't despair. We have Magic.'

"The monster was destroyed by a New Wonder and the man from West Texas who fell in love with the curly-haired woman lived forty-five more years. After he recovered, he and the curly-haired woman taught school in an oil-boom town and then he became a superintendent there—they taught geometry, Latin, English, Spanish, basketball, football. They had two boys, a silent tinkerer of engines, and the other, a lover of words, who followed his mother everywhere until she introduced him to *The Hardy Boys*. The serious man taught himself the law, passed the bar, and moved his family from the dusty plains of Lubbock to the edge of an orange grove near Mexico. They were very happy because they had escaped tornadoes and could eat sweet grapefruit and papayas every day. Much later, a nastier monster with a distorted face returned, and the shoulder and arm had to be severed. He drove his Karmann Ghia with one hand. The wheel flew free while he shifted. Sometimes the car was driving itself. I was fifteen and loved riding in the Ghia. It was like *Chitty Chitty Bang Bang*. I am the daughter of the son who loved words and read every *Hardy Boy* mystery.

"Lucas insisted that I continue with the story. And he asked what happened to the one-armed man."

"What happened to him?" Samy asked.

"I couldn't tell Lucas. So, I said, 'Let's play poker. *Blindman's Bluff. Go Fish.*' Anything. We had made playing cards from little pieces of cardboard. But Lucas didn't want to play cards: he wanted to listen to the rest of the story. I said, 'Look, Lucas, you can't force someone to tell you a story. I'm not in the mood.'

Lucas stopped talking to me for five hours! Even a man as good as Lucas could be flawed. He was human."

"So, you never told him the rest?" Samy said. "It never came up?"

"No."

"Why not?"

"The one-armed man tottered, teetered, and then finally toppled over. And the curly-haired woman was dwarfed from carrying him on her back."

"So, he died?"

"Yes," I said. "It was a terrible death. But you see, we had to keep our spirits up. We had to think about living, not dying. Anyway, the boy with the stutter appeared at the right moment that evening. His name was Adel. He brought us *makdus*, those baby eggplants stuffed with walnuts and chilies. 'My grand-mother made them,' he said. 'My grandmother simply doesn't believe you are Imperialists of the Universe,' he said. This struck us as funny and we laughed and laughed until tears came into our eyes. We hadn't laughed for a long time."

"One day Adel disappeared. No more treats," I said. "No more homemade Lebanese food. Just dry bread and olives."

"Do you think Adel died? Was killed?"

I shrugged. "Could be. That's the way it was in the civil war. People just disappeared. Sometimes they were killed in the street on their way to buy bread. They just never came back. We kept asking the other guards, but they were vague. They refused to tell us. I drew a picture of an eggplant on the wall with a nub of lead: the 100th day. Our halfway mark."

"When were you released?"

"Easter. 1986. Lucas saw this as significant. Maybe it was."

"I think I remember…."

"Maybe. There were a lot of hostages at that time. Grisly. So many didn't make it. Died in captivity. Tossed in ditches."

"You were lucky," he said.

"Oh, yes," I said. "We were."

"Tell me again about how you were released."

"One day some men we had never seen before came and blindfolded us. For the second time, I thought that was it. But they dumped us near the Ameri-can Embassy in Beirut. We looked awful. But we were alive. It had just rained. I remember the smell of jasmine."

I held up my glass. I was a little tipsy. "A toast. To being alive." I hiccupped.

Samy laughed. He raised his stein. *"Fee Sehetik."* To your health.

"Salud," I said. We clinked our glasses. For a moment, I felt I was looking at a rainbow.

But I had had too much drink and couldn't stop talking.

"You wouldn't believe it but one more terrible thing happened. The weekend after we were released, Lucas flew to Cairo to meet his wife, Ruth, and their daughter, Maggie. Maggie was teaching school in Alexandria. After they had a wonderful reunion, Maggie left. On the way back to Alex, her bus crashed into a train. She was twenty-four."

The smile disappeared from Samy's face. He looked genuinely distressed.

"I'm sorry," I said. "I'm drunk. This is very sad. Absolutely the wrong thing to say after a toast. Tactless."

He shook his head. "You didn't do anything wrong." But soon after, he called for the check. The following week, he canceled our meeting.

The Barrel Bar was decorated with red tinsel. They had put up a real pine tree. When I went over to inspect the decorations on the Christmas tree, they were tiny amulets of Tutankhamen. I thought this was a little strange, but the Barrel Bar was a crazy place. When Samy strolled in, he had a present tucked under his arm. Somehow, he looked more serious than the first time I had met him, even though he was wearing casual clothes, baggy Levis and a flannel shirt. There were dark circles under his eyes.

He had wrapped the present very carefully. The wrapping paper was covered with a jolly Santa Claus and decorated with a big red bow. I tore open the wrapping paper. It was a large leather book with rough handmade paper. My name was engraved on the spine in gold letters.

"Write down the stories, please," he said. "For each link in the chain…"

"It's beautiful," I said. "But I'm not writing. I'm only a journalism teacher. A supervisor of *The Daily Mirage.*"

He laughed. "*The Daily Mirage?*"

I giggled. "It's appropriate."

"Did you give the newspaper the name? It's your humor."

"No, the kids came up with it. Some of them are pretty good. They really hustled and came up with some good stories, especially before the Iraq War. 2003."

"Anyway, put the pen on the paper. You might be surprised," Samy said.

"I don't have a present for you."

He shrugged. "I don't care about things. It's really a goodbye present."

"Goodbye? Are you leaving?"

Gaby had become more and more insistent that Samy was a fraud. She was hectoring me: if he hasn't told me his story by now, he must be dishonest.

"Yes, I am," Samy said. "I have to go back to North Carolina. Living here was temporary. I had to get away."

I just knew that there had to be an honest explanation. "So, you're married?"

He looked genuinely surprised. "No," he said. "I'm not. I mean, I was. Oh, I see," he said. "It's just that I couldn't talk about it before." He gestured with his hands and opened his mouth, but the only thing that came out was a croak.

"What happened?"

At last, he spoke, "My wife died of ovarian cancer last year. She was only forty."

"Oh," I said. "I'm really sorry." Words seemed inadequate for grief. But what else could I say?

He cleared his throat. "I came back to live with my parents. But I am too old for that. My mother is overfeeding me with her grape leaves. And trying to introduce me to virginal girls in their twenties. I prefer the American way of life. I like to be alone. Here—there's no privacy."

"I understand," I said. "Do you have any children?"

"No," he said. "No babies. We planned on it." His voice croaked again. "It's just that…." He waved his hand. "We didn't expect…"

"I'm sorry."

"I didn't want to tell you another sad story. I didn't want to bother you," Samy said. "It was never the right time."

"No one has the corner on sadness."

"We'll keep in touch," Samy said.

And he sent me the occasional postcard with captions like: *Visit the Rocky Mountain Park*. On the back, he scribbled: "How's your tooth?" Underneath he signed his name with a flourish. Beside the signature, he drew a caricature of a dentist, extracting a tooth from a panicked patient.

A year or so after our meetings at the Barrel Bar, the postcards dried up. The bad dreams had almost disappeared. I moved back to Beirut and fell in love with one of my Lebanese colleagues, Elias, from our old AP office. He was now running a wonderful restaurant in Ashrafiyya called Filomenke. I was never tempted to join a card game with our customers, but I hung around and listened to their stories. I started writing a novel.

But I never saw Samy again.

9

Tiger

NAME'S HALE, DUDE. I REACHED OUT AND offered my hand. His hand-shake was soft. Suppose they don't shake hands like we do in Alabama. Since the time I was a little kid, my folks always taught me to shake hands and say, "Pleased to meetcha." In fact, my father always yelled at me if I didn't shake hands with firm conviction. He used to say, "A successful business-man always knows how to shake hands." And here, this dude is shaking hands just to please me. A very soft handshake.

"Meetcha?"

"Meet you," I said. I slowed down, "Nice to meet you."

"Oh," he said. "It is my good chance. My name is Adel." He raised his beer. I was fried and hadn't slept for days. I had just lost my teaching assistantship at the University of Mississippi. "Inappropriate behavior," the Dean had said. The fact was, Ole Miss couldn't deal with Goths. Now, I'm in the land of the pharaohs for two whole weeks—very cool. I always wanted to see the Pyramids since the time I was six. Mom and Dad wouldn't let us go anywhere but England and Disneyland.

My father was yelling, "You look like a loser. If you're staying under my roof, you'll get that hair cut."

I have a purple mohawk. It would be better if I had a top hat, like Dracula. But Adel was saying, "You are from America?"

I was really tempted to say, "No shit, Buttafuco." But why should I be mean?

"Alabama," I said. I picked up the bean in the dish. "What do you call these little critters?"

"Tirmis," he said. "You don't eat the cover." He sucked on the bean and took off the skin and then left it in the metal dish.

They were bland. I was hungry, but it didn't look like there was any food at this bar, except these beans. At some of the other tables, people were smoking water pipes. A few were nibbling on peanuts. Some dude just walked in with a big bulbous-looking guitar. I had never seen an instrument like that before. You could hear the clicking of chess pieces.

"Alabama is in the South. Where they killed the black people. Had the manifestations."

"Lynching. Things have changed."

I still didn't have many African-Americans in my classes, although there was the occasional Tyrone, a quarterback who was interested in gospel music. Did this Egyptian dude want a lecture on the Civil Rights movement and Martin Luther King? Anyway, I was getting my Master's in Southern Culture—my specialty was rock-'n'-roll—Elvis Presley. Or was… Maybe I'd be working at *Hairy Man's Barbecue* when I returned to Tuscaloosa. How many pounds of pork ribs for you, sir? An extra order of taters? My father said, "You'll end up just like your Uncle Bill. Nothing to show for all that education."

I'd muttered, "Just because he doesn't drive a white Caddy."

Dad had shouted, "If you have something to say to me, son, you say it loud and clear. Face reality."

Was reality a white Cadillac? "Whatever."

I was so bummed about getting kicked out of grad school that I called up Uncle Bill and he sent me a ticket to Cairo. "It'll do you a world of good," he said. "To explore some. See something new."

"I have my Master's degree in American Literature from Cairo University," Adel said.

"No shit," I said. "I'm sure you're in great demand." What was he supposed to be doing? Selling electric lawnmowers in his Dad's hardware store, like me?

How about a little syrup for your hummingbirds? Although Goths, like me, need not apply. You'll scare away the customers. Heh! Heh!

He raised his beer. "To William Faulkner. My preferred book is *As I Lay Dying.*"

"To William Faulkner," I said, raising my glass. I was ashamed to say, I had never read *As I Lay Dying.* I dug Anne Rice. If you were going to go for corpses, why not vampires?

"Who is your favorite character in *As I Lay Dying?*"

"Well, er," I said. "It's been a long time since I've read that novel. Actually, I love Mark Twain. He cuts through all the baloney."

"Yes, I have heard of bologna business."

"Hypocrisy. You know, when people say things they don't mean."

"I would love to go to America," he said. "It's a free land. But they never give us the visas."

"It might not be as free as you think," I said. My mother had driven me to the Birmingham airport and her parting words were, "You've broken our hearts again, son!"

"Give me the fuckin' violin," I'd shouted after her, but she floored her white Caddy away and didn't hear me.

I had first broken their hearts when I refused to go to Baptist Sunday School. My Sunday school teacher, Miss Letty Lou, went into a diabetic coma when I told her that Jonah could never have been swallowed by the whale. "The whale would vomit," I said. "It's logical." I had started a campaign to sell possum BBQ for the Boy Scouts. Had almost burned down our local Boy Scout meeting place with explosives. I had gotten a tattoo of a vampire doing the deed with a pig on my ass my freshman year instead of pledging Sigma Chi as the men in my family had done for the last one hundred and fifty years. To hear my mother tell it, I murdered grandma with an axe—that's when I started listening to those heavy metal bands like *Bauhaus, Joy Division, the Cure*—I couldn't take all the copycat mindlessness of our family. Next, I got a few wicked piercings in my nose. So what? Yo, I put on a feather earring and wore a spiked dog collar on the day of the dynasty family photo. Ha! That did the trick. I was not allowed in the plantation for two weeks. I told my business professor: *This sucks Big Mammoth Thing!* Hold on to your britches: I wrote a ninety-page paper on images of violence and evil in *Deliverance* for my senior thesis. Graduated with honors in Southern Culture and Film, but it was yet another heartbreak for my Dad because it wasn't BUSINESS. I said, "Dude, don't you understand that I'm a free thinker?" My father said, "You will call me Dad." Meanwhile, my brother was taking accounting classes. He even parted his hair on the same side, like Dad. He was real cute and was dating a nice girl, as my mother said. Gag. It made me want to plant a dead crow in his book bag.

"Hey, Adel. Is there anything to eat around here besides these beans? I haven't eaten for twenty-four hours."

"*Kosheri,*" Adel said. "You will love *kosheri*. It's delicious."

"What's *kosheri*?"

"An Egyptian dish. Let us try it," Adel said. Adel made a motion with his hand for the check and the waiter came over. He had a pencil behind his ear.

I barred his hand. "No, I'll pay."

But Adel said something in Arabic and the waiter ignored my money. Adel motioned to me, "In our country, guests do not pay. If you will allow me to take you to the most famous *kosheri* shop in Egypt, *Abu Tarek.*"

"Bitchin'," I said, following Adel out of the bar. *The Lonely Planet Guide* had said that the *El-Horreya* was a hangout for local intellectuals. I had visited Faulkner's house, but never bothered to read Faulkner's stuff, except they made us read *The Bear* in high school. Poe was my man. I was into darkness and evil. The heart beating under the floorboards. Although I remembered "*A Rose for Emily,*" the old lady who sleeps next to her dead lover for years.... The smell must have been rank!

"Bitchin'," Adel repeated. "Actually, the word 'bitch' is a shameful word in our language."

I laughed. "Dude. It means 'cool' in Goth. Awesome."

"Awesome," Adel repeated. It sounded weird when he said it. He couldn't get the "aw" right.

We picked our way through a street that specialized in car parts. Silver tire rims decorated the outside of one shop, like huge donuts. Shops featured different parts: mufflers, tires, tire rims, bolts, fan belts, steering wheels, even old car seats. A woman on a street corner was selling round pieces of bread off a plate of braided wood. Men were sitting at rickety tables on the sidewalk, playing backgammon. They were slapping the backgammon pieces down with great force. One man hooted. The hood of a blue Fiat was popped open, but no one appeared to be working on it. We passed a boy with grimy, oil-stained hands, who dipped a plastic spoon into a container.

Adel gestured, "That's *kosheri*."

"Looks like spaghetti to me," I said. "I was expecting lamb. Don't you eat lamb in this part of the world?"

"Meat is expensive," Adel said. I followed him to a two-story *kosheri* shop crammed with people. In fact, I didn't even see how we could enter the shop—people were pushing and shoving to get inside.

I peered in the window of the shop. A man was dishing up macaroni and rice into small plastic containers from a huge metal vat. In between were brown dots of something. Next, I saw bits of brown floating in a smaller vat of grease. After the man put the macaroni and rice in the plastic container, he poured red sauce over the mixture and added the browned tangle. A mob stood in front of him, waving tiny bits of paper.

The moment we entered the shop, everyone started staring at me in horror, as if I were a concentration camp victim. Nobody at the bar had acted this way.

"Hey," I said. "Why are they staring at me?"

"You have violet hair," Adel said. "Maybe they have not seen anyone with violet hair."

Yeah, right. Spiky, purple hair. And the mohawk. Since I was following Adel into the shop, they were asking him about me.

"What are they saying?"

"They want to know if you're Russian," he said. "I told them you're American, but they don't believe me. They said Americans would never dye their hair violet. They think you look like a Russian gangster."

"Oh," I said. I wished they would stop staring at me. At home, I gloried in the attention—I was not a frat boy wearing an IZOD tee-shirt with top-siders at Ole Miss, but a Goth who rejected dogma and tradition. I cranked the band *"In the Reptile House"* at my apartment on football game days. A Goth who crashed fraternity parties, dressed in vampire attire with a top hat. But I felt out of place with my combat boots here. I was wearing my favorite tee-shirt, which said, "Eat a bag of shit." I wanted to crawl into a hole.

An Egyptian woman in a long black cloak was pointing at me—she had the Gothic look, but she was spooky. She had the black cloth over her face, too. Was she hexing me? I restrained myself from giving her the finger. Don't they call that the *burqa*?

Adel pushed his way through the crowd. He called out something and the crowd let him through. I had slept through high-school Spanish, but now could suddenly see how Undead it was not to be able to communicate. Without Adel, I was a helpless moron.

I tapped Adel on the shoulder, "Dude, I'm a Goth. That's why I have purple hair."

"We are going to eat upstairs," Adel said, gesturing to a spiral stairway.

Why did it matter if I were a Goth or not?

"Tell them I'm a Goth. I'm not a Russian gangster," I said.

"Follow me," Adel said. "You will taste the *kosheri*. Do you want some chilli sauce on the top? We call it *shatta*."

I was now starting to feel the effect of the jet lag—this place was pissing me off.

"I'm not a Russian gangster," I said. My teeth clenched. "Tell them."

"Those people already left the shop," he said.

"Oh," I said, feeling stupid. I followed him up the stairs.

We sat down at one of the tables. A waiter arrived with two bowls of spaghetti in metal plates. He was staring at me so much he almost dropped the plate of food.

"What's his problem?" I asked. "I am not from Mars."

Adel waved his hand. "But we have never seen anyone like you."

"Maybe he should get over it," I said. I remembered those Pakistanis I had seen in 7-Eleven in Birmingham who spoke weird English. Was this how they felt when people stared at them?

Adel handed me a fork. "What's a Goth?"

I didn't know how to explain what a Goth was. Someone who wears black? Has a taste for Goth music? Why did I have the purple hair? To piss off my Dad? I mean, to be a strict Goth, I should have dyed my hair a pure black. The Goths around Oxford told me I wasn't a pure Goth since I hadn't gone for the black.

"It's a movement in the United States. People wear dark colors and adopt a Gothic look."

"You are assuming the character of *Dracula*?"

I took a bite of the *kosheri*. It had a peppery flavor mixed with rice and macaroni. I was sure this guy had probably read Bram Stoker's novel, *Dracula*. I had only seen the movie.

"This is good," I said. "You could say that. If I look like Dracula, I won't have to work in my father's hardware store."

Why didn't I just tell Dad that I didn't want to work in his store?

"I wish I had somewhere I could work. Even if it was a store. I have no job. I can never marry my darling without a flat," Adel said. "It will take me a hundred years to buy a flat. A hundred years of solitude."

Now he's quoting Marquez. I didn't want to admit that this was another thing that I did not know or had not read! The dude was much more knowledgeable than I was.

"Too bad," I said. "Can't you teach?"

Adel shrugged. He was despondent. "I give private lessons. But the students are so dull and so spoiled, you cannot believe how much. Her parents want her to marry an engineer."

"Do you love her?"

He brightened. "Of course. Do you have a girlfriend?"

I laughed. "Are you kidding? The girls laugh when I pass by. You know, the purple hair." Of course, there had been Darla. I heard her say, "Gross. Hale, are you trying to make yourself ugly?" Darla had really been into me, when I had been doing the Elvis Presley look-alike contests. She had thought that was cool and had come to all the contests. Anyway, when I dyed my hair purple and became a Goth, Darla broke up with me. I heard she was dating a guy in his last year of law school.

"You could wear a hat," Adel said.

I laughed. "That would defeat the purpose."

"What is the goal?"

I played with my nose piercings. "To look like the Undead. To be cool. Look, man, I'm getting tired. Maybe I should go back to my uncle's apartment."

"Of course. Do you know your way back?"

"Look, it's no biggie. I can figure it out. You don't have to go with me," I said.

But Adel insisted. I was kind of relieved, like, sometimes you just want to be ferried to the place without worrying about how you're going to get there. I sank back into the back seat of the taxi. I closed my eyes for a minute—I really needed to crash. My eyes felt grainy and I had a headache. When I opened them, I realized our taxi driver didn't have any legs. If Marilyn Manson had planned it on his show, he couldn't have come up with a more Gothic taxi ride. Driving without toes.

Adel was sitting up in the front seat. I tapped him on the shoulder and whispered, "How is he driving the car?"

"The brakes have been changed to the hand signals," Adel said. "He was a truck driver in Iraq. Lost his legs in a roadside explosion."

"Wow," I said. "That's terrible. Can you tell him I'm sorry?" That was definitely not 'bitchin'.' Adel said something to the driver, but I wasn't sure he translated what I had said.

Adel nodded. "It is sad. But we must say *al-Hamdulellah*. We must thank God for our blessings."

Thank God for what? Dad forced us to say the blessing before each meal. "Dear Lord, for these our many blessings…Thank the Lord for this fried chicken and mashed potatoes."

"I don't think God comes into it," I said. I lay my head back against the seat of the taxi. A blue eye dangled back forth from the mirror. "Hey, what that's blue thing hanging from the mirror?"

"It's the evil eye," Adel said. "It protects us from harm. Bad luck."

I thought of the costume shop in Oxford where the Goths went to buy their clothes: monster clothes, black mesh, pointy boots with studs, top hats, belts with etchings of Satan.

"Where do you buy those things?" I asked. Those would be cool souvenirs to take back to some of my Goth pals—not that I had that many friends, but we had a tiny club of the Undead at Ole Miss. We could wear them around our necks. Dude, I said, your ass is out of Ole Miss.

But Adel was saying, "We are passing over the Nile." Two huge lion statues marked the beginning of the bridge. But traffic was blocked. People had gotten out of their cars. I heard shouting.

The taxi driver had turned off the ignition of the car.

"What's going on?"

When he turned around to gesture to me to the stalled cars on the bridge, I noticed the taxi driver had a wart on his nose. Lord, I heard my mother's voice echo in my ear. Not only was he missing his legs, but he had a mongo wart on his nose and a wandering eye. "Lord, Hale, why are you wearing those awful outfits?" I heard my mother again. "Why don't you spruce yourself up? You've got movie-star good looks."

Adel got out of the car and I followed him. A crowd of people were peering over the side. From where we were on the bridge, we couldn't see what they were looking at. A few small boats hovered down below in the river. Another small blue boat was blocking boats from going underneath the bridge. The boats with the large sails were turning around.

"Police boats," Adel said.

And then, we suddenly saw a rope that had been tied to one of the iron poles on the bridge.

"Shit!" I said. A man was swinging back and forth, below—his head lolled forward. I felt nauseous.

I had only seen one dead person in my life and that was my grandmother in McElroy's funeral parlor—they had put pink lipstick on her that had seemed so phony. The Egyptian guy looked young. Maybe in his twenties. What had made him...?

Adel was very upset. "I am sorry you are seeing this. You are a visitor to our country. This is not usual. It's against our religion."

"Yeah," I said. I thought I was going to barf up the *kosheri* over the side of the bridge. "No religion cheers for offing yourself. You'll be buried in the potter's field."

"Potter's field?" Adel asked.

I felt exhausted. How to explain it? A graveyard for the losers? Poor people. Beggars. Suicides? Of course, Marilyn Manson did a lot of death stuff on his show, *Flesh of Monster Flesh*—I had thought that was cool when I had watched it on video—that he had pushed the limits of convention. A row of baboons, hanging by ropes, execution style. Real skeletons in deck chairs. Death masks.

The body dangled just a few feet short of the boat so it wasn't going to be that easy to cut the rope. A man in a white uniform on the bridge was shouting to the police below—they waved back. Was he a cop? What had he said?

Cars that were trying to get onto the bridge had started honking. When one stopped, another began. And then all the cars seemed to be honking in unison—it was deafening. I felt dizzy. Adel was pulling me back toward the taxi. "No, Adel, please," I said.

Before I knew what was happening, I was barfing red grunge all over my tee-shirt, "Eat a bag of shit."

Adel looked sad beyond belief. "This is a terrible first day in Cairo. Let me get you a Kleenex." Adel ran back to our taxi and brought me the whole box of Kleenex. I really couldn't believe my folks told me that I shouldn't come to Cairo because of terrorists.

Uncle Bill would regret inviting me to his place in Cairo—had I screwed that up, too? Well, anyway, if I ever got back…. If I ever went to bed. I think I had now been awake for, like, two days. They were now saying in the family that I was manic depressive and I needed to be on lithium. Even though no one had bothered to take me to a psychiatrist—just because I had purple hair and wore black. Bill's girlfriend, Rose, would probably greet me with her hands on her hips, "Darlin', who spiked your balloon?" Last time I had seen Rose was at the Bounty Hunter Bar in Tuscaloosa, Alabama, after fifteen beers. She said I was a sexist pig. I told her to go play with a few rattlesnakes.

"Dude," I said. "I am sorry. You are probably wishing you never met me." But Adel didn't answer. He was looking up at the sky. "I'm unlucky," I said.

The sky had turned orange and the wind started to blow hard. The body was slapping back and forth against the bridge now. The air became filled with sandy dust. Twigs whirled through the air. The palm trees were bending, as if it were a hurricane—the wind became fiercer.

Adel pointed to the sky. "*It's a khamaseen.*"

"What?" I said. I couldn't hear because of the wind.

"A dust storm," he said. "Get into the car. It's not safe to be outside."

The crowd disappeared from the bridge. People jumped back into their cars. Cars started to move across the bridge.

"What will happen to the dead man?" I asked.

Adel said. "They will bury him today." Adel said something to the taxi driver. I remembered being in the Dean's office. "Now, son, do you think you used good judgment in the classroom?" Well, maybe it hadn't been such a good idea to moon the daughter of the football coach of Ole Miss. She didn't want to share when I'd ask them to make a list of their favorite television shows. I had told her over a hundred times not to play on her cell phone. But maybe she was a brat and deserved to be mooned—all of this seemed trivial, compared to what I had seen on the bridge. And to think that I was so down that I had considered taking drastic measures…Don't even go there. Yeah, well, working at *Hairy Man's BBQ* was not the end of the world. Not the apocalypse. I could eat as many free pork ribs as I wanted to. If I had to, I could sell bird feed and lawnmowers at my Dad's—not my idea of a good time.

We had pulled up to my uncle's building. A guy in a long robe and a turban was standing at the entrance.

"If you need any help……" Adel was saying. He handed me a card. "I have to work now. I'll take my cousin home and then I drive the taxi for the next six hours."

"He's your cousin. You knew him all along?" I asked. I felt lost. I never knew what was going on. "You're a taxi driver?"

"It's something I do to earn money," Adel said. "Do you have a job?"

I was too embarrassed to tell him that I had lost it because I had pulled my pants down and showed my tush to a girl. He would think I was a real dumbass. Worse than being a Russian gangster.

"I'm on vacation," I said. "Don't you want to come in and meet my uncle and aunt?"

Adel put his hand on his chest. "Another day? Maybe we could go to the Pyramids on Friday? I will contact you."

"Cool," I said. "Awesome." I didn't know if Adel would want to see me again. The wind continued to whip up leaves. Even the porter's stool blew away. Loose boards and trash were flying off the roofs of the buildings.

Adel said something to the porter of the building. He nodded and he pulled me towards the elevator. "Mister Bill?" he said. "Mister Bill. Good," he said, giving me the thumbs up. Then, he followed me out of the elevator and pressed the doorbell—it made an odd chirping sound.

Rose answered the door and I could see the worry in her eyes. I had expected her to be a smart aleck. But she shouted out, "He's here." She enveloped me in a bear hug. She smelled lemony. "Are you all right, darlin'?" Her dog, Scarlett O'Hara, wouldn't stop barking.

Uncle Bill put the phone down. Who was he calling?

My cheeks felt wet. I didn't feel like telling them about the Egyptian man we'd seen hanging from the bridge—it was too much. What had made him so desperate that he had done that? I imagined how his mother would wail and I felt sorry for her—her heart would splinter into shards of purple glass. I was such a blabbermouth and felt that I had to tell everything that wafted through my mind, but I wouldn't this time. A little silence wouldn't be bad for a change. Maybe stop talking about being a Goth. Just be quiet.

"It's better to be indoors during a sandstorm. You can get hit by flying objects," Uncle Bill said. "How did you find your way back? Who brought you home?"

"A nice Egyptian guy I met in a bar," I said. "Adel."

Uncle Bill nodded. "The people are real nice here." He said, "Anyhow, Tiger, I think you need some shuteye for now." When I was small, my uncle had called me "Tiger."

For once, I didn't disagree.

10

Pure Water Part I

SO WHAT ARE YOU IN HERE FOR? You got to be kidding. Stealing bathing suits from gym lockers at your school? That's a howler—a small-time klepto... What do you do with the bathing suits? Tell me, I'm curious. You jerk off into them? That's a scream!

Actually, this place isn't half bad for a loony bin—I'd almost swear I was at the Miami Hilton... Except, of course, if you look at that high wall with the barbed wire. Listen, can I hang out with you? Okay, thanks. What? I'm more fun than heroin addicts? Gee, thanks a lot!

Hey, just between you and me, know how we might sneak out of here? You know, vamoose. Ha! Fly the coop. I've got to proof my novel—those fuckers won't wait. They're just dying to find any excuse to reject me. Contaminated water in Egypt. Oh, yeah? So, you don't think anyone'd want to read it? Get this: we're already negotiating with translators from all over the world.

Why am I here? Because I got a truck to dump a ton of contaminated fish at the front gate of the university. My students lugged the fish in and piled it in front of the food court: a protest against polluted water. Yeah, pretty extreme. Those fuckers think I'm a loose cannon and they want me out of the way. A little like your dad. Behave or we'll put you away...

Why would I make it up? It's true. Who cares? Shut up? Shut the fuck up? How dare you! No, I won't shut up. They're all trying to shut me up.

My God, did you see that? The KFC delivery boy just rode his scooter into the garden. You ordered it? You shouldn't eat the stuff—it's shit and really bad for your system. Well, if you insist. Spicy wings are my favorite.

Look, I'm sorry. I didn't mean to get aggressive. Well, just one French fry, although they're like Doritos, you can never just eat one!

"THERE'S A RAT IN MY KITCHEN. WHAT AM I GONNA DO?"

No, I won't stop singing. "*There's a rat in my kitchen. What am I gonna do?*" Am I embarrassing you? So sorry! The manic depressives are giving us the finger. Come on, what do you care? You're the outsider. Why don't you tell them to scram? Hey, that's awfully nice of you to share your KFC with me. If it were me, I probably wouldn't share!

By the way, did you hear about the revival of the plague in Libya? The Black Death? Okay, I'll shut up this time. You want to know? No, I won't tell. Only if you beg me. What happens to you is grisly. Huge bruises burst up under the skin—buboes. Fever, headaches, vomiting. Then diarrhea runs down your legs—you shit on yourself. Delirium. Coma. Death. Aren't you sorry you asked?

I'll just have a swig of your Coca-Cola and then I'll scoot off...Thanks for the wings! I'm going back to my room.

Well, well, this is very nice for a damned prison. Have to overlook those hall guards lurking about. Hey, this is almost as nice as my university flat. Cool down. Come on, Gary, why don't you think of this as a sabbatical? Take it easy. Of course, you choose to be on sabbatical. Nice watercolors—Egyptian stuff. Not bad. Whoever decorated this place has good taste. That picture is lopsided. Straighten it up. There—that's better. Who's the painter? David Roberts—that nineteenth-century painter. Khan el-Khalili. Ibn Tulun. Everybody takes home his paintings to their friends. Nice Oriental souvenirs—but that's what people like back home. Twin beds. They haven't said anything about sharing. Surely they won't put some loony in with me. Let them try it. Go ahead, buster. Sit on the bed—usually the beds are too soft. Hey, what ya know? It's perfect!

Actually, maybe it's a blessing I'm banished from that place. I'm working in a kindergarten. *"Please, doctor, can I go pee-pee and wee-wee?"* Give me a break! *"Doctor, I don't need to bring paper and pen to class. I'm a genius."* Listen up, brats, even Einstein took notes.

So, Gary, look at it this way. At last, you can catch up on your reading. What books did I bring with me? Fuck. Not even a John le Carré. I was so drugged out, I only brought *The Encyclopedia of Disaster Management*. Smart! The same day the fish were dumped at the food court, they jabbed me in the ass with a needle and hauled me off. Now that's a good story. It would be funny, if it weren't happening to me! Look on the bright side, Gary, you had some very nice chats about hepatitis and bilharzia with that doctor who jabbed you with the needle. The security guards didn't know what to do with all those stinky fish. I mean, my biology students started putting the fish on the belt of the x-ray machine. Come on, Gary, that's something to be proud of. Contaminated fish as potential terrorists. That's an original way of thinking about it, isn't it? Terrorized by bad food and water? Can I help it that I'm a high achiever? Well, yeah, if I want to survive in a university, I'll have to go back to cranking out more scholarly articles. But to get promoted, you have to list every little thing you publish, even two-line encyclopedia entries. Why be obsessed with promotion? Isn't there something called having a conscience? You know, I'm not cut out for this. I worry too much. Somebody might take me out. Now, come on. That's paranoid. No, I'm not. Think about it. The Big Guys don't want themselves exposed.

It's stuffy in here. I'll put on the fan.

So, reading is out. Oh, well. No bulb in the lamp, anyway. Hey, there are mosquitoes in here. Awww. That hurt. I swat my cheek. I'm going to get you,

you devil. And not just one. My God, a whole posse. God, look at the wall—a mass of bloody spots. Surely they have repellent tablets. Here we are. Crap! The packet is empty. Who should I call? Right. No phone, either. Maybe I could just put the covers over my head. I was getting sleepy, anyway…

I woke up. Someone was slamming a door. A mobile was going off: Louis Armstrong's "*What a Wonderful World!*" ANSWER YOUR PHONE.

The light was switched on.

"What's going on here?" I said, sitting up in bed.

I confronted the doctor. He'd been the one who'd interviewed me when I was brought in. He'd gotten rid of the white coat. This time, he was wearing a silk suit—looks like an Armani. He must be some hotshot. "Dr Gary, we are most sorry for the inconvenience. Mr Kharalombos' stay will be temporary. We had no other place to put him."

My new roommate stood in front of me. My God, where did they get this guy? He's huge—a real giant. Did that make me a shrimp? I stared at his belly—it was enormous. If he were pregnant, he would be giving birth to sextuplets. He had dishwater-blonde hair and blue eyes. Was he Egyptian? Some foreign blend?

"I'm not sharing," I said. "That's final."

"Thank you for understanding," he said. He smiled. "I knew you wouldn't mind."

"Don't you do anything in the daytime? It's three-thirty in the morning," I said, looking at my watch. Really!

The doctor said, "Ve are creatures of the night. Rest well, Dr Gary."

"This is not a fucking joke," I said, as he closed the door.

"Pleased to meet you," said my new roommate, extending his massive hand. His handshake was crippling.

"Dr Gary Williamson. PhD Yale," I said. "Hell-raiser. Liberator of the world. Fighter of environmental injustices."

"Yanis Kharalombos. Teacher of ballroom dancing. Waltz. Foxtrot. Salsa. Samba. Tango. At your service."

I laughed uproariously. Suddenly, Kharalombos was whirling me around the room in a waltz. So, he could dance. Even though he was large, he was very light on his feet. "You know how to follow," he said.

"It's not hard," I said. "Do you get paid well?"

"They pay very well," he said. "And not just in money." He winked at me.

I imagined him dancing with an anorexic girl. Her waist would be as wide as his ankle.

"Seems like life is treating you well, Yanis. Why are you here?" I asked.

Suddenly, he started weeping.

"God, what did I say? Why are you crying?" I asked. "Don't cry. I hate it when men cry." I patted him on the arm since I couldn't reach his shoulder.

"No more pork patés," he said.

"What? I don't understand." What on earth was this guy talking about? We were joking and having fun a minute ago.

"I have an addiction to pork paté," he bawled. Tears rolled down his cheeks. Mucus had started to run from his nose. This was getting messy. Did we have any Kleenex in the room?

I handed him a Kleenex. "Please don't cry."

"Please," he said, getting down on his knees. "Do you know someone who can bring me pork paté from Europe? Even a single pork chop would do."

"No, I don't know anyone," I said, pushing him away from my crotch. He was getting a little too close for comfort.

He instantly stopped crying. "Impossible. You must know someone," he said. "Aren't you even married?"

"No. Not married. No kids," I said.

"Not married? How can you not be married?" Kharalombos said. He was very surprised.

"I'm just not. That's the way my life turned out. Not everyone is married. Are you married?"

"Me? I'm too big," he said.

"There are plenty of big people out there," I said. "What's the problem?"

Kharalombos picked himself up off the floor and sat down on his bed. I looked at his enormous bulk. Where did he buy his clothes? Plenty of tailors in Cairo.

"So, you have an addiction to pork paté?"

As he moved, the bed springs squeaked. Yikes, would the whole thing collapse? "Pork patés are like my mistress," Kharalombos said.

He was sweating profusely—he mopped his brow. Poor guy, he was distressed. The Kleenex had disintegrated into a wad of goo. I handed him another.

"Now all the pork butchers have gone out of business in Egypt. No pigs." He wept.

"You could eat other things. Chicken. Lamb. Fruit and vegetables," I said. I had to cheer him up. "Lentils," I ventured. Really, why did I say that? Lentils wouldn't be a big draw for this guy.

Kharalombos barked. "Vegetables? You think I'm some kind of a rabbit. I need flesh."

"Well…." I said. "Yeah, I see what you mean." I resisted the strong urge to guffaw again. This guy would have to eat a ton of vegetables to sustain him. I needed to lighten things up. It wasn't my thing, but I could ask for salsa lessons.

"Why are you here? You seem okay," Kharalombos asked me.

"Got into trouble with the authorities," I said.

"What?"

"Well, I dumped a ton of contaminated fish at the food court at the university," I said.

"Why?"

"To make a point," I said. "Pollution is destroying the Nile."

Kharalombos laughed. "Everyone complains about the pollution."

The next minute, he was snoring. I put the pillow over my head, but it did not mute the snore. If whales snored, this is exactly how they would sound: a snorting bellow.

I have to get out of here. What am I going to do? Five o'clock in the morning. Kharalombos is driving me crazy. Hang out in the garden? Okay, why not? I closed the door to the room. There's Wanker Boy. He's waving at me. Dude! I cringed. I hated the word *dude*. Call me anything but dude—friend, man, guy, pal—but not dude. Wanker Boy was surrounded by a group of characters— I stared at the skeletal anorexic girl who rested her head on Wanker Boy's shoulder—My God, you could see her bones. Had she mutilated herself? She had nasty cuts all over her arms. Hey, there's that famous Egyptian singer? What's his name? Abdel Wahab Kebab. What's he doing here? "Yo," Wanker Boy said, "Dude. Dr Gary. Please. Tell your fish story. Please. Hey, listen up, everybody. This is awesome." And so I told them about how I booked the dump truck, how I recruited the students, how I contacted the newspapers…. At the end of the story, everyone applauded. Abdel Wahab Kebab whistled. We started singing,

"Don't kiss me in the eye." When I returned to the room, Kharalombos was still snoring away, curled up in a fetal position, smiling, as if he didn't have a care in the world.

Count Dracula opened the door. A lackey followed him in with a tray.

"So, what's the secret recipe today?" I asked.

"Fried tilapia," he said. He gestured for the lackey to put the tray on the table.

"Oh, no. Fish. Please, no. Seafood for breakfast? Is there anything else? Fava beans?"

"We ran out of beans. Well, why don't you at least try a bite?"

"No thanks. This fish is stuffed with lead," I said.

Even so, I was getting hungry. Without sleep or food, my legs felt wobbly. My head throbbed.

"No. Dr Williamson. You're an intelligent man. A Yale graduate," Count Dracula said, smiling. "Sooner or later, you'll have to eat."

Kharalombos stirred. "*Kalimera. Kalimera.* Good morning," he said, smiling.

"Yeah," I said. "It's a great morning." I had been the center of attention in Wanker Boy's group for hours and I was on a high. I felt like the Pied Piper.

The bed creaked when Kharalombos got up and he started unzipping his fly. He staggered to the bathroom. His pissing sounded like a Niagara waterfall.

"Did you bring me some bottled water?" I asked Count Dracula.

He handed me the bottle. "Here, you are."

"You know, a lot of people are interested in hearing my fish story. I know you think I'm dangerous. But I was only trying to make a point..." I said.

"You've really got to be more persuasive than that," he said.

"Look, I'm a professor of biology. Pollution is a serious problem. People are consuming contaminated water and food—it's screwing up their health. Their kidneys."

Kharalombos stood at the door; his fly was still open. He was putting his dick away. My God, no wonder he couldn't find a woman. He wasn't kidding. He really was too big.

Kharalombos grabbed the huge bottle of water. He drank it in one gulp. What a monster—reminded me of that character on *The Addams Family*. What was his name? Lurch? God, this guy's grocery bill must be horrendous.

Count Dracula made for the door. "Listen, I'll think about what you've said. But now, I have to check on some of my other patients. You know, we've had a few patients on hunger fasts that we had to put on IV's."

"Are you threatening me?"

He didn't reply. He closed the door.

I surveyed the tray. Overcooked carrots and green beans. Some watery mashed potatoes. A packet of salty crackers.

Kharalombos said, "I wish there was bacon."

"Get off the bacon, will you?" I said. I was hungry as well.

He was weeping again. I really couldn't take any more crying. I was still elated from my performance in the garden. Abdel Wahab Kebab thought I was funny!

"Listen, Kharalombos. I'll make a deal with you. You can have some of my lunch, if you stop crying."

With one of his paws, Kharalombos grabbed the entire fish.

"Let's make a plan to escape from this place," I said. "Vamoose."

Kharalombos' mouth was full, but he nodded vigorously.

Kharalombos picked up the book, *Disaster Management*, sitting on my bedside table. He handed it to me. "Our escape plan?"

"Not a chance," I said, throwing the book against the wall. "The answer is not here. Only charts and graphs." I sat on my bed. My toenails were in awful shape—I picked up the nail clipper and started trimming them. "Let's say you don't escape, how long do you think it will take you to get cured from your addiction to pork paté?" I asked.

"I don't know," he said, wiping away the tears with his paw. "I have other problems."

The room was quiet, except for the sound of my nail clipper. My toenails were thick, like the horns of a sheep. It was very difficult to clip them.

"Really? Like what?" I said. Maybe he was worse off than I was emotionally. There was nothing wrong with me. I just went too far. Was an anarchist.

"A love affair," he whispered. He unbuttoned the tight collar of his tux. How unobservant I was. Had he come from a party last night? His Adam's apple bulged. He had started sweating.

"Oh?" I said. I handed him the Kleenex. "What happened?" Maybe this guy was not what he seemed to be, either.

He continued whispering, "Can I trust you?"

"Sure, why not? Well, yeah…What happened?"

"Swear," he said.

"Come on. Where's the big bad wolf?"

"You never know with those people," he said. I couldn't hear him. His voice was barely audible.

"Which people? What are you talking about?" Maybe I shouldn't get involved with this guy. Keep a distance. He was acting as if some big Mafioso was after him.

"I had to disappear for a while. The only woman I have ever loved in my life."

"Who was she? Not a minister's wife?"

"Let's just say, he was an important man in this country and he asked me to do him a favor. To teach his only daughter how to waltz on her wedding night. We became very close…Quoted poetry to each other. 'She walks in beauty, like the night/Of cloudless climes and starry skies/And all that's best of dark and bright…'"

"Who's the poet?"

"Lord Byron."

"Go on. What's the rest?"

"One thing led to another…." Kharalombos voice trailed off. He was surveying the rest of the vegetables on my tray. I snatched the crackers off the tray.

"Go ahead," I said. "I don't want it. Help yourself." He shoveled the rest of the overcooked vegetables into his mouth. It made me want to gag.

"She was so different. I had never met a girl who loved the Romantic poets. The other girls I teach to waltz talk about their designer clothes. Their iPods."

"I still don't understand why you're in any kind of danger," I said. "Why is this dangerous?"

"I think she might be pregnant," Kharalombos said. This was much better than the plot of my novel. A Greek dancing teacher impregnates an important person's fiancée.

"Not good," I said. "Who's her father?"

Kharalombos started shaking. "The kid will be a giant," he said. "And then what?"

I was tempted to say, you better leave the country.

"Do you have any relatives in Greece?"

"Stavanger, Norway. They run a restaurant there," he said. "They already said I could teach dance."

"Well, what are you waiting for? Go!"

"I need a visa," he said. "Do you know anyone at the Norwegian Embassy?"

I shook my head. "Norway? Norway. No. Can't say that I do. I have a few contacts at the American Embassy."

Kharalombos shrugged. "I had to submit millions of pages of documentation. I suppose it shouldn't be a problem. I have a lot of money in my account."

"How long do you think you'll be in this place?" I asked.

"I don't know. Maybe a few more weeks," he said. "Why are you letting the pollution get to you?"

"I don't know. Ever since I was a little kid, I feel like the world is just getting worse. The world is beautiful. We're destroying it. I have started having panic attacks. I mean, just look at the Red Sea. It's being ruined by developers."

I looked up. "Kharalombos?"

He was snoring again. My stomach growled.

Hey, what if Kharalombos were working for the *Mukhabarat*? First, his ridiculous story about the pork patés had been a ruse. And then he had told me another story, equally preposterous, about impregnating an important person's son's fiancée—what if he had been sent by the secret police to watch me? See what I was up to. Okay, be rational, Gary. Didn't the Egyptian secret police have bigger problems to worry about? Like real terrorists. If I keep my cool, I can get out of this place.

First things first. I was hungry. I had to eat. I'll go find Wanker Boy. There he was: sitting at the picnic table with his headphones on—listening to his iPod. He rocked back and forth. I sneaked up behind him. He was singing along, "*We don't go out to eat. All we ever do is play in the sheets.*" I tapped him on the shoulder. He held up the KFC box and pointed, smiling. Now, let's see. The picnic area/snack bar is close to the entrance. Could one just sashay out the door? Four guys, having tea, right smack in front of the gate. On the other side, there is a group playing dominoes. The walls are too high to climb unless you had a nine-foot ladder. Eight guards at the gate. Getting out of the cuckoo's nest was not going to be easy.

Listen, Wanker Boy, I'll get you a year's supply of bathing suits if you order me a box of KFC. Wanker Boy took off his headphones. What? You'd rather have a recommendation to Harvard? Sure. Could you also get me extra coleslaw? "Eat, eat," he sang, swinging his wild, curly mop of hair, back and forth. An extra-large Pepsi. "Freak. Freak."

Abdel Wahab Kebab jumped up on the picnic table and started singing, "Cleopatra, which are the dreams from your beautiful nights?" He used a twig for a microphone. A crowd gathered.

Less than five minutes later, the KFC delivery boy roared through the entrance without even showing his ID. Kicked the stand to his bike. When he saw Abdel Wahab Kebab, he ran toward the table. Like a small child, he stood there, mesmerized.

The keys dangled in the ignition of the bike. This was my chance—no one was paying attention to me. I climbed up on the seat. I had no idea how to ride a scooter. I looked down. Didn't you kick something to get it started? Why wasn't I a more macho guy?

Suddenly, the delivery boy rushed toward me, waving the bill. One eye was covered with a filmy white. "Extra crispy, sir. At your service." How could he see to drive the bike?

I had to get off the bike so I could fish the money out of my pocket. "I always wanted to learn how to ride one. Ever since I was a kid." My lie sounded lame. But maybe it never entered his head that I might steal his bike.

"No problem," he said, handing me the KFC bag. The smell was heavenly.

Wanker Boy called out, "Hey dude!" He beckoned for me to join the group.

"You'll get your recommendation to Harvard," I called out. I ran back to the room as if I were a thief. I didn't want to share my three pieces of fried chicken or Pepsi with anyone in the garden or even with Kharalombos.

I sneaked back into the room on tiptoe. Kharalombos started sniffing the air. Maybe I should eat my fried chicken in the bathroom. Quick, before Kharalombos could wake up and snatch my precious chicken, I rushed into the bathroom and slammed the bathroom door. I opened the box: my mouth watered. Look at all that spicy crust. I lifted the drumstick to my mouth. Kharalombos must have recently taken a dump—the smell was disgusting. Air, air. Let me breathe some fresh air. I was gagging. I had to get out. I put the dinner box on the cistern on the back of the toilet. Turned the handle of the door.

The screws were loose. Shit! Why hadn't I tried the lock before I locked myself into the bathroom? The handle came off in my hand.

I banged on the door. Bang. "Kharalombos." Bang. Bang. "Open the door!"

I was getting edgy. I couldn't stand being in elevators or enclosed places with crowds—a rash was breaking out on my neck.

"Kharalombos. Please." I banged harder on the door. "Wake up!" I put my ear to the door, but could hear nothing. Why didn't he answer? Suppose he had left the room. That was ridiculous! He was in the room when I came in. Why was I always imagining the worst? But why didn't he answer? My face started feeling hot and I scratched my neck. I started to feel dizzy. Calm down. Breathe deeply. A fat roach skittered up the wall. I gagged again. I felt myself slide down the wall. My ears started ringing.

Suddenly, the door was lifted away.

"It's okay," he said. "It's okay." He set the door to one side.

A whoosh of air came into the room. I gulped the fresh air.

"God, you're a lifesaver," I said. "How did you…?"

"The hinges were rotten," he said. "No problem."

He smiled. "Oh. Look. Yummy. Yum. Yum," he said. He stretched his arm towards the cistern. At the same time, I grabbed his arm. The KFC box teetered on the edge of the cistern, before it fell into the toilet bowl.

"Shit!" I said. I lost my appetite. The bottom of the bowl was clumped with crap. Kharalombos fished the box out of the water. It was soggy. He handed it to me. "No thanks," I said. "Not now."

There was a light knock on the door. Count Dracula entered.

"Ah, it looks like you're eating. Good. I love KFC."

"Be our guest," I said.

"Hello, Uncle," Kharalombos said. "Any news?"

"Uncle?" I said. So, the doctor was his uncle? Maybe that's why he had come in the middle of the night. Maybe his story was true—incredible.

Count Dracula put a finger to his lips. "There's been a change in plan. Norway won't work. You're going to Malta. Tonight."

"Tonight?" Kharalombos asked.

I wondered if Count Dracula had a name. He didn't seem like a bad guy. I was being silly. He had probably told me before, but I wasn't listening.

"The people who must remain unnamed are looking for you," he said. "The Dragon Lady wants to learn how to do the tango. Or that's what they're saying."

Sweat rolled down Kharalombos' cheek. He was shaking.

"By the way, what happened to the bathroom door?" Count Dracula asked.

"It's me. I got stuck inside," I said. "I'm claustrophobic. Your nephew rescued me."

Count Dracula said. "Oh, yes. That's right. Your chart said you were claustrophobic." He moved back into the bedroom. "Why don't you sit down? I have some bad news."

"Go ahead. I can take it. I'm ready." I plopped down on my bed, as if I were a kid at summer camp.

"From our first interview, I know this is something that is very dear to your heart," he said.

"My novel," I said. The publisher had been bought out? They were not going to publish it after all. My agent had reneged on the deal. Those fuckers always weaseled. My mind was racing.

Count Dracula sat down on one of the rickety chairs. He crossed his legs. "I've just had an email from your publisher. The novel that you sent your publisher had a virus. It's destroyed all the documents in their company."

"That's terrible. I'm sorry to hear that. I can send them another copy of the novel."

"No. No. It's worse than that, my dear fellow," he said, unwrapping a Hall's mint. "The new virus is called Pure Water. And it was in your email attachment. It sailed through the virus protection of the publishers."

"I don't know anything about that. I didn't know I had a virus," I said. "That's not my fault."

"Well," Dracula said. "We know that. But the US government is looking for you. The virus was traced to your computer in Cairo."

"But that's ridiculous. I'm inept when it comes to computers," I said. "I don't even know how to do a computer scan!"

"Maybe. But you do have a history with the *Earth Liberation Front*," Count Dracula said.

Kharalombos said, "Yes, it's obvious. Clearly, it's the people who must remain unnamed…What's your novel about, anyway?"

"A water conspiracy. Set in Egypt," I said. I just echoed part of my usual pitch for agents. They usually gushed, "How interesting."

Kharalombos shook his head, woefully, as if I were already a dead man. "You better disappear."

"What? I refuse to be intimidated. I would like to contact the US Embassy," I said. "I have a right to a lawyer."

"Of course," Count Dracula said. "As a matter of fact, some officers from the *Regional Security Office* from the US. Embassy are coming to visit you tomorrow."

"This is outrageous. Absolutely outrageous. I haven't done anything wrong," I said. "Did they give you any details?"

"No," Count Dracula said. "They said it was a security issue."

So maybe they thought I was guilty. What if they didn't believe me? Okay, Gary, you are innocent until proven guilty in the United States of America. Yeah, but what about those guys still languishing in Guantánamo? How many years had it been? They had been detained because they were "suspicious characters." No trial. What if it took years to prove my innocence? I had nothing to hide. If I tried to escape from this loony bin, would I look like a suspicious character?

"Are you going to be at the meeting?"

"No," he said. "They insisted that they meet you alone."

"No lawyer?" I asked.

"Lawyers were not mentioned," Count Dracula said.

Those security officers would not believe me. I didn't want to hang around for my interrogation.

"Did you tell them I was harmless?" I asked. I was now desperate.

Count Dracula shrugged. "I don't think you're harmless. But I don't think you're a cyber-terrorist."

"A cyber-terrorist!" I said. A rash was starting to break out on my neck.

"That's the new term they're using to describe internet crime," Count Dracula said.

"Those fuckers are going to do something to me," I said. "Anything's possible after the Patriot Act."

I had to get out. I couldn't be trapped in a loony bin or a prison forever, trying to prove my innocence. I would go bonkers, then.

"There might be another option," Count Dracula said. "Don't ask me why I'm helping you. But it's a chance to get out."

"What?" I asked. Instead of becoming a celebrated novelist as I dreamed, I was now an internet hacker on the run. But why not? Did I want to wait around for the verdict of the security officers from the American Embassy? Were they no different from the people who must remain unnamed?

"Kharalombos'll need a companion."

"I'm in," I said.

Kharalombos said, "My uncle's right. You're in danger now." Kharalombos gave me a thumbs-up. God, his thumb was huge.

"You'll have to go in disguise, of course. You can go as Kharalombos' husband. He'll be completely veiled. We have a television makeup artist. She's agreed to help."

"This is real cloak and dagger," I said. Were they both playing me? But why? They didn't need me.

Count Dracula smiled. "London. MI5 at your service."

"Are you joking?" I asked.

But Count Dracula didn't answer.

And that is how I came to be living in Malta. Had to lie low for a while. I don't know about the future, but I feel looser—not suffocated by schedules and meetings and titles. I feel like a kid on a high tree swing, flying through the air, before he jumps into the water. Kharalombos got me a job as a cashier at the *Palace of Knights Museum* in Valletta. I really didn't know if I'd ever get another tenure-track job at a university again. But was that such a bad thing? I became a WANTED MAN. The *Chronicle of Higher Education* ran an article on me: "Professor Tanks Career over Contaminated Fish. Creates Dangerous New Water Computer Virus. Still Missing." I would never, ever have to force myself to read books on *Disaster Management* and *Deluges* again—that made me gleeful. I had taken up other hobbies, like teaching myself Maltese. If I'm not taking tickets from tourists, they have me in the back, making wax knights. Two days a week, I go to yoga classes—I'm not as angry anymore. I don't go around calling everyone a "fucker." Kharalombos and I got rooms in a cheap pension, The Roma, by the sea. Every morning I sit on my balcony and watch the sun come up and enjoy the view. The tourists I meet at the Museum in Valletta are retired Brits, who are genuinely interested in the *Knights Hospitaller*. So, I'm still teaching, in a way. And then one day, when I was taking salsa lessons with Kharalombos, I met you, Boriana, my lady of the trapeze. You make me laugh. That's my story, dear. Believe it or not. Hang on.

"Waiter! Waiter! Two brandies, please. Tell me, was there a bearded lady in your circus?…"

1 1

Pure Water Part II
"On the Run"

"**A**RE YOU CRAZY?"

Kharalombos bellowed, "I'm a father. I want to see my son."

"Congratulations!" I said. "That's wonderful. But how do you intend to get into the royal palace?"

Kharalombos laughed. "You're such a joker."

"I'm not joking," I said. "How are we going to sneak back into Egypt? Our disguises worked before when we had to get out of Egypt. But the same game doesn't work twice. Why don't you go by yourself?"

"I'm not going without you," Kharalombos said. "We're a team." He threw his arm around my shoulder.

"Absolutely not," I said. "Now people think I'm the one who brought down the Israeli stock exchange. Malta is the best place to hide."

"You're like my brother," Kharalombos said. "I taught you how to dance salsa. Anyway, things are not going well in Egypt. The American Embassy is going to be distracted."

"Maybe you're right. Maybe I'm overestimating my importance," I said. Going to Yale had done that to me. But even a Yalie could be unimportant!

I felt myself weakening. I missed the idiosyncrasies of Egypt. The unpredictability and spontaneity of the place. And, I had been in such a hurry to leave the country that I had left a copy of my novel behind. Of course my publisher blamed me for that nasty computer virus, Pure Water, and had definitely deleted the electronic copy I sent them. They would never publish it now! I had left behind a hard copy under my bed—maybe it was still there. I secretly hoped that the next occupant of my flat had not thrown it away. Maybe he was a slob?

"We can stay at my uncle's place," Kharalombos said. "He has an empty flat in Garden City."

"I'm blacklisted," I said. "Do we tap dance right through Immigration?"

"My uncle has connections at the airport," Kharalombos said. "*Wasta.*"

"The guy will whisk us through without checking the list on the computer? Give me a break."

"No," Kharalombos said, his gigantic arms folded. He was confident now. "There is a way around it."

"Aren't you afraid of the people who must remain unnamed?" I said. "You're on their black list, too."

"False passports," Kharalombos said. "I have a Romanian friend here in Valletta who specializes in this."

"In the US that's a felony."

Kharalombos guffawed. "Interpol already wants you. What's a false passport?"

Forget about Interpol. Was I now on the rosters of Mossad? And what would they do to me if they caught me? I felt a knot in my stomach.

But here I was, at Cairo airport, dressed in a loud Hawaiian shirt, wearing Ray-Ban sunglasses. Kharalombos was wearing a Panama hat and a white suit, as if he were a British colonial. I was sure that we were so obvious that the police would appear with handcuffs the moment we got off the plane—straight into the box. I didn't relish the idea of an Egyptian jail. My new identity: a textbook salesman from Ames, Iowa, who was going on a once-in-a-lifetime Nile cruise. Kharalombos was a Greek national who owned an olive-oil factory. We had met on the island of Santorini at a motor scooter shop and had become fast friends. To my surprise, the hall was empty and we sailed through Immigration. The customs officer, in his white pressed uniform, stamped our passports without even blinking an eye.

When we went down the escalators to pick up our luggage, there were very few passengers next to the belt. Next, we picked up our bags and headed through customs. Nothing to declare. The officer seemed surprised to see us, but waved us through. He made a movement with his hands that indicated we were crazy. Did he know who we were? Yet he didn't care? Before I had been accused of being a cyber-hacker I was paranoid, but now, the anxiety had quadrupled. I popped a Tums in my mouth. Practice yoga breathing now. Deep breaths. Feel the breathing in my lungs. Om Shanti. Om Shanti. Om Shanti.

"Hey, Kharalombos," I said. "Something's wrong. The airport is never empty. Not even at three o'clock in the morning."

"There have been demonstrations," Kharalombos said. "Didn't you see the monitor at the Valletta airport?"

"So *Happy City Tours* is picking us up?" I said. Like him, I had seen the clashes on the monitor.

He didn't answer. A bad sign.

When we dragged our bags through the airport and exited the hall, the parking lot was completely deserted. Usually the place was mobbed with relatives, hasslers, and the enterprising opportunist who called himself a taxi driver. Tour guides with signs, who intoned strange-sounding names. They raised their banners high. No drivers with signs. No *Happy City Tours*, either. And even the fleet of torn-up black and white taxis that usually lined up to harass the weary traveler to death had disappeared. I felt nostalgic for them.

Kharalombos pulled out his mobile phone. "I'll call my uncle." He kept redialing.

"What's wrong?"

"No line."

"Maybe there's something wrong with your phone," I said. "You need another SIM card."

"No," Kharalombos said.

He sauntered over to a policeman, who was smoking a cigarette.

"You'll blow your disguise," I hissed. "You're a wanted man."

But Kharalombos was unconcerned and ignored me. He lumbered back to where I was standing. "They cut the networks. There's a curfew."

"What?!" I said. I should have stayed in Valletta. I felt a nasty mood creeping up on me. Why had I let Kharalombos talk me into returning to Cairo? For the sake of a little adventure, I was going to be arrested for a crime I didn't commit! No one would believe me that I was not the mastermind of the computer virus, Pure Water.

"The policeman said he would drive us to Garden City for three hundred dollars," Kharalombos said.

"That's highway robbery! It usually costs twenty dollars to get downtown," I said.

"The demonstration against the BIG MAN and HIS MEN has become violent," Kharalombos said. "Anyone who disobeys the curfew will be shot."

Just at that moment I heard a voice behind me say, "Good heavens, are we the only ones here? They did say they were sending a car?"

Just behind us were a couple. He was wearing a Panama hat, much like the one Kharalombos had perched on his head. Had they bought their colonial attire in the same shop? And he was also wearing a white suit, but his was a more expensive linen. A little light for January. However, he was wearing a pair of pointy leather green shoes. I felt queasy—they looked suspiciously like crocodile leather. He was wearing huge white plastic glasses that enveloped his smallish weasel-like eyes. His wife was even stranger-looking. Her hair was done in a pixie cut, dyed a bright orange. While he was tall and slim, she was tall but very round, and her middle ballooned like the Pillsbury Doughboy. Her outfit was even more outrageous: she was wearing a muumuu with huge purple hibiscus flowers against a yellow cotton print. She carried an enormous green leather purse, the size of a Hefty garbage bag.

"Ja-aa," she said, opening her purse. She pulled out a gigantic lighter, placed a cigarette in a black holder, and lit the cigarette with a huge flame. They took away lighters at airport security; how had she gotten that monster through?

The man was clutching two plastic bags in each hand from the Duty-Free shop and he clinked whenever he moved. "Oi," he said, suddenly noticing me. "Could you assist us, mate? We're newbies."

I couldn't control myself. "Killing crocodiles for a pair of shoes is morally reprehensible. Outrageous!" Crocodiles weren't charming reptiles, but they didn't deserve such a cruel fate! Neither did the animals who were killed for their fur—mink and foxes. Wasteful, selfish people were destroying our natural world! Dumping poison and sewage into the rivers—destroying the fish.

Kharalombos put his finger to his lips. Yikes. That's right—I was supposed to be Joe Smith, a textbook salesman from Ames, Iowa. For selling the most textbooks in the Midwest, I had been awarded a Nile cruise by the company. It was harder than I thought to be a yahoo!

"Ja-aa," the lady with the carrot-red hair said. "They have these wonderful sneakers in America." She showed me her purple Keds. "Cheap." They were basketball sneakers.

The man chuckled. "She's off her trolley." When he smiled, he had two fangs. He cleared his throat. "Bollocks. I don't see the sign for the Conrad Hilton. Have they given us the elbow? Or maybe something is happening."

Kharalombos said, "A revolution."

"You're mad," the man said. "The hotel assured us that the demonstrations would be over in a few days. That'll spoil our Nile cruise."

"Things look bad. Our ride hasn't shown up, either," I said.

"Ja-aa," the lady said, sighing, "I told you we should go to India, *Liebchen.* You never listen."

"This is most inconvenient," the man said. When he moved, he clinked. "Allow me to introduce myself. I am Viscount Triksky," he said, at last setting down the bags. "For restoring the tissues."

"What?" Kharalombos said, puzzled.

Kharalombos' English was almost perfect, but he sometimes missed idiomatic expressions.

Viscount Triksky gestured towards the bags. "Spirits."

"Oh," Kharalombos said, but he was gazing at the large lady in the muumuu with the purple sneakers. She was twenty years older, but she was exactly his height and size. Never had he met another giant his size. He had been dancing with upper-class anorexic Egyptian girls for years.

The lady laughed. "We are in a large pickle. Isn't that what you say? My English is so bad."

Viscount Triksky was still extending his hand to Kharalombos. I suddenly blanked and forgot Kharalombos' fake name. How were we going to get into the city? Where were we going to go? We had no way of getting in touch with Kharalombos' uncle. Hard to believe he was the one who had checked me into the mental hospital before; now, we were desperate to find him.

I shook his hand vigorously because Kharalombos couldn't take his eyes off the large lady. It was as if he had seen Cinderella. "Joe Smith," I said. "Nice to meet you."

Viscount Triksky winked at me. Was he hitting on me? "You look like a good American egg. Any idea how we can get to our hotel? Looks like you've done this before."

Did this character see through my disguise? God, coming back to Cairo had been a terrible idea. Why had I let Kharalombos talk me into it?

"This is our first visit to Cairo," I said. "We signed up for a Nile cruise."

Viscount Triksky shrugged. "Thought you looked like old hands."

The giantess was smiling at Kharalombos. She was saying, "This is Gudrun Luckenbach from Schulenburg, Texas. I was from Munich, but I moved to Texas near a big river. And I have a camp for girls called *Clover Flower*. Ja-aa, we do archery. Have you been to America? Their sausages are terrible, but I love it."

Kharalombos was entranced and had forgotten that we were in trouble. "They killed all the pigs here," he said. "I love pork paté."

I cleared my throat. "Zorba," I said. "Zorba." Kharalombos was supposed to be a Greek tourist. He would blow his cover if he started talking about how the pigs were dumped into pits in Cairo and covered with lime during the swine flu panic.

Suddenly, a sleek black limo stopped in front of us. The door popped open and a head peered out. The man was wearing an *Indiana Jones*–style hat. Could it be? I felt as if I were on a movie set.

The Egyptian man hissed, "Quickly enter the car. Before anyone sees Ramses. Everyone will recognize Ramses. Want to rob Ramses' hat."

"Do you know him?" I asked Viscount Triksky. I had seen him in the Egyptian newspapers, in the English newspapers, and on the History Channel. He received more publicity than the Big Man.

"Of course. We studied mummy preservation together at Oxford. Although my doctorate is on ancient pottery. Amulets…"

I didn't remember that Ramses el-Kibir was an Oxford graduate. I pushed that doubt to the back of my mind. Kharalombos was giving me the thumbs-down sign. Ramses el-Kibir was one of the Big Man's cronies. Now it was Kharalombos' turn to be paranoid. Was this a trap?

"I thought you were being picked up by the Conrad Hilton," I said. Who was Viscount Triksky? And why had Ramses el-Kibir come to pick him up? I thought anyone out on the streets would be shot.

"I'm a consultant for his television show," Viscount Triksky said. "*The Marvelous Adventures of Ramses el-Kibir, the World-Famous Archaeologist.*"

Kharalombos almost guffawed. Then he covered his mouth with his huge hand. Instead, he acted as if he were coughing from Gudrun's cigarette smoke.

"What about your Nile cruise?"

Viscount Triksky smiled, baring his teeth. "We're combining business with pleasure."

Gudrun said, "Nein. Nein. I don't know this man. Where is the Conrad Hilton? You didn't mention any business appointments."

So, Gudrun didn't know what was going on, either. Did she know Viscount Triksky very well? Was he even her husband? Er, probably not.

"Get in the car. As soon as people recognize me, they will want my autograph."

"The airport is empty," I said.

"Who are you? You keep acting like you are someone big," she said. "Big. Big. Bigger than the Pyramids, ja-aa." She waved her cigarette holder in the air.

Kharalombos started twirling her around, as if he had a dance partner. "This is a waltz. One-two-three. One-two-three."

What was he doing? Why was he suddenly teaching her how to waltz? Gudrun had not asked to learn how to waltz.

"Zorba, we will dance later," she said, waving her cigarette at him. She acted as if she had known him for years. Was this another one of Kharalombos' secrets?

"I am Ramses el-Kibir. World-Famous Archaeologist," Ramses said. "One of the Great Explorers of the World."

Gudrun snorted. "Never heard your name. But then, I am in the nature and never turn on the television. It's mostly useless. I am helping the girls shoot arrows, ja-aa." She turned to Kharalombos. "You could teach dancing at my camp. You know Latin dance? The young people want to learn that. Samba. Cha-cha-cha."

Viscount Triksky had already loaded his own suitcases into the backseat of the car. "I say, old girl, let's vamoose. Before Ramses changes his mind. We've got to make hay while …."

Ramses was gesturing for Gudrun to get in. Unfortunately, she didn't travel lightly and had two enormous steamer trunks: one pink and the other orange. Neither man offered to help her. They acted as if we were the porters and should load the trunks into the limo. I asked Kharalombos to help me lift it. What did she have in there? Five hundred pair of basketball shoes? What could she possibly need for a ten-day trip to Egypt except muumuus and underwear?

"Open the boot, ja-aa," Gudrun said, gesturing to the driver. However, the driver ignored her orders.

Ramses said, "The trunk is full."

She snorted. "Ja-aa. Don't tell us. Gold treasure from the tombs. GELT!"

Ramses sniffed. "Equipment for archaeological expeditions. For shooting my show, *The Marvelous Adventures of* ….."

I gestured to Kharalombos. "Set it down." I felt as if my arm might break. Actually, Kharalombos was so strong he could pick up the trunk with one of his pinkies. I don't know why I insisted on helping. I was a shrimp compared to all of these Jolly Green Giants.

Viscount Triksky sighed. "Don't be a plank, Gudrun. Get in the bloody car. We're wasting Ramses' time."

Ramses said. "Yes, you're wasting Dr Ramses el-Kibir's time. Tomorrow we have a shoot at the Pyramids."

Did he always talk about himself in the third person? If I ever returned to academia, this might be an effective way of getting attention in committee meetings.

"Ja-aa," Gudrun said. "So, you are going to film yourself tomorrow?"

The driver had gotten out of the limo. I suddenly noticed that he was a soldier, wearing fatigues. Why was a soldier driving Ramses el-Kibir around during a military curfew?

"I will have to leave the trunks here," Gudrun said. "There is not enough room for all of us."

Ramses said, "All of us? We are only taking you and the Count."

Gudrun said, "Ja-aa, so the ship is sinking and you leave your friends to go down with the ship. What kind of man are you?"

Ramses' face turned red. "My honor as an Eastern man has been insulted. No one talks to Dr Ramses el-Kibir like that!"

But she was! Go, Gudrun! She was fearless! Taking on Ramses el-Kibir. Many world-famous archaeologists had to kiss his ass to get their dig permits approved.

The Viscount peered out. "My dear girl, they are mere acquaintances. I say, get in the car. I could use some kip."

A minute ago, before Ramses had arrived, the Viscount had been very chummy with us. Now that he had a way into town, he had dropped us like hot potatoes. I glanced at Kharalombos, who gave me the signal to keep quiet.

Gudrun was sitting on her trunks and refused to budge. She lit another cigarette. Kharalombos was gazing at her with pure adoration. He had forgotten that he was supposed to be in love with the Big Man's daughter and had risked his life to come see his newborn son.

Gudrun gestured for us to get into the car. After we had gotten in, she squeezed herself in on the outside. The tiniest person in the group, I was sandwiched between Gudrun and Kharalombos. The thin Viscount was sitting to the left of Kharalombos. However, his Duty-Free bags took up so much room on the floor that there was no room for our feet. This was a huge vehicle. Why were we all crammed in the backseat? The third seat was full of crates: For Export: written on the sides in Arabic. What was in the crates?

The driver turned on the engine. Gudrun's trunks sat, woeful, on the sidewalk.

The Viscount said, "What do you propose to wear during our holiday?"

Gudrun frowned. "I can always buy new clothes."

We glided out of the airport easily. The few cars parked in the parking lot were stationary. The driver stopped to pay the toll for the airport. As soon as we hit Salah Salem, we flew through the streets. Not one pedestrian in sight. No cars. No donkeys. No street sellers. No cleaners. No street urchins. No bicycles. No motor scooters. No pizza delivery. We passed under a bridge. A tank was positioned there. The soldier peered out, alert, waiting for a surprise attack: at the absolute ready.

Ramses el-Kibir was saying, "Tomorrow the crew will meet us at the Giza Pyramids to shoot the last show for the season. Did you read the script? Ramses saves Madonna, who is trapped in the Pyramid, from bats and tomb robbers."

Viscount Triksky said, "Smashing. It's simply brilliant. First class. A1. Do you think you could also add some camels to the scenario? Maybe a chase across the desert?"

Was the Viscount really a Hollywood producer?

"Excuse me, but the situation looks really serious. How do you think you are going to film a television show?" I asked.

Ramses straightened his Indiana Jones hat. "The Big Man's army will clear the city by tomorrow. No problem. Never underestimate the power of the Big Man."

I worried about Kharalombos. What would happen to him if the Big Man's men discovered he was back? Straight to Tora prison. Or worse…

"Ja-aa, this is ridiculous. We will not be going on any cruise down the Nile," Gudrun said. "In fact, look at the tanks everywhere. Viscount, we should return to the airport and go to Bombay immediately."

I had attended a conference on Contaminated Water and Cholera in Bombay… Maybe there were more felicitous cities in the world to flee to? Was she looking for relaxation?

"Pssst, old girl," the Viscount said. "You've been saying you wanted a grand adventure. Archery is a bore. The girls' camp. Here you go. Actually, I was fortunate to be in Ethiopia when Haile Selassie was deposed in 1974. Great fun. Arse-over-tit in the hotel bars."

What was he doing in Ethiopia in 1974? I peeked into the Duty-Free bags: Viscount Triksky had expensive taste: Hennessey, Jameson, single malt whiskey. He had a thousand dollars' worth of booze here. You were only allowed four bottles on your passport when you came in. He had fifteen. I wondered how he had managed that.

Kharalombos was saying to Gudrun, "I could also teach rumba at your camp. It's the dance of love."

Kharalombos and Gudrun were holding hands over my chest. Wasn't this a little premature? What had happened to his passion for the Big Man's daughter?

I cleared my throat. "You know, Zorba, the quality of the extra-virgin olive oil at your farm is excellent. We should have brought some extra bottles to give out as presents to the other passengers on the Nile cruise."

Kharalombos looked at me strangely. And then realized he had dropped his disguise.

Gudrun reached into her enormous bag and fished out a bag of Reese's Peanut Butter Cups. I was absolutely starving. I had not eaten anything except a gluey cheese sandwich in the Valletta airport—that was eight hours ago.

She did not give Peanut Butter Cups to either Ramses or Viscount Triksky. "Nein. Nein. We cannot hear another word about the Marvelous Adventures of Ramses el-Kibir. We are fed up."

Ramses said, "Please. I have not eaten anything since my wife's okra stew. I have to keep my strength up for my shoot tomorrow."

Gudrun shook her orange head, vigorously. "NEIN. NEIN."

"I promise," Ramses said. For a Reese's Peanut Butter Cup, he had suddenly turned into a lamb.

We passed a minibus, which looked like a pretzel. The driver swerved to avoid burning tires in the road. I felt my stomach lurch. We should have spent the night at the airport.

She threw Ramses a piece of chocolate. He caught it. As soon as he popped it into his mouth, he began another monologue, "Ramses el-Kibir gave Barack Obama a tour of the Pyramids. He has lectured to kings, queens, and other important dignitaries about important Egyptian treasures…"

Viscount Triksky said, "You know, Ramses. It might be better if Madonna meets the mummy of Tutankhamen in the Pyramid. Americans know about King Tut. You know how woefully ignorant they are about everything else…"

A mob of young men were blocking the bridge. The driver slowed down. I heard the doors lock electronically.

Ramses el-Kibir, who was in the passenger seat, was saying, "Count, you know I am the hero of the show. I have to save Madonna from the tomb robbers and the bats."

I turned around and looked behind us. A huge truck was bearing down on us from behind. The men were waving machetes, clubs, and scythes—strange. Who were they?

Not too long ago, almost everyone I met said, "*Welcome to Egypt.*"

"Kharalombos," I said. "Turn around." He was wedged so tightly in that he couldn't turn his head.

We were no further than three feet away from the mob in front of us. They were playing chicken with the driver.

"Nein. Nein. Stop the car! Stop the car!" Gudrun was shouting.

Instead, the driver gunned for the boys. At the very last second, the boys jumped out of the way of our car. Suddenly, I heard a loud crashing noise. Someone had thrown a huge rock through the back windshield. We were showered with small bits of glass. The wind whipped our hair across our faces.

The soldier said, "It's war."

He was now driving over a hundred kilometers an hour. We had lost the truck. No one said a word. Even Ramses had stopped talking about his shoot.

As we came nearer the city, we saw a building on fire. A government building. And then, in the distance, we saw the flames in the sky: The Big Man's Headquarters.

Ramses el-Kibir moaned. He took off his hat. "We must protect our national treasures. Go to the Museum immediately."

The driver said, "The guests should be safe first."

"Are you disobeying Dr Ramses el-Kibir? That is an order."

The driver ignored him and continued to drive at lightning speed. We flew past burning tanks. Trashed cars. Ambulances whined past. Packs of men stalked past us with clubs. Light was just starting to break.

Suddenly, the car whirled to a stop in front of the Conrad Hilton. Armed men stood in front of the hotel lobby.

After we exchanged phone numbers with Gudrun, we set off for Garden City. She begged us to stay in the hotel. But we couldn't be registered under our real names anyway. However well-intentioned she was, we couldn't explain who we were. I didn't have credit cards in my new name—we didn't have that much cash with us. We had to find Kharalombos' uncle, our only hope. Or at least the key to his empty flat.

The streets were deserted. No taxis, even. We would have to walk to the building in Garden City. Dozens of tanks surrounded the television building. Armed soldiers were posted at all the entrances. A soldier was stringing barbed wire directly in front of the building.

"No police on the street. Not even traffic cops," I said. "Why?"

He suddenly started to cry. "I don't think I will get to see my son."

I wanted to reassure him, but this looked like it might be the end for the Big Man. His daughter would be stashed somewhere safe—maybe she had even left the country already. I didn't want to make him feel worse so I kept my mouth shut.

We continued to walk down the corniche, not exactly a pleasant stroll by the Nile.

Flames continued to shoot out from the top of the Big Man's headquarters. No fire trucks in sight. Were they going to let it burn out?

A kid about eighteen was taking a picture of his friend who was sitting on top of a burned-out car in the parking lot of the Big Man's headquarters. The kid was taking a picture with his phone, as if he were a tourist taking a picture of a castle in a distant land—a visit to the Louvre. An expensive jeep still smoked from burning embers.

A mob of young men streamed out of the Big Man's headquarters, like frantic ants. Some were carrying chairs over their heads. Others had their arms full of bars of chocolate—taking whatever they could carry from the building. How odd—a twelve-year-old boy was strapping boxes of Chivas Regal to a donkey.

"Keep walking," Kharalombos said. "I don't like the feeling."

Out of the corner of my eye, I saw another gang of men, armed with machetes.

"Stop!" one of the men called out. "*Spies! Infiltrators!*"

He waved the machete at Kharalombos. It barely missed his ear.

"Thugs. Filth," Kharalombo spit on the ground. "Run! Now!"

For someone so large and heavy, Kharalombos was very light on his feet—all those years of teaching ballroom dancing. He was able to run as fast as a soccer player. Once I dared myself to look back; they were still chasing us, waving their machetes at us. I had a cramp in my side, but scarcely felt it. I felt as if someone had injected me with a heavy dose of sugar. We kept sprinting.

At last, Kharalombos raised his hand. "You can stop now. They won't follow us into Garden City. Too many embassies."

"Are you crazy? Did you want to get us killed?"

"They are the dogs of the Interior Minister."

"Sure," I said. I had never seen any people like this in Egypt before; they had been kept discreetly out of sight. I had led a sheltered life as a professor before my escape from Egypt the first time.

"*Baltagi*," Kharalombos explained. "They do the dirty work for the police."

"We have to avoid the American Embassy," I said. "Although I am sure they are under lockdown. They won't be looking for me."

Garden City was silent, except for the occasional sound of gunfire. Where was it coming from? God. My stomach knotted.

When we reached Kharalombos' uncle's building, I couldn't have been more surprised. "This is my old building. Why didn't you tell me before that your uncle's flat was in this building?"

A group of men were huddled around a small fire.

One of the men aimed a shotgun at us. We moved forward with our hands over our heads. Please, don't shoot. I muttered under my breath, "That's not for killing rabbits."

"What?" Karalombos said. "Just keep your hands up."

"That's Am Sayed," I said. "The *bawab*."

Another man with a full head of white hair advanced with him. He was carrying a baseball bat. He had an odd-shaped body, very short legs with a long torso. He was wearing an *Atlanta Braves* tee-shirt—probably an American.

Kharalombos called out, "Ya, Am Sayed. It's me, Kharalombos."

Am Sayed lowered the shotgun. He ran forward and exclaimed, "Kharalombos. Kharalombos. We haven't seen you for such a long time. You light up our day." He kissed him on both cheeks. "Are you all right?"

Kharalombos said, "How are your boys? Are they married yet?"

Am Sayed sighed. "Yes, thank God, they are all married. They are working as minibus drivers. It is not what we dreamed of. But we must earn our bread."

Another man was fast asleep in a La-Z-Boy chair behind Am Sayed. His snore sounded like the wheezing of an elephant. Yet it was clear he was ancient—maybe about eighty-five. When I looked closer, I could see that he had a great many medals pinned to his green IZOD cardigan. He was clutching a sword.

Kharalombos said, "Who is that?"

Am Sayed smiled. "The landlord's uncle. A general. He wanted to help us guard the building. He has been telling us jokes and stories all night. He told us how he ate snake for breakfast in Sinai during the '73 war."

Kharalombos brightened. "Where is my uncle? Do you know?"

"At the hospital with the patients," Am Sayed said. "No one else would go. He's on call day and night. He's a hero."

Am Sayed shook his head sadly. "What's wrong?" Kharalombos asked.

Why did Am Sayed look so forlorn? I felt panicked. Felt gritty from lack of sleep. His uncle had sold the apartment?

"You can't believe the chaos. Someone stole the plant," Am Sayed said.

"The plant?" I echoed. What was he talking about?

"My uncle keeps the spare key in a plant," Kharalombos said. "It was always safe before. That was our hiding place for years."

"*Salamtak*, Dr Gary," Am Sayed said, turning to me. He kept shaking my hand. We had never kissed on the cheeks—I had never felt comfortable with that. An American man thing. "How is your health?"

He meant, are you still cuckoo? Cuckoo. Buckoo. Woo. Woo. Of course, Am Sayed had been there the day I had been sedated by the university doctor and taken away to the bin. An ugly scene.

"Wonderful," I said. "I shine. I've fully recovered." No one believed me, but I wasn't crazy to begin with. Granted, I should have fully calculated how persuading students to dump a ton of contaminated fish at the gates of the university would ruin my career, but I was trying to make an ethical point. I wondered if Am Sayed also knew that I had been accused of cyber-crime. Was wanted by Interpol. Probably—*porters* knew everything.

"Where are we going to stay?" I asked Kharalombos. "What now?"

A man offered his hand. "The name's Bill...I'm a visiting professor in Human Rights Law. We were here nine years ago. You're quite a character." He chuckled. "Legendary."

What had people said about me? I was a nut? A loon? Deserved the punishment I got? My imagination and ego started to run wild. Can it, Gary, will you?

I laughed. "No," I said. "I've become bland. A domesticated cat without any claws. I'm now a textbook salesman in Ames, Iowa."

Surely, he didn't believe such an outrageous fib. Wasn't it a bit gratuitous to keep up the disguise? Back at my old building everyone knew who I was.

Bill said, "By the way, Gary, we are living in your old flat."

Had they found my novel? Was it still under the bed? I was dying to know. Just when I was about to ask, we heard the whirring of helicopters overhead.

Am Sayed pointed to the sky. "People have been angry for a long time. They want their rights."

"Do you remember what happened in 1986? When they burned down the Holiday Inn. Many died," Kharalombos said, shaking his head.

Who were they? Frankly, I decided it was BETTER NOT TO KNOW. Or ask.

Am Sayed sighed, "This is much, much bigger. I hope it doesn't become bloody."

We should have stayed in Malta. But that was the risk of adventure: sometimes things backfired. And how! They had backfired badly. The hint of draconian doom was making me anxious. I had not been to the bathroom for twenty-four hours; I needed a bathroom very soon. At the mental hospital, I had suffered from bouts of diarrhea. Of course, who could eat contaminated tilapia from the Nile? I would rather starve! I heard the voice of my yoga teacher, "Breathe. Feel the air in your lungs. Stay calm."

Bill was saying, "Y'all come on up and have a cup of coffee. Sample some good ol' pe-can pie. Meet Rose, my wife. She's a firecracker."

We left Am Sayed and the snoring general to guard the building and followed him up the stairs.

The door suddenly swung open. Rose was saying, "Now, Scarlett O'Hara, darlin', you've already had your sugar for today. Don't be a wart." A tiny Chihuahua was barking ferociously, as if she were a lion. At the most, Rose was in her late thirties or early forties—tall and svelte. She had terrific, tanned legs. She was wearing a pair of flimsy shorts with a red Alabama tee-shirt: *The Bloody Tide*. She had eschewed the cheerleader look; instead of long blonde hair, her hair was cropped short in a spiky cut. What surprised me even more was the tattoo of a whale on her arm: *SAVE THE WHALES*. A woman after my own heart, another crusader for the environment.

"Baby, we have visitors…." Bill said. "Put on the coffee. Get out your pecan pie. She makes the best pe-can pie."

Kharalombos reached down to stroke Scarlett with one of his giant hands. Rose said, "Darlin', I wouldn't do that if I were you."

But it was too late. Scarlett had sunk her teeth into Kharalombos' hand. "Awwww! Shit!"

Rose pulled at the rat-like Chihuahua. "Scarlett O'Hara, I'm counting to three. One. Two. ...Stop being con-trary. Right now...I mean it."

Bill cleared his throat, embarrassed. "Baby, you better put her in the back room. She doesn't like..."

When Rose scooped up the dog in the crook of her arm, her breasts jiggled. She wasn't wearing a bra. The dog kept barking furiously.

Bill raised his hands in the air, exasperated, as if he were imploring God for help. "Rose said she wouldn't come to Cairo without her baby. It has been challenging...Scarlett is diabetic. A very high-maintenance dog."

I couldn't resist laughing. First, Viscount Triksky and Gudrun. Now, a diabetic dog named Scarlett O' Hara. I felt I was hallucinating on mushrooms.

Bill didn't think it was funny. "I'm dead serious. The dog goes with us everywhere. We even had to take Scarlett on a Nile cruise. She jumped into the Nile. They had to stop the boat." Was the sex with Rose so great that he tolerated this nasty dog? I would be tempted to strangle it in the night. But maybe that's why I had very temporary girlfriends—I refused to compromise. I wondered if Boriana, my Bulgarian girlfriend, would really wait for me to return to Malta. I hadn't promised her anything.

Drops of blood oozed from Kharalombos' giant hand. We had escaped from all sorts of threats on our way here.

Rose sauntered back into the foyer. She said to Kharalombos. "I'm so sorry, she can be a real pill at times. She hates men. The animal shelter told me she had probably been abused as a puppy."

"Baby," Bill said. "Aren't you forgetting your manners? This is Kharalombos. He is...I'm sorry... did you tell me what you do?"

Kharalombos who was in a lot of pain, gasped, "Olive farmer."

Bill looked puzzled. "Do they raise olives in Egypt? I didn't recall..."

Kharalombos continued. "I'm a retired olive farmer. Now, I teach ballroom dancing to movie stars."

What was wrong with Kharalombos? Had he gone off his rocker?

Bill chortled. "You don't say. That's quite a career. I'm an expert on torture!"

Yeah, right! Surely, he wasn't serious.

"I think he might need something to stop the bleeding on his hand," I said. We didn't need to talk about Kharalombos' real identity. About how he had done the deed with the Big Man's daughter. How he had returned to see his newborn son.

"Baby," Bill said. "Bring the first aid kit. It's in the bathroom."

"Oh, darlin', I am so, so sorry," Rose said, taking Kharalombos' hand in hers. "Will you look at that? Bleeding like a stuck pig."

Scarlett was yapping loudly in the other room. Did she ever stop yapping?

Rose went to the bathroom to get the first aid kit. Bill said, "I think you fellas might need a cup of coffee. I'll put on the coffee. Maxwell House, okay?"

"What are you doing?" I whispered.

"We're dead men," Kharalombos said. "Why should we hide?" His eyes were bloodshot. His back had suddenly become hunched. He seemed to be losing confidence. Was I supposed to pick up the slack?

Rose suddenly appeared with peroxide and a long bandage. "Oh, darlin', you won't die from one of Scarlett's bites. You sit down right there and let me doctor you."

A few minutes later, Bill was bringing in two mugs of steaming coffee. "I didn't introduce Gary. He used to live in this flat."

"Why, I'll be..." Rose said.

"You didn't by any chance find a novel when you moved in? I think I left it under the bed. It was called *Pure Water*."

"No," Rose said. "Don't think so. Don't believe we did. Our maid cleaned the place when we moved in." She was spraying Kharalombos' bite with disinfectant. "Bill, darlin', did you see a novel anywhere? Under our bed?"

"Naw," Bill said. "Never saw a novel. No siree."

Rose wrapped a long bandage around Kharalombos' hand. "That okay? Well, darlin', what's your novel about?"

"An American scientist thrown into the Nile by the Egyptian secret police for exposing corrupt water companies. They're selling contaminated water."

"Sounds like a real page-turner. Don't you think, Bill?" She fondled the brass ring in her nose.

Bill cleared his throat. "Do you think that's plausible? I don't mean to knock your idea, fella. But don't you think that's a little paranoid? Something out of Dan Brown?"

"Why not? Even the strictly factual is fantastic. Soad Hosny, an Egyptian movie star, was thrown off a balcony in London by the secret police."

Kharalombos' face had turned white. How tactless of me: this was going to make Kharalombos feel that his time had come. Sometimes I couldn't resist showing off my knowledge.

"Rose is a writer in her own right. She is working on a novel about snake handlers in Alabama."

I laughed. "Snake handlers in Alabama? That sounds bizarre. Fantastic. What an original idea!"

Bill added, "She's mighty talented. Her first novel was about a grisly murder among carnie people. Say, would you fellas like a piece of homemade pe-can pie?"

"I don't want to talk about my characters," Rose said. "It's bad luck. Spoils the incubation process. People start telling you how to write your story. That's damned annoying."

Bill smiled. "Those fellas think if they don't get bitten by the snake, that shows their faith. They even drink the poison in their services. That's the Pentecostal Church for you. *The Church with Signs Following*."

We could hear gunfire in the distance.

Rose said, "Bill…That's enough. I think we need cheerful thoughts right now."

Kharalombos said, "Where is Alabama in America? Wasn't that part of what they called the Confederacy? They lost the Civil War. Thousands died."

Bill said, "Darn right. It was bloody. Over six hundred thousand men from both sides."

The phone rang. "Rose's Bar and Grill," she said, cheerfully. But she suddenly became serious and covered the mouthpiece of the phone. "Citibank is being looted."

Bill was saying, "The worst battle was Gettysburg. Fifty-one thousand men died on that battlefield alone."

Scarlett was barking. "What? I can't hear you. Can you speak louder? You know Scarlett makes too much noise."

She covered the mouthpiece again and said, "A shootout at the prison in Maadi. They can hear the machine-gun fire."

She hung up the phone. She said a little too brightly, "Well, anyone for pe-can pie?"

We were shown into the living room. The atmosphere was funereal. What was going to happen to us?

"Please," Bill said, gesturing to the huge chairs. "Have a seat. Rose has done a real nice job of decorating the place. She put her heart and soul into making the place a home."

Kharalombos settled into one of the giant chairs, which was next to the sofa. I sat on the couch. To my surprise, Bill sat on the floor in an Indian-style pose, facing us.

He said, "I'm an old hippie. Smoked a lot of dope in my time. A Vietnam vet."

Rose had hung orange tent-work material on every wall. I felt as if I were hallucinating again—too many vivid colors and geometric shapes. And yet it wasn't unpleasant: Oriental fantasy—geometric designs of reds, greens, yellow, and blue. When I had lived in the flat, I had done nothing to decorate the place; the walls were a plain white. I was obsessed with my work and had not paid much attention to domestic details. I couldn't believe that this was my flat; it was like I had never even lived here.

Kharalombos gestured with his bandaged hand. "This material is used for funeral tents."

"Uhhhuh. Do you really teach movie stars how to dance?" Bill said. "Any famous people that I know?"

Kharalombos said, "Omar Sharif."

"Geez," Bill said. "Omar Sharif. Anyone else...?"

"And a very beautiful girl named..." Kharalombos sighed. And his eyes looked sorrowful. He looked as if he just might break down in tears. He was thinking of Yasmine, the Big Man's daughter, and his newborn son. Did Kharalombos even know the boy's name?

"I'm sorry. I didn't mean to offend."

"You know, Bill," I said. "We haven't slept a wink for hours. And now we have no place to stay since we don't have the key to Kharalombos' uncle's apartment."

"Y'all are welcome to stay here for a few days. Experience a little Southern hospitality. See how we cook with Crisco."

When Rose returned from the kitchen, she plunked down a bottle of *Maker's Mark* bourbon in the middle of the coffee table. She plopped down next to me on the couch, tucked her legs underneath her, like a mermaid. She was very flexible. I couldn't resist staring at her legs. I caught Kharalombos staring, too. I wondered what she could do with her pelvis in bed.

"Bourbon with pe-can pie at eight in the morning?" Bill asked. "You'll get higher than a Georgia pine."

She smirked. "Okay, Pa, if that don't put pepper in your gumbo!" She stuck out her tongue at him. God, she had a brass ball in her tongue! I wondered where else she might have piercings. On her nipples? "Maybe these fellas need a drink."

"Not for me," I said. I took a bite of the pie. Too sugary, but I was hungry so I kept eating it. "Pie's delicious," I said.

Kharalombos poured himself half a glass. He rarely drank. He must feel awful.

Bill looked serious. "Baby, you know what we agreed. We shouldn't even have it in the house. Where did you hide it?"

Rose said, "That's for me to know. And you to find out. I need this. Rome is burning. You want me to drink lemonade?"

"Are you sure you didn't find a manuscript when you moved in?"

Rose took a swig of bourbon. "Let me tell you, we have this maid, Zennuba. Dumb as a bucket of rocks. She either moves things or throws things away. She used to cook for us. Baked chicken with the head still on it. Gross. How does she expect us to eat that? It would be easier to fry the chicken myself. Except I'm trying to write a book…"

"Rose, he is asking about his book." Bill said. "Could you just answer…"

Rose threw her hands up in the air. "I told you there's no fuckin' book."

"Don't go off like a pistol half-cocked. Everything will be all right," Bill said.

"You're lying like a legless dog," Rose said, gulping the bourbon. "All of us are shit scared. I don't know why I let you talk me into coming to this godforsaken place. It would have been much easier to stay in Tuscaloosa. Now I'm never gonna make Knopf's deadline!"

I said, "Maybe it'll turn up." I felt a little sick. I imagined how my novel had been carted away to be recycled at Moqattam Hills with all the huge mounds of trash in Cairo. I had slaved away on that book for seven years—not a single trace of it was left. Gone. Poof. Like I had never even written it. I imagined myself in Moqattam Hills, rooting around like one of the pigs they raised there, through

Pepsi cans, Kotex, bits of gristle, pizza boxes, leftover macaroni—desperately searching for my five hundred pages that I had hoped would one day become a book. Even if I found the greasy manuscript among the trash, no publisher would take me on—I was a pariah. Who had gotten into my computer and created that nasty virus? And why? Okay Gary, listen up. You know why. You are exposing some big factories in Egypt who dump their chemicals into the Nile. Bad publicity. Bad for business.

Bill said, "Well, hell, I'm writing a book, too. About how Bush had anyone he suspected extradited to foreign countries. Where they were tortured. A clear violation of human rights. Plenty of innocent people were tortured. Plenty."

"Please spare us," Rose said. "This is a need not to know."

Kharalombos' face had turned green. He looked as if he might be about to throw up. "Do you think I could lie down?"

"Of course, you can have the master bedroom. Scarlett has her own room," Rose said. "Come with me."

In the next three days, we had to adjust to long curfews. Five hours a day, we were allowed out. I walked in circles in the neighborhood, very close to the building—in fact, I circled one block thirty times. I invented expeditions to the Blue Nile grocery store for candles, *Bounty Bars*, cigarettes, and cheddar cheese. When I heard gunfire, I scurried back to the building. Once indoors, I played solitaire for hours in the main living room since Scarlett had the spare bedroom. She never, ever, stopped barking. Kharalombos spent most of his time outdoors, with the group guarding the building: he never got tired of listening to the general's stories. Or maybe he was avoiding Bill? He took Bill's place on night duty—his weapon was one of the general's golf clubs. During the day, he was so tired he slept on the couch in the living room: a loud bellowing snore. Without any internet, we floated between rumors and phone calls. Rose always had a drink in her hand; and was always talking on the phone. She announced: "They are saying we better have a bag packed." Or, "They let all the convicts out of jail." Bill was nonplussed. "I was in Saigon when it fell." He sat cross-legged on the floor in the living room, cracking his teeth on pistachios and drinking huge glasses of Pepsi with ice. When Rose became hysterical, he said calmly, "Everyone has to learn to deal with their own fear. Don't you listen to them, baby."

Bill seemed outwardly calm, but he behaved strangely, too. As soon as you sat in the living room, he talked compulsively about the different ways victims could be tortured—hung from the balls, pointy objects rammed up the anus, feet roasted over a fire, face dunked again and again in water. On the third day, he started telling me about how they used rat torture in the Elizabethan era. "They used to encourage the rats to eat the flesh of the prisoners. Hung the prisoners near the river Thames so the rats would eat them."

I started reading Rose's copy of *The History of Alabama Football* in the bathroom—it seemed the only place where I could find peace in their flat. Or I volunteered to help Rose make fried chicken in the kitchen. We ate fried drumsticks and rat cheese for breakfast, lunch, and dinner—if we ate.

Suddenly, the networks came back on. I wondered if it might be better to float between rumors and phone calls. On the television, we could see the huge crowds swelling in Tahrir Square. People shouted with their fists raised, "Out. Out. Out. Get Out Big Man!" One afternoon, fighter jets streaked across the sky; they made a frightening, squealing sound.

Whenever the living room was empty, Kharalombos sneaked phone calls to the Big Man's daughter.

I whispered, "Are you calling the landline of the royal palace? They've split, I'm sure. *Left town. Hit the road, Jack. Ain't comin' back. No more. No more.*"

Kharalombos was despondent. "It's not funny. I'll never get to see Nunu now."

When he called Yasmine's mobile number, someone seized the phone and said, "This is her father speaking. Who is this?"

"Are you sure you have the right phone number?" I said. "Do you honestly think it was the Big Man?"

We stood fixated like zombies in front of the television. Rose became more and more anxious, watching the huge crowds. From lack of sleep and too much booze, she became feverish. "I'm telling you, darlin', it's gonna be a bloodbath."

Even Bill became jittery from drinking too much Pepsi. He'd say, "Now baby, don't rush to conclusions." After he said something calm, he usually launched into his monologue about the different ways victims could be tortured.

So much hysteria was wrecking my stomach—I had watery diarrhea. I wasn't sleeping, either. Who could sleep with Scarlett barking? And the television was on at full blast, day and night. Were they going to start bombing the Square? What if Rose were right?

I began to dread the ring of the phone.

Rose covered the mouthpiece of the phone and said, "Obama is sending planes. All Americans should get out."

"What? Are you sure?" I said.

"Positive," Rose said. "Pack your bags."

"Baby," Bill said. "We don't know that for sure. We haven't heard anything from the university."

Rose was now drinking Scotch neat; she had long ago finished the Maker's Mark. "Where the hell are they? Hello!"

"I have an idea," I said. "Why don't we turn off the television? Kharalombos will teach us how to waltz this evening."

We had to think about something else or we really would go nuts.

Bill chuckled. "That's a fine idea, Gary. Good thinking."

Kharalombos looked at me as if I were crazy. Then he said, "Why not? We'll need to clear the living room of the furniture so we have a space."

We pushed all of the furniture into the dining room so that the living room was clear.

Kharalombos said, "Now, the first thing to remember if you are dancing a waltz is to count, especially if you are leading…."

We waltzed the evening away until late into the night. And that was the only night we slept.

The next morning, the phone rang at seven am. A music professor in the building was leaving the country. Would Rose take care of his ferret, Wolfgang? What an odd pet! Why didn't he have a cat? Cats were more than plentiful in Cairo. He could have given a street cat a home.

"Surely, darlin'. I know how much Wolfgang means to you," Rose said, rubbing her eyes. She had not even washed her face yet. "Be safe."

Bill was saying, "Baby, do you think that's a good idea? Scarlett doesn't like to share her territory."

Yeah. We were sleeping in the living room since she had the guest bedroom! Kharalombos was on the couch; I was sleeping on a pallet on the floor.

The doorbell rang. The cage with Wolfgang was passed through the door. I just noticed that he had long, slender fingers—a pianist?

Two hours later, the doorbell rang again. A woman with wild, red, curly hair stood in the door with a parrot in a cage. I answered the door. Bill was taking a shower. Rose was in the kitchen, making coffee. Kharalombos was fast asleep on the sofa.

She screeched, "Her name's Ophelia. No milk. No junk food. Just fruit and veggies!"

Rose poked her head around the corner. "Trudy, why don't you come on in? Have a cup of coffee, darlin'."

Trudy said, "The driver's waiting downstairs. Have you seen the lines at the airport? You better get out while you can."

We had avoided the television. "I think I have my hands full...."

Trudy called out, "Bye! No caffeine. No booze. Bad for the bird."

I was standing in the foyer, holding the cage. "Where should I put her?"

Rose was holding a cup of coffee. "Hell's bells. Wolfgang can't be with Scarlett. Ophelia can't be with Wolfgang. The bathroom?"

So every time I was sitting on the john, I would have to stare at the parrot? That was my haven in this flat—now gone.

"Bill's in the shower," I said.

"That so?" Rose said. "Hmmm," she said. "Living room."

"Wolfgang's there," I said. "On the coffee table."

When Bill came out of the shower, he was not happy to see the parrot. "For crying out loud, baby, this is not a zoo. Say no to the next one...We can't take care of all these animals."

The next person knocked with a pitter-pat. "Ah, que bueno," the short, petite woman said when I opened the door. She handed me the cage: a pure white rabbit. She gave me a kiss on both cheeks. "I am Abril. This is Blanca. Where is Rose?"

Rose and Abril kissed each other on both cheeks. "You will take care of Blanca, my *chuela*. She trusts you. She thumps when she is scared. I am only going to Madrid. Not to America."

The door closed. When Bill saw me holding the cage, his face turned red.

Rose shrugged, "I couldn't say no to Abril. She's a good gal. Helped me buy a coffeemaker. And a microwave. Come to think of it, the vacuum cleaner, too."

"Who's she?" Actually, I was thinking that Abril was the only nice person who had rung the doorbell.

"She's a translator," Rose said. "Fluent in three languages. Puts us to shame."

Bill had turned on the television. "Baby, come look at this."

Thousands of people were leaving Egypt in droves.

The next morning Bill cornered me when Rose was in the shower. "Gary, can I talk to you privately?" he whispered.

"Why are you whispering?" I asked. He acted as if he were about to tell me a big secret. Kharalombos was snoring away on the couch—deep in slumber.

He put his hand on my shoulder. "I've arranged for us to go on an Embassy plane to Cyprus. You can see what kind of shape Rose is in. She's fragile. Acting like a chicken with its head cut off. I have to get her out of here."

"Oh," I said. "Sure. What about all these animals?"

"Well, buddy, I know we just met. I was wondering if you would do us a real big favor. I know it's a lot to ask. But you need a place to stay. Maybe in exchange...?"

"You want us to take care of them? You're taking Scarlett?"

Bill shook his head. "I'll have to break it to Rose. Embassy's orders. One small carry-on bag. No pets."

"I thought she couldn't be separated from Scarlett. She'll never go," I said. God, was I going to be stuck with nasty Scarlett, too?

"She'll go," Bill said, confidently. "She's a drama queen, but she'll go."

With the rest of the bailouts from the other expatriates. I should have seen it coming. I was still stunned. "You're coming back?"

"I wish I could say we were. We've had a great year here," Bill said. "But you can see for yourself that things are getting bad. Nobody knows what will happen."

"When are you leaving?" I asked. I had really thought Bill would stick it out for the long haul, especially since he kept mentioning his experience in Vietnam. How tough he was. Was that a bluff?

"A few hours," Bill said. "The last seats on the plane."

"Rose doesn't know?" I asked.

When she got out of the shower, doors slammed. I could hear her yelling, "You're not my daddy. How dare you! I won't go!"

But in the end, she had a tiny carry-on bag over her shoulder. She was holding a small computer bag. She was sobbing. "Scarlett, darlin', I'm so sorry. But momma'll be back real soon. In a jiffy. You behave for your Uncle Gary. Gary, can you give shots?"

My stomach took another dip. I might be able to write books and organize massive protests on the environment, but giving shots to irascible pets was not one of my many talents. Come on, Gary. Stop being a wimp. How hard could it be?

"Shots?"

"Gary, darlin', Scarlett is diabetic. She absolutely has to have two shots a day of insulin. Let me show you where I keep it."

I followed her into the kitchen and peeked into the refrigerator—an absurd number of packets of insulin took up the entire second shelf of the refrigerator. The third shelf was entirely devoted to Stella beer.

"What happens when the insulin runs out?" I asked. I didn't want to be responsible for the demise of Scarlett O'Hara.

"Cross that bridge when you come to it, darlin'," Rose said. She opened a drawer and took out a shot. "Let's have a lesson before I go."

Like an experienced nurse, she inserted the insulin into the shot, scooped up Scarlett, and gave her the shot in the rump before I could blink. Scarlett whimpered. "See, easy as pie."

Bill was calling out, "Baby, driver's honking. Gotta go. We're gonna miss the plane. Stop dillydallying."

"What about the other animals? Did the owners leave instructions? I don't know anything about ferrets. Rabbits. Parrots. Once I had a beagle named Oliver when I was a kid. But that's it."

"Well, darlin', you love the natural world. You'll do just fine. Check the internet. All the answers are there."

"But we don't have a computer," I said. "Aren't you taking yours?"

"Yep," Rose said. "My book....Snake handlers..."

Bill yelled, "Rose!"

Rose pinched my cheek. "You're a smart man. You'll figure it out."

Kharalombos woke up an hour later. He stretched his long arms, and yawned. "Where is everybody?"

"Flew the coop," I said.

I started combing the flat for my novel. I was obsessed. Bill and Rose were gone; I didn't have to be polite anymore. First, I would start with the place I was sure I had left it—under the bed in the master bedroom. And Ophelia and Blanca would stay in the master bedroom with me. They were the least offensive creatures in the menagerie. I carried their cages into the bedroom. At least I wouldn't have to sleep on the floor on a pallet anymore. My back was killing me. All that work with yoga in Malta; I still couldn't make myself do the exercises without the teacher. Did I just go to the class for her sexy, calm voice? *Breathe deeply. With control. With control.* Maybe we could keep Wolfgang imprisoned in Scarlett's room. He looked like a weasel. Was he part of the weasel family? Scarlett's barking was annoying, but she could not have full rein of the apartment. She would have to be separated from the others.

I threw the bedspread over the side of the bed and peered underneath—I pulled out a pair of handcuffs. What in the hell? A nasty black cuff for the neck. A leather whip. Paddles. *Please spank me! I'm the maid!* Bungee cords. For tying up your partner? A strap-on dildo. Bubble wrap. *Oh, please, Big Daddy, wrap me tight! Now, I'll put some pepper in your gumbo.* Maybe I should suggest this to Boriana. Skewers. What were those for?!

Okay, no manuscript here. But wait! I saw a few pieces of paper. First Baptist Church of Tuscaloosa newsletter—Rose's address was written on it. Did she really attend? A Warning Letter from the Daughters of the Confederacy: "You have not paid your dues for the last three years. You will be dropped from our society if you do not pay immediately." I could hear Rose say, "Frankly, I don't give a damn."

I heard sporadic gunfire outside. My stomach knotted up. I pulled out the thick magazines. *Screw. Juggs. Hustler's Taboo.*

Kharalombos stood in the doorway. "I tried to call Yasmine again. Now the phone is out of range. Maybe you're right. They've left the country."

"Look at this. Incredible," I said, showing him the insert. "Have you ever seen such big tits?"

"Do you think it's right to go through their things?" Kharalombos said.

"I'm looking for my novel," I said.

Kharalombos snorted. "That doesn't look like your novel."

Blanca was thumping again.

"I think Blanca might be hungry. Could you bring me some carrots?"

Kharalombos returned with the entire vegetable bin. He handed it to me. "No carrots."

"How about some lettuce? Potatoes might be hard to digest. Cauliflower?" I said. "You know, *chuela*, cauliflower is boring without cheese. Okay. Lettuce will do."

The doorbell twittered.

"Could you get the doorbell?"

I quickly shoved the porn magazines back under the mattress. Maybe Bill and Rose had not been able to get on the plane after all.

Kharalombos reappeared. "Nobody there."

"Are you sure? Do you think somebody knows we're here?" I asked.

"I don't know. Somebody could have easily followed us," Kharalombos said. "Traced the phone call."

"Do you think Am Sayed is really going to be able to stop those guys if they come after you?" I asked.

"No," he said, hopelessly. "They'll stick a hose up my ..."

"Do you think you could feed Blanca?"

When Kharalombos opened the cage to put in a piece of lettuce, Blanca hopped out. She started jumping up and down around the room. Boing! Boing! Boing! Up on the bed. Boing! Boing! Boing, towards the door.

"Quick, close the door. Scarlett will have her for lunch," I said.

He said, "I'm going to have tea with the general." Then he slammed the bedroom door shut. My eye wandered to the bedside table. Hey, here's a copy of Rose's novel: I read the jacket cover: A dwarf in rural Alabama takes revenge on his lover in a story of betrayal and passion. A thrilling whodunit in a carnival camp. A blurb from *Publishers Weekly*: "*An exciting voice from the New South.*" This made me a little jealous. Where was my novel? Give me mine! "An imaginative creator of a universe." That's me! "In the footsteps of Carson McCullers." Is that so? I tossed the book on the bed. Blanca jumped off the bed. Boing! Boing!

"You know, Blanca," I said. "You can't jump around the house freely. There's Scarlett. And Wolfgang. Two very nasty creatures."

I hadn't heard Scarlett barking for a while. At some point, I would have to give her a second shot of insulin. I dreaded the moment.

Ophelia flapped her wings, but didn't make any noise. I had forgotten about her.

I heard a loud explosion outside. Shit! What was that? Shouldn't I see what was happening? I switched the channel to El-Gezira. The local Carrefour superstore had been looted. A thug was carrying out a mannequin from the store. Why did he want that? The jewelry store in the mall had been stripped completely—even the cases were gone. Had the whole city gone haywire? El-Gezira then showed a series of clips of police stations on fire across the country. BREAKING NEWS: *Ten thousand convicts were released from three prisons in Egypt.* God! What was going to happen to us? Maybe we should have gotten on the plane. Too late now! What time was it?

I had put it off long enough—I would have to give Scarlett her second shot. Come to think of it, she was awfully quiet.

First, I congratulated myself on putting the insulin into the shot. A major victory! Hurray! I tiptoed into the living room. That sneaky dog. Never to be fooled, she must have heard me coming. I chased her around the coffee table. Up on the couch, off the couch. Through the dining room, into the kitchen. The chase continued for over an hour. At the end, she yapped as if she had won. And she had!

"You die!" I shouted at her. "Without this sugar."

But she yapped at me happily. If she did die, I dreaded facing Rose.

It had been one week since we had landed in Cairo. In the next few days, we developed a routine which revolved around feeding the animals. We put a limit on how much television we watched. No more than three hours a day. Another rule: we did not watch television when we were eating. It wasn't exactly Italian gourmet dining: canned tuna, Mars Bars, sardines and saltine crackers, liver sandwiches and fava beans from the cart down the street. Images of grocery stores and banks that had been looted, burned-out cars, bleeding people, were not good for your digestion.

Kharalombos often came in, breathless, to tell me what was happening in the street. "Am Sayed stopped a minibus full of thugs with his shotgun. They had Molotov cocktails. They were going to throw them at our building! The old general made them break the bottles and told them they should be ashamed of themselves."

Another night, Am Sayed shot out the tires of a motorcycle that tried to break through the barricaded street.

During the daytime, the tear gas floated in from the Square and made my eyes burn. I was always running to the bathroom, to douse my face with water.

At last, the Big Man gave a speech about his love for the people and his own heroism for the country. The people in the Square had long awaited this moment and they were sorely disappointed. The Big Man certainly wasn't Santa Claus, but he looked tired and sad on television; I almost felt sorry for him.

I heard the loud booing from the Square from our open window. Imagine a million people BOOING…BOOOOOOO! Did the Big Man still believe the people loved him? Soon after, angry chants started, "Out. Out. We want the Big Man out," they shouted.

Tanks surrounded the Square; the army seemed to be with the people. But were they? Could they kill all the people in the Square if they wanted? We didn't say this out loud. I thought of Rose's prediction, "Darlin', it's going to be a bloodbath."

At night, someone kept calling the flat. Deep breathing. Or a sinister voice, "We know who you are." Was it the Big Man's men? But weren't they too busy to worry about small-time imposters like us?

Besides the anonymous phone calls, someone kept ringing our doorbell in the middle of the night. I opened the door; no one was there. Who was it? Everyone had fled except for the old general and Am Sayed.

I heard shouting outside the building. What was happening now? Had marauders gotten past Am Sayed, the old general, and Kharalombos? Suppose they broke down the door. I should start boiling water. Really? Maybe I just had to deal with my fear. Breathe deeply. Take valerian to calm down.

One morning when Kharalombos came in to sleep, I said, "Could you stop calling Yasmine? It's putting us in danger. They are probably tracking the call."

He said, "I haven't called her for days. Maybe it's a prank caller."

I had one last place to search for the novel. Scarlett's bedroom was a monument to kitsch. Rose had collected a lot of Egyptian junk from tourist shops: perfume bottles, statues of Osiris, King Tut, papyrus with gold designs. On the bedside table were a stack of coffee table books on Egyptology. I picked one up. Ramses el-Kibir in his Indiana Jones hat smiled back; he pointed a finger at me. "Gotcha." The title of the book: *Explore One of the Seven Wonders of the World with Ramses el-Kibir*. I turned over the cover: "If you like this, check out Ramses el-Kibir's television show: *The Marvelous Adventures of…*" We had heard that Ramses el-Kibir had single-handedly beaten off looters of the Egyptian Museum with a ball-point pen. At least, that was what the Arabic newspapers reported!

Wolfgang's cage was set on an uncomfortable-looking, ornate Louis XIV chair. He bared his teeth at me. I shuddered. Why on earth would anyone have such a wild creature as a pet? I wondered about the musician who owned him. Was he deranged?

He hissed at me. He had ferocious-looking teeth. Terrible, malicious eyes.

I got down on my knees and flipped over the bedcover. Nothing. Just a lot of dust and hairballs from a cat. A cat? Zennuba had not done her job, no. I'd say she was a good hoodwinker, not a dumb bucket of rocks.

I was suddenly thirsty. I wandered into the kitchen. I was getting hungry, too. Maybe I should cook something. I picked up a recipe book: Southern desserts. A piece of scrap paper marked the page: Mississippi Mud Pie. I turned it over—the title page to my novel, *Pure Water*. On the other side, scribbled handwriting. A list: sponges, toilet paper, Dettol, garlic, lemon, Coca-Cola.

The phone rang. "Hello. Hello. Hello?" Some small child giggled, "Hey, mister, fuck you." My eye wandered to the scrap paper next to the phone. Don't do it! Phone numbers in block letters on each scrap of paper: Drinkies. VET in red Magic Marker pen. The tailor. I dared myself to peek. I turned over each scrap: random pages from my novel. Page 323. Page 13.

Surprisingly, I was not enraged. When I finished it, I had thought: what could be a better whodunit than an American scientist dumped into the Nile for his exposure of a grand conspiracy by water companies? Maybe, just maybe, the novel was not as good as I thought it was. No! Sacrilege! My darling just might have a few warts, or a pimple here and there; God forbid, a disfigured face. Or maybe she was bloated and needed to go on a crash diet. Or she needed a scalpel.

I had a better idea for a novel than the whodunit. A man on the run who hides from Interpol dressed as a Crusader knight in a Hospitaller museum in Valletta. A man who finds himself when he walks away from his ambitious career. A man who was so driven that he never allowed himself the time to get close to women—who finds love at last with a beautiful Bulgarian acrobat. My real life sounded like fiction. Anyway, if I wrote my autobiography I would surely be caught by Interpol! Why hadn't I called Boriana? Shouldn't I be worried about other suitors? Had someone kidnapped her in my absence? Afraid of commitment.

Commitment could wait. Could I eat another can of tuna or sardines? Maybe boredom would overcome laziness! I was not known for my culinary talents, but I had plenty of time while we were waiting for whatever happened after the Old Man's speech—the unmentionable. What would the people who must remain unnamed do now?

I wandered back to the master bedroom—I felt lonely and wanted Blanca's company. I glanced into Ophelia's cage. God! Her poop had turned watery. She had diarrhea. But why? Were we feeding her the wrong thing? What was her breakfast today? That was the problem. We were just feeding them random veggies, hoping it would be all right. I would have to call a vet. Do something! Maybe Kharalombos would know what to do. But he didn't know any more than I did about parrots. Well, who would have guessed that Scarlett would take her insulin shot if she got a bite of Egyptian parmesan cheese? Okay, maybe I could delay dealing with this crisis until after dinner.

Scarlett had stopped barking. I carried Blanca's cage into the kitchen and then tiptoed into the living room. All clear. Scarlett was curled up asleep on the couch; she was so tiny she looked like a small pillow. Blanca could jump around the kitchen freely if I closed the door.

Blanca was standing upright in her cage. "Be a good girl," I said. I opened the trap and she leapt out. Blanca was bouncing up and down with happiness. Boing! Boing! Boing! She jumped down from the counter. Boing! Boing!

I started singing, "*Those were the days, my friend. We thought they'd never end. La. La. La.*" For a moment, I felt happy.

Suddenly, something shot underneath the kitchen door. A large sewer rat. God, it was Wolfgang! He had gotten out. Shit! How? He was lunging at Blanca. Where was the broom? Broom. Broom. Yes. Cleaning closet. Quick. Blood. God, no! Drops of blood dripped on the tiled floor. I flailed the broom at Wolfgang, but he was quick. Brushed him back with the broom. With the other hand, I opened the back door and Blanca sprang out. I started beating Wolfgang with the broom. You bastard! But he darted past me and ran back to Scarlett's bedroom. In the meantime, Scarlett had started barking. I had forgotten to close Scarlett's bedroom door. But how had Wolfgang gotten out of the cage? I ran down the front stairs and around the side of the building, tracking the drops of blood. But the trail suddenly stopped.

After the disaster with Blanca and Wolfgang, I was too upset to cook. That nice Spanish translator would be devastated about Blanca. Such an impractical boob. I might love nature and the environment, but I couldn't take care of animals.

Kharalombos said, "Maybe we should see what is happening. We have to know. By the way, do we just have any plain tuna in a can?"

One hour after the booing from the crowd in the Square, the Big Man and his family had fled to Libya. He was embracing the Clown Man, the ruler of Libya. The Clown Man was wearing a purple jester's cap with a long purple tunic and Turkish-balloon pants. His face had been disfigured by bad plastic surgeons.

Kharalombos gasped. "But he hates the Clown Man."

"He doesn't have a choice," I said.

"Asylum has been offered to the Big Man's family by the ruler of Libya," the announcer continued, suppressing a smile. Surprising, since this was state television.

The image flashed to the roaring crowd in the Square. Another image flashed back to the Big Man and his family—willowy Yasmine was standing next to a handsome young man. She was carrying a white bundle in her arms. "That's Nunu!" Karalombos shouted. "Yasmine! I will never see my son. It's over. I can never get into Libya."

The announcer said, "The Big Man is accompanied by his wife, the Dragon Lady, his two sons, daughter, her husband, and his first grandson."

Kharalombos had started to sob. This was much, much sadder than watching him cry about all the dead pigs in Cairo.

"She married Eeek Junior!" he said, sobbing. "He was a terrible dancer. I tried to teach him how to waltz for three years!"

"Eeek?"

"Eeek, the son of the most famous businessman in Egypt. He owns all the mineral water companies," he said. "You know that."

"Eeek. Oh, yes," I said. "Eeek." Seeing how skeletal Yasmine looked reminded me of Ophelia. God, I had better check on her. "Ophelia is sick," I said. "The fava beans."

But Kharalombos wasn't listening. He was distraught, understandably. How could I console him?

Ophelia's condition had gotten worse. The newspaper of her cage was covered with a yellow liquid. She was slumped in a corner. Oh, God! I'm sorry. She barely lifted her beak and made a sound, as if she wanted to tell me one last thing. The faint twitter of our doorbell. "It was you," I said. "You were the one imitating the doorbell." Then she was silent and still. Was she…? I put my finger in the cage. She didn't stir. What would I tell…? Who owned Ophelia? What's her name? The Shakespearean scholar with the red hair. "I'm sorry. I fed Ophelia some oily fava beans and they killed her!"

The phone was ringing.

When I came back into the room, Karalombos said, "Of course, we'll be there as soon as possible."

"Ophelia…. Who was that?"

Kharalombos had stopped crying.

"Gudrun. She wants us to come to the Conrad Hilton immediately."

"Is it an emergency? What happened? Is she all right?"

"She didn't say," Kharalombos said. "She said she must see us. We should hurry."

I was suffering from cabin fever. I felt as if I was trapped in Noah's ark. I didn't flatter myself that I was Noah with two casualties. We would have to do something about Ophelia's corpse, but not now.

On our way out of the building, Am Sayed offered us some rabbit and *mulukheyya* with rice.

I suspected it was Blanca. I decided not to ask. I couldn't face any more unpleasant truth today.

When we arrived at the Conrad Hilton, there was a huge entourage waiting for us in the lobby. Many of them were carrying camera and filming equipment. Gudrun was wearing a red *galabiyya* embroidered with gold thread. She was wearing a black pharaonic wig, a gold crown slightly askew on top. The last time we had seen her she was wearing a purple muumuu with Keds sneakers.

Kharalombos hugged and kissed Gudrun. "I will never get to see Nunu," he murmured.

"Nunu? Who is the Nunu?" Gudrun asked. She pinched Kharalombos' cheek.

"It's a long story," I said. "We thought you were in trouble. Is this an emergency?"

"His majesty demands your presence, ja-aa." Gudrun snorted. "He wants you to play in his television show. It's going to be fabulous. Don't laugh, ja-aa. I am the great Cleopatra! Madonna is not coming."

"Surprise!" I said.

Gudrun pinched Kharalombos' other cheek. "Kharalombos will be the perfect Mark Antony. You will be a servant. Or maybe Cleopatra's son. All the foreign actors flew the nest."

"It's always been my ambition to be in a reality television show," I said.

But Kharalombos didn't laugh. He was gazing at Gudrun. "As long as I get to dance with you." God, he was a sap.

Gudrun said. "What have you been doing all these days? I thought I might never see you two alive. It's good you are still ticking."

"Taking care of pets of the people who fled the country," I said. I decided not to tell her that two of my charges had passed on to the next world. "Kharalombos was guarding the building."

"Such a brave man," Gudrun said, adjusting the gold tiara on her black wig. "There are so many cowards in this world, ja-aa."

Kharalombos stood tall, as if he were a knight from the Middle Ages. Only one hour before, he had crumpled before my very eyes. He had so much emotional elasticity—I envied him.

Ramses el-Kibir suddenly appeared in front of us with a retinue of ten minions. He clapped his hands. "Silence! Silence! To fulfill my duty to the nation, I must finish my current obligations to the BBC. That is why we must film the final episode of *The Marvelous Adventures of Ramses el-Kibir*, today."

Gudrun winked at me and whispered, "I have never seen such tantrums as this man can throw. He is a baby. Don't take him serious. Nein."

I raised my hand. "Is it okay to be out at the Pyramids? I mean, is it safe for YOU?" Of course, what I meant was—was it safe for any of us?

"No problem. The army gave me permission to film." Ramses clapped his hands again. The entourage headed to their vehicles—a crazy mélange of black and white taxis, a blue American Chevrolet, film trucks, tanks, jeeps, and Datsun pickups.

Gudrun, Kharalombos, and I were crammed into the back of a little Datsun pickup. Kharalombos' head hit the roof. Our convoy, headed by a tank, made our way down the empty streets toward the Pyramids. Something strange: we saw a huge posse of camels and horses riding in the opposite direction.

I said, "Where is Viscount Triksky? I thought he was a film consultant."

Gudrun snorted. "He drinks too much, ja-aa. Almost a bottle. Snoring like the Kaiser when I left."

Once we arrived at the Pyramids, it took hours to get dressed. The make-up artist spent over an hour curling my hair and painting black kohl on my eyes. I was wearing a Roman toga—I was sure I looked ridiculous.

I stood in front of Ramses el-Kibir. "By any chance, do you have a script?"

"No script," Ramses el-Kibir said. "This is reality TV."

"But doesn't reality TV imitate reality?"

Ramses waved me away, as if I were a fly. He pulled his Indiana Jones hat over his eyes. "Improvise. I hear you are good at it." He bellowed, "Mustafa. Mustafa. Where is my camel?"

The small thin man coughed. He had a bad smoker's cough and couldn't stop coughing. Finally, he said, "Effendim, there are no camels."

Ramses said, "Impossible! No camels at the Pyramids! How can that be? Summon all the owners of the stables in the area."

Another couple of hours passed. At last, the small thin man appeared. "They say," he began and he started coughing, as if he might choke. One of the men brought him a bottle of mineral water.

Ramses said, "Speak, man. What is it?"

"There are no camels and horses today," the small thin man sputtered. "They went to the Square."

"Why? I demand to know," Ramses shouted, stamping his foot. I suppressed a desire to laugh. Gudrun guffawed. "A big baby," she said.

One of the cameramen offered the small thin man a wooden stool. He started to sit down. "You will not sit in my presence, Mustafa. Why are the camels and horses at the Square?"

He looked as if he might collapse from emphysema. He whispered, "Someone paid."

Ramses said, "Ramses el-Kibir will not be defeated! Instead of the battle scene with the camels and horses, we will film Mark Antony killing himself.

And then, Cleopatra killing herself. Gary, you will deliver the snake in a basket!"

A huge crowd of people from the nearby village had appeared to watch the shooting of the scene—it was like a carnival. Who would have guessed that huge demonstrations were going on in downtown Cairo? Small children from the stables skittered around the cameras. Sellers had set up carts: they were selling water, KFC dinner boxes, peanuts, Egyptian flags, postcards of the Pyramids. A few of the army soldiers who had escorted us to the Pyramids were nibbling on fried drumsticks. They lounged against their tanks.

Ramses el-Kibir clapped his hands. The cameramen stood at attention. "Let's get ready. Kharalombos, you will fall on your sword when you realize that you have lost the battle."

Kharalombos was imposing in his Roman toga and breastplate. He had a spear and a sword. "I thought this show was about your discovery of ancient treasures."

Ramses laughed. "Of course, it is. I will point out Cleopatra and Mark Antony's grave at the end of the re-enactment. We are wasting Ramses el-Kibir's valuable time." He clapped his hands. "Move."

Ramses was never satisfied with the way Kharalombos fell on his sword so we did the scene over and over again for two hours. Kharalombos did it perfectly, but Ramses wanted him to look more distraught. "NO! NO! Just look like you've lost everything! You look too cheerful." It was true—Kharalombos looked like he was having fun. And every time he plunged the sword into his side, he grinned impishly.

Finally, Ramses exploded. "Cut. Cut. Cut. We will do Cleopatra's scene. Gudrun, you lie there. Look sad. Gary, you will bring in the basket with the snake."

"It's not a real snake, I hope," I said.

"Of course! This is reality TV." Ramses el-Kibir said.

I panicked. Besides agoraphobia and claustrophobia, I also had a profound fear of snakes. I felt my stomach heave.

Gudrun said. "Ja-aa, we will not endanger our lives. What kind of snake do you have in that basket? I demand to know."

Ramses el-Kibir said. "It's a cobra. Don't be scared, though. He doesn't have any teeth."

One of the children from the crowd flicked open the basket. He poked the huge snake with a stick. The cobra reared its head. The crowd roared.

"I don't think I'm the right man for the job," I said. "Maybe you can get someone else to…"

Ramses el-Kibir shouted to the crowd. "Silence! This is serious. I'm warning you. Get that boy off the set. Not another word."

Kharalombos towered over Ramses el-Kibir. He clenched his spear. "I swear to God, on my honor you will not endanger the life of this visitor to our country. This is against our tradition of hospitality."

The crowd hooted and hollered. They clapped.

Ramses el-Kibir's nostrils flared. "Out of my way. We will shoot the scene. Gudrun, lie down on the couch. That is an order."

She snorted. "Ja-aa, do you think I am a fool? A nincompoop, as the Americans would say. Get another Cleopatra!"

Someone in the crowd shouted, "Look, the cobra has teeth!" The cobra looked as if he were about to strike.

The crowd panicked. The sellers wheeled their carts away. The Bedouins who had been lying on their carpets packed them up.

Suddenly, I felt a heave. I started to throw up—green stuff. Bits of tuna. A pickle. My ill-fated tuna salad.

Ramses shouted, "At your places. Get ready to shoot. We are wasting Ramses el-Kibir's precious time."

But the cameramen were also packing up their equipment. They lugged their heavy cameras to the film trailers. The soldiers were revving their tank engines.

Gudrun was saying to Kharalombos, "Sometimes, God is merciful, ja-aa. Kharalombos, my darling, you are so brave. How can we ever thank you?"

Ramses' phone rang. I heard him say in Arabic, "What? I am coming at once! Defend our national treasures!"

When I finally finished throwing up, the desert was empty except for two lone figures, Gudrun and Kharalombos—they looked as if they belonged together.

"Where is everyone?" I asked. "I feel terrible."

Gudrun dabbed my forehead with a wet handkerchief. "Ja-aa, this is awful. Poor man. At least, we didn't have to film with the cobra."

I wiped my mouth with my hand. Kharalombos handed me a bottle of water. "What happened to the cobra?"

Gudrun chortled. "Some fearless man killed him with a club."

I had a sip of water. Then, I started throwing up again—dry heaves this time. Kharalombos patted my shoulder. "I think the tuna was bad. Where is everyone?"

"Ramses went to the Square. Camels are riding through the Egyptian Museum," Kharalombos said. "I don't know about the others."

Gudrun threw her black wig down in the sand. She put the gold tiara in her purse. We headed back to the main road. The streets were empty. We walked about seven kilometers before we got a ride back to the Conrad Hilton. A man in a red Toyota with bananas piled high in the back stopped for us. Gudrun and Kharalombos crammed in the front; I balanced on top of the bananas in the back. Kharalombos tried to pay the driver, but he refused to take any money.

Viscount Triksky was not asleep when we returned to the Conrad Hilton. He was watching something on television—it sounded like an American football game. When he saw us trooping into the suite, he quickly switched the channel to the BBC News. He was drinking a Heineken beer.

"Crikey!" he said. "It doesn't look like it was a blinding success."

Gudrun said, "Ja-aa, I have never seen such a fiasco. This was why you came to the Egypt, for that Ramses el-Kibir? We can forget the Nile! Tomorrow I am making my reservations to leave for the Taj Mahal."

"Well, he is a bit of a barmpot. Did he have you beavering away? Tell me, I am dying to know what transpired."

Kharalombos sank into a large chair. He closed his eyes.

Gudrun said, "Kharalombos was Mark Antony. Gary was one of Cleopatra's servants. He was going to bring me a cobra in a basket so I could kill myself."

The Viscount smiled benignly at me. "Nice kit." He winked at me. He must be gay. I had forgotten that I was still in my Roman toga outfit.

"The snake escaped. I have a terrible fear of snakes. I got sick," I said.

"Sorry, old chap. Should we order a boiled potato for you from room service?" Viscount Triksky said. "Or some brew? Maybe a fizzy drink?"

"I want to lie down," I said.

Gudrun waved her hands. "There was no script! Weren't you talking about the script on the way from the airport? You are always talking the nonsense."

"There was a script," Viscount Triksky said. "But everything went a bit pear-shaped. You know, he's a prat. He changes his mind all the time."

Kharalombos said, "We walked back to the hotel. Almost ten kilometers. They left us there."

"Bollocks!" Viscount Triksky said. "Ramses is a cad. What can we do to cheer you all up? What about a game of Snakes and Ladders?"

Gudrun snorted. "Nein. You play the Snake and Ladder. I want a glass of your whiskey."

Viscount Triksky's beady eyes narrowed. "I am afraid to say, someone nicked every bottle. It's vanished."

"You must be joking me, ja-aa." Gudrun said. "You had ten bottles a few days ago. We didn't even have room for our feet in Ramses' car."

Kharalombos was playing with the remote control. He suddenly stopped at state television: A man in a green beret was standing in front of the camera, reading a communiqué. "While the Army acknowledges the service of the Big Man to the Nation, they accept his honorable resignation. The General will now head the Nation. The crowds at the Square are kindly urged to go home."

Gudrun said, "What is the man saying in the Arabic language? What does it mean?"

Kharalombos sighed. "The Big Man's Men will take over. There will be another Big Man."

Gudrun yawned. "Ja-aa, there will always be a Big Man. I slept very bad for three nights."

"Can we stay here?" I asked. "I don't think I can face the animals." What a wuss I was—I couldn't face a ferret and a Chihuahua. Maybe we should call Am Sayed to feed them. I was tired. Anyway, they could last one day without food.

Gudrun said, "The Viscount will give you his room. He can sleep on the couch."

"Well," the Viscount laughed lightly. "You are making the arrangements. In '74, when Haile Selassie was deposed, I got some kip on a bar table. Nightie-night."

In the middle of the night, I woke up, thirsty. A small hall light illuminated the hallway on the way to the bathroom.

I could see the Viscount's back. He was tiptoeing towards the door. He was carrying a huge duffel bag.

Gudrun rubbed her eyes. "Ja-aa, so maybe the Viscount is downstairs having his breakfast."

"Afraid not," I said. "I think he's cleared out."

Kharalombos said, "I was never convinced by his English accent. It reminded me of P.G. Wodehouse. I used to read those books when I was a boy."

I laughed.

Gudrun said, "Ja-aa, he's a rat. I wasn't sure of him from the beginning, but I was lonely at the camp. And he kept flattering me. He came to pick up his niece at the camp. He kept hanging around."

Kharalombos said, "Did he rob you?"

She sighed. "Only the price of a ticket to Egypt and a Nile cruise. I wanted a companion."

"You could have lost more," I said. "What are you going to do now?"

Gudrun smiled and said to Kharalombos, "Could I have this dance?"

Kharalombos bowed. Gudrun and Kharalombos started waltzing around the small living room while I watched. After the short dance, she said, "I'm hungry. Maybe we should have the breakfast downstairs and celebrate."

"What are we celebrating?" I asked.

Gudrun said, "You are invited to America as my guests, ja-aa. You will come, won't you? I am not ready for Bombay now."

Gudrun described her girls' camp on the river. We could float on tubes and rafts for hours in a cool river, drink beer, and eat brisket barbecue.

We both agreed to go to America the next day, provided we could sneak out of Egypt.

Kharalombos said, "What happens when the holiday is over?"

Gudrun shrugged, "We will see, ja-aa. You can teach the salsa or the cha-cha-cha to the girls. And Gary can teach the yoga?"

It sounded like a plan.

Acknowledgments

I WOULD LIKE TO ACKNOWLEDGE THE MAGAZINES that first published these stories individually: *Storyglossia*: "The Wedding Guest"; "The Empty Flat Upstairs"; "Taken Hostage by the Ugly Duck." *Story South*: "A Little Honey and a Little Sunlight"; *Mediterranean Poetry*: "The Charm"; *Gowanus*: "Fatma's New Teeth."

The American University in Cairo granted me a Professional Development Leave for the fall of 2006. This gave me uninterrupted time to work on all of the stories. The university also supported funding for many writers' conferences, where I received valuable feedback: *Squaw Valley Community of Writers*, *Tin House Writers' Workshop*, and *Dzanc Books International Lisbon Literary Program*. *The Vermont Studio Center* granted me a partial scholarship for a residency in 2006. *The Valparaiso Foundation* in Mojacar, Spain granted me a month residency in 2011, to finish the manuscript. A Mini-Grant from the university supported the book project *Shahrazad's Tooth*.

Note to the Reader

I STARTED WRITING THE STORIES FROM THIS collection in 2005, after I had lived in Cairo for five years. Originally, my fiction was realistic; however, learning Arabic, meeting so many colorful characters, and living in Cairo transformed the way I told stories.

This short story collection, *Shahrazad's Gift*, was originally published in 2013 under the title *Shahrazad's Tooth* in Cairo by Afaq Publishers. They had also published my first book, *Three Stories from Cairo* (2011), a bilingual story collection in English and Arabic, translated by Mohamed Metwalli, the Egyptian poet. *Shahrazad's Gift* is the same except for the addition of two stories that I had written at the time, but did not include: "Ice" and "Fatma's New Teeth."

Many thanks again to Jody Baboukis for her careful editing and proofreading.

I had always wanted this collection of stories to reach a wider audience. After Scott Davis accepted my novel, *Confessions of a Knight Errant*, he decided to publish this collection. Sadly, he died unexpectedly the month the novel was published, October 2022. Many thanks to his wife, Mary Davis and Brenda Pierce for their dedication and support at Cune Press.

About Cune Press

Cune Press was founded in 1994 to publish thoughtful writing of public importance. Our name is derived from "cuneiform." (In Latin *cuni* means "wedge.")

In the ancient Near East the development of cuneiform script—simpler and more adaptable than hieroglyphics—enabled a large class of merchants and landowners to become literate. Clay tablets inscribed with wedge-shaped stylus marks made possible a broad intermeshing of individual efforts in trade and commerce.

Cuneiform enabled scholarship to exist and art to flower, and created what historians define as the world's first civilization. When the Phoenicians developed their sound-based alphabet, they expressed it in cuneiform.

The idea of Cune Press is the democratization of learning, the faith that rarefied ideas, pulled from dusty pedestals and displayed in the streets, can transform the lives of ordinary people. And it is the conviction that ordinary people, trusted with the most precious gifts of civilization, will give our culture elasticity and depth—a necessity if we are to survive in a time of rapid change.